HIS CURVY MUSE

A SMALL TOWN CURVY GIRL ROMANCE

BOOK BOYFRIENDS WANTED
BOOK 15

MARY E THOMPSON

His Curvy Muse

Book Boyfriends Wanted, book 15

Copyright © 2023 Mary E Thompson

Cover Copyright © 2023 Mary E Thompson

Cover Photo from depositphotos, Copyright © matusciac

Cover background from depositphotos, Copyright © tomert (lights) and Milanares (blue)

Cover watercolor stripe from depositphotos, Copyright © ronedale

Published by BluEyed Press, All Rights Reserved

Ebook ISBN: 978-1-953879-62-2

Print ISBN: 978-1-953879-63-9

Audiobook ISBN: 978-1-953879-64-6

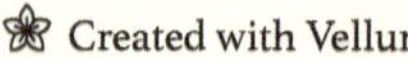 Created with Vellum

BOOK BOYFRIENDS WANTED

Someone new has come to town. He has a few secrets, but he's a good guy. We think. He's definitely going to make the summer hot, especially for our favorite introverted maintenance woman. Sofia has met her match in this story, and I'm so happy you're here for it, because I sure am!

Of course, all your favorite couples are enjoying the show, too. MacKellar Cove is happy to have you visit. Check out Finley's store, Hudson's bar, the bakery where Valentina works, and Ian's boat shop. There's something for everyone in this small town.

Never miss a thing when you sign up for Mary's newsletter. *Romancing the Curves* comes with subscriber exclusive freebies, sneak peeks, and a first look at everything Mary has to offer. Be the first to know about new releases and sales and all the curves ahead!

SUBSCRIBE NOW AT MARYETHOMPSON.COM

Happy reading!

For Jessica, Christy, Suzanne, and Krista...
Thank you for your support, your ideas, and your friendship

1

SOFIA

I WIPED THE FLOOR OF THE BATHROOM CLEAN AS I BACKED OUT of it, careful not to leave any marks on the floor. It was perfect. As perfect as it could be in a week. It was good enough for the new tenant who would be living there for the next three months.

The rest of the place was functional. The stark difference between the newly remodeled bathroom and the rest of the apartment was almost laughable, but it was going to have to be okay.

Piper insisted the tenant said they were fine with something that wasn't fancy, so I went with it. If they didn't like it, Piper would let me know. As my boss and best friend, she wasn't shy about telling me the truth.

I was the one keeping secrets lately.

I took one last pass of the apartment and let myself out the door. The cleaning crew would be in first thing in the morning, and the new tenant would move in tomorrow afternoon.

And in less than two weeks, my dad was coming.

I had to stop thinking about my dad. I was dreading the

visit, but like everything else that came with him, catastrophizing only spun me tighter than a professional ice skater at the Olympics.

"Hey!" Haley said, startling me as I made my way to my apartment.

"Hey, Haley. How are you?"

Haley was a good friend. We'd gotten to know each other over the last year, and she was the only one who knew my dad was coming for a visit. She got it out of me a week ago, and I'd been avoiding Piper since because I felt guilty for telling my new friend and not my oldest friend.

"I'm good. How was your day?"

I shrugged. "Good, I guess. I finished the bathroom, so it's ready for the tenant to move in once it's cleaned."

"Nice. How about the other thing?" Haley knew talking about my dad upset me, so she tiptoed around the conversation. Which wasn't really any better.

"Fine. He's supposed to be here a week from Sunday."

"And he's staying with you?" she confirmed again.

I nodded. "He said he's not sure how long he'll be here. I thought about asking Piper if he could stay at MacKellar Cove Inn, but I felt bad asking since he's not always the most considerate guest. And summer is busy. I don't want him taking up a room that someone else could use."

"That and you haven't told her yet," Haley said, her voice lifting in question at the end.

"Yeah, that, too."

Haley sighed. "Sofia, you need to tell her."

"I will. I need to get through the new tenant moving in, and then I'll think about my father."

"Are you sure?"

I nodded. "Yeah. But right now, I need a shower. Have a

good night, Haley." I waved and hurried away before she could invite me to have dinner with her or something.

Yes, that was a bitchy move, but I didn't mean it that way. I had a limited capacity for people on any given day, and some days my capacity was the size of a thimble. On a good day, it was closer to a bathroom cup. Haley? I don't think she had a unit of measure. She was one of those people who was blessed with the gift of communication and was never at a loss for words. It made it easy to be friends with her, but exhausting when it was a thimble day.

It was definitely a thimble day.

I let myself into my apartment and let out a breath. My apartment was my sanctuary. When Piper lived with me, my room was my space to decompress and let out all my emotions, but since she moved out a few years ago, the entire apartment became mine.

And in under two weeks, that would change again.

"Ugh."

I shook my head and stepped away from the door. I locked it and pushed away from the door, tugging my tee over my head as I walked toward my room. I tossed my dirty clothes in the hamper in my bathroom and turned on the shower as hot as it would go. Steam filled the space as I tried to think of what I'd eat for dinner.

Takeout would be nice, but that would mean talking to someone. Maybe there was a frozen meal somewhere in the back of my freezer.

I stepped under the hot stream of water and let it wash the day away. Something crusty was in my hair, hopefully leftover grout and not something from the garbage disposal I replaced first thing that morning. I scrubbed my hair twice, just in case, then dragged conditioner coated fingers through my hair, working it to the ends.

I leaned against the wall of the shower and sighed. My bathroom needed a remodel, too, but not when my dad was there. I had a two-bed-two-bath apartment, but there was no way in hell I was going to share a bathroom with my father.

Shaking free of the thoughts, I finished my shower and dried off. I wrapped my hair in a towel and grabbed my fuzzy robe. I'd worry about clothes before I went to bed.

I lucked out with one frozen dinner left. While it heated up, I found a sappy rom-com that I knew would leave me in tears, but it was a happy cry kind of night. Happy tears were better than sad or frustrated tears.

After the movie, and the tears, I tossed my plastic tray in the recycling and put myself to bed. Tomorrow was another day, and I would only be ready for it if I got lots of sleep.

"Sofia! Sofia!"

I rolled over and groaned. Weird dream. Piper was calling me.

My bedroom door burst open. "Sofia! Are you okay?"

I jerked upright, looking around my room to figure out what the hell was going on.

Piper sat on the edge of my mattress, her gaze assessing and concerned.

"What are you doing here?"

"The new tenant moved in today."

I nodded. "Yeah. He's supposed to be here at ten to sign the paperwork."

"It's noon, Sof."

"What?" I threw the covers back and jumped up, making Piper jump at the same time.

"I already met with him," Piper said, stalling my frantic movements.

"You met with him?" My brain was fuzzy, like I went on an all-night bender. Except I knew I hadn't. What the hell?

"He was staying at the Inn last night. When he checked in, he mentioned he was renting a place, and we ended up talking. He's really nice. Cute, too."

"You're married."

"Happily. But you're single."

"And not interested."

Piper sighed. "Are you feeling okay?"

I shook my head. "Just frazzled. So, you gave the new tenant his keys yesterday?"

Piper shook her head. "When he checked out, he said he was on his way here to meet with you. He called when you weren't around. Said he called and texted you, even knocked on your door, but you never answered."

I shook my head. It was not like me to sleep through my alarm. At all.

"Are you okay? You've been out of it lately."

I looked up at my best friend and knew I needed to tell her everything. The guilt was eating me alive, and she would find out soon enough anyway.

"My dad is coming here in two weeks."

"Your dad?" she blurted. Piper knew the significance. Mostly, at least.

I nodded, the fringes of my hair getting in my face. I pushed them back and searched for a hair tie. "He called a few weeks ago. Wanted to come see me."

"Why didn't you tell me?"

I laughed mirthlessly. "You know why."

"Because you didn't think he'd actually show up."

I nodded. It wasn't the first time my dad said he was

going to come visit. But this time, he had flight arrangements and a rental car. Not that he couldn't cancel both, but it was more than he'd done before.

"And you think he's actually coming this time? Where is he staying?"

"With me."

"And then I added this new tenant and made the time before crazier, and eliminated your escape. Shit, Sof. I'm so sorry."

I shrugged. I finally found a hair tie and wrapped my loose blonde locks into a ponytail. "It's fine. You didn't know. And he still might not show up. But I've just been a little all over the place lately."

"I can understand. Well, don't worry about the new tenant. Gavin made sure the apartment was all set up. The cleaning crew did a great job, and the movers had everything loaded in as soon as the cleaners were finished. The apartment is fully furnished and Daniel is moving his stuff in now."

"Now?"

Piper nodded. "Yes, which means you're fine to relax."

"I should go apologize to him."

"Gavin apologized and explained this isn't like you. Everything is fine. I'm sure you'll meet him soon. And don't think I don't know what you're doing." She leveled me with a look that said she saw through my attempt to get out of the conversation we needed to have.

I scowled at my best friend and accepted that I owed her better than I'd been giving her lately. "Fine. But I have no food, and I'm starving."

"As it happens, I know where we can find some food. Just Tacos?"

She knew how to get me. My stomach rumbled in response, and Piper chuckled.

"Get dressed and we'll go. You can tell me all about dear old dad's impending visit."

I cringed. There was so much to tell her. And I was out of time. She needed to know the whole story.

I just didn't want to tell it.

PIPER'S TACOS sat on her tray, untouched and forgotten. My story was that good.

Or bad, depending on your perspective.

"Okay, wait. So, your dad is a famous musician. Your mom had a fling with him on the road one night, and you were the product of that one-night stand."

I nodded. "Yep. He denied it, refused to give her anything. When I started middle school, something changed. I'm not really sure what, but maybe he grew a conscience or found religion or something. Anyway, he started coming around. Said he was sorry. Agreed to a paternity test. Set up a custody agreement that included back payments for child support."

"Wow. That's kind of impressive."

"I guess. My mom never spent that money. She saved it for me. Wanted me to have it. She was angry, and hurt. She was doing her best to take care of me. The night she died, she was going from her day job to her night job and was hit by a drunk driver. Since I was only fourteen, the state made me go live with my dad."

"On the road?" Piper confirmed.

"Yep. There was proof he was my father, but only a few people knew who I was."

"Was it fun? To be on the road and tour with a band?"

I thought back to that time. My feelings around it were so muddled that I wasn't sure I could answer that question without telling her the rest.

"At times, yeah. The first year, I was pretty lost in my grief over losing my mom. She was my best friend, and going from having her there to having her stolen from me was hard. I was nasty to my dad. Our relationship was tentative at best anyway, and I didn't make it easier."

"I would think that's how almost anyone would have handled what you went through."

"Maybe. After a year, I got some help. One of the guys got married. His wife was really sweet. She and I would spend time together. She'd lost her mom when she was young, too, and she helped me to heal. She also helped me to see that I was treating my dad as the bad guy instead of accepting that he messed up and was trying to be there for me."

"She sounds pretty great."

"Maddie was amazing. I don't think I would have survived without her. When I turned seventeen, Maddie had a baby, though, and she stopped touring as much. I was still in school, so I had to go with them. I couldn't stay home alone as a minor. That's where I met Nate Catalan."

As predicted, Piper's brows shot up. "You know Nate Catalan?"

I pursed my lips into a smile. "I knew him. Or, I thought I did."

"What happened?"

"I fell victim to the oldest trick in the book. The starstruck kid falls for the sexy, alluring rocker and gets her heart broken."

"I feel like there's a lot more to the story than that."

I laughed. "So much more. We were kids. He was eighteen. He joined the tour as a backup singer for one of the opening acts. But it was obvious he was going to be a star. He had that presence that everyone knew would make him famous eventually. And he liked me."

The sourness of that time in my life turned my stomach. The regret and pain and hatred seeped into my bones.

"What happened?" Piper asked softly. She lifted her taco and took a bite.

I watched as a piece of chicken slowly tipped over and fell from her taco. It hit the tray with a soft splat. "I fell in love with him. I thought he felt the same. He was my first, and I was sure we were building a life together."

"But?"

"But on my eighteenth birthday, the night we were going to tell my dad about us, I caught him with someone else."

"No."

I nodded. "He tried to tell me she didn't mean anything. That all the guys screwed other women all the time. That it was just a part of being on the road and I would have to get over it if we were going to be together."

"What an asshole," Piper breathed.

"He wasn't wrong, though. I'd been on the road long enough to know how it was. No one was faithful. Maddie never came back to the tour because she knew what she'd find. She was bitter and angry the next time we talked. Anyone who tried to settle down with any of them were the same."

"Oh, Sofia."

I drew a breath and let it out slowly, willing to pain to go with it. "I left after that leg of the tour. My dad no longer had an obligation to keep me there. He said he wanted me to stay, but it was too hard for me."

"You were heartbroken."

I nodded. "I was. And I was stupid because I fell in love with a man who would never love me back. He was a great actor. Talented and smart and magnetic. All the things that are said about him now."

"Well, I'll never watch another one of his movies or go to one of his concerts."

"He's one of your favorite actors," I said, knowing she'd never stick to it.

"Not anymore. Not now that I know what he's really like."

"It was more than twenty years ago," I said.

"Once an asshole, always an asshole. I just wish I'd known. All the times I begged you to watch one of his movies with me."

"I was so ashamed. I hated myself for falling for his lies and for believing he cared about me. But when my dad shows up..."

"You're not going to be able to hide everything. And you know I'm not going to judge you. We all fall for someone we shouldn't at some point in time. There's nothing we can do about that."

"I'm just happy I was never part of his behind-the-scenes stories or something. I was hidden. But that's part of why my relationship with my dad isn't better. He never understood why I left like I did."

"You never told him?"

I shook my head. "He knew parts of it, but I don't think he ever really understood the whole story. Nate was a friend before we started seeing each other. My dad was the one that introduced us. When it ended, I was just his ex. I had no claim to him, and even if I did, what difference did it make? I asked my dad to kick him off the tour, but he didn't.

I told my dad I couldn't be around Nate anymore and that it didn't make sense for me to stay on the road with him when I was a legal adult. He didn't try very hard to change my mind."

"Shit," Piper whispered. "I'm still baffled I never knew any of this. I never knew your dad was famous, or that you dated Hollywood royalty."

"I wish none of it were true. I wish I were just an ordinary person who lived in a small town and no one knew me at all."

"Well, your secret is safe with me. As far as anyone else knows, that's exactly who you are."

"Until my dad shows up. Then everyone will know."

Piper scowled. She knew I was right. And that there was nothing I could do about it.

2

TREY

DAY ONE, AND I ALREADY MISSED MY FIRST CHANCE. OF course, it makes me think she's as flighty as her father that she slept through my arrival. No wonder the place was vacant and could be rented out at the last minute if that was how they did things.

I walked around the apartment that I was going to call home for three months and debated packing it all in and getting the hell out of the podunk little town. I was already going stir crazy after twenty-four hours there. Three months was going to be painful.

At least the weather was good, though. And the water was pretty amazing. And Piper and Gavin seemed okay.

But they weren't why I was in MacKellar Cove. I was there for one reason only. And as soon as I got what I wanted, I could get the hell out of dodge and move forward with my life.

It took me all of five seconds to settle in since I only brought clothes and my guitar with me. The guitar was locked in my trunk while I was staying at the Inn, but being in the apartment, I had to bring it in. I felt more myself with it in my hands. Like I knew who I was.

The apartment building was vacant and dead when I walked outside. The street parking was less than ideal, but the location was the best in town. With Sofia Frank as the building manager and maintenance person and all-around welcome wagon, it was where I needed to be.

I grabbed my guitar and the notebook I'd been trying to write songs in from the trunk, then turned back to the building. Two women were approaching from the other direction. One was blonde, curvy, and made my mouth water. My fingers itched to touch her the same way they did to pick up my guitar when a song ran through my mind. Like if I didn't get my hands on her in a few seconds, I would lose that feeling forever.

The other woman, a brunette, waved. Shit. It was Piper. Which meant the blonde was the woman I'd moved there for.

Sofia Frank.

I wasn't expecting her to be beautiful, or for her to have curves that made me want to forget about getting out of there in three months.

I shook my head. Fuck that. I wasn't the settling down type. And I sure as hell wasn't going to settle down in a town that barely had a decent bar, let alone nothing in the way of entertainment. A movie theater with two screens? A few tiny restaurants? The biggest stage was two hours away. Same with the hospital and nightclubs and women who would be easy to slide into bed with.

"Daniel! Hi!" Piper said, catching me mid-daydream on the sidewalk in front of the apartment building. She smiled that big, cheerful grin of a woman who slept with the man she loved every night. That was the smile my music inspired. The smile that said I'd done my job.

"Hey, Piper," I said, ignoring the twinge of jealousy that tightened my gut. I didn't want what she had. Never did. Never would.

"I'm so happy we ran into you. Now you can meet Sofia," Piper said, shoving her friend toward me.

"Hi, Daniel. It's so nice to meet you. I apologize for not being available earlier. It's not like me at all. If there's anything I can do to make it up to you, please let me know."

She shook my hand with a grip that shocked and impressed me. Most women preferred to bat their lashes at me and pretend they were helpless and needed me to care for them. Not Sofia. If her grip was anything to go on, she could not only take care of herself but kick my ass if it came down to it.

"It's nice to meet you as well. And nothing to apologize for. Things happen. Piper and Gavin were nice enough to run over and get me the keys, so all good."

"Well, thank you for being so kind. Piper's been singing your praises."

I glanced at Piper, trying to get a read off of her. Did she recognize me? Was Sofia trying to tell me something?

"What's your favorite song to play?" Sofia asked before I could answer the questions in my head.

"Excuse me?"

She nodded to my guitar case. "I'm assuming there's a guitar in there and not a really big gun."

"The gun's in my pants," I said without thinking.

The three of us were silent for a long moment. I wanted to melt into the sidewalk. What the hell was I thinking?

I wasn't. That was the problem.

Piper burst out laughing, bending over and laughing so

loudly the sound echoed off the building. Sofia glanced at me, then at her friend, then started laughing with Piper.

I chuckled, trying to not feel like a douchey asshole for throwing a line at them. I needed to stop being the dick I was out on tour and act like a human being.

"Oh shit, that was good. I like that one," Piper said, wiping tears from beneath her lashes. "That was just smooth. I needed that laugh. Thank you."

"I aim to please," I said, smiling at her, and getting another giggle out of her.

"Well, that was good. But I need to head home. Please let either of us know if there's anything you need while you're here. And I hope you take Gavin up on the offer to meet at O'Kelley's tomorrow night. There's a group of guys who meet every week. I think you'll like them." Piper stopped and shook her head. "Sorry. I didn't mean to presume. I have no idea who you'd like. But they're good guys. Since you're going to be here for a few months, it can't hurt to meet some people, right?"

"Of course." I smiled at her even though I had no intention of buddying up to the locals.

Except one.

"Good. Okay, I'm gone. Love you, hun. See you soon." Piper hugged Sofia warmly, Sofia's lids falling closed as the two embraced. Piper released her and waved to me, then retreated down the sidewalk back toward where they came from.

"Can I get the door for you?" Sofia asked, moving toward the building.

It took me a second to realize what she was asking. I finally nodded and followed her. "Thanks."

"You're welcome."

I proceeded her into the building, feeling like an ass for

not holding the door for her. Didn't women like her expect that?

"Nice meeting you," she said as soon as she was inside the building. She headed toward the mailboxes on the ground floor without a second look at me.

I stared after her, wondering how in the world I was going to get her to tell me where her father was if I couldn't get her to have a conversation at all.

A door closed somewhere down the hall, and I sighed, accepting defeat. Again.

I carried my guitar and notebook upstairs and let myself back into my apartment. I locked the door as soon as it was closed, then took the guitar to the living room. I laid the case on the floor and flipped it open.

Now, I could consider myself unpacked.

WHAT THE HELL was I thinking? Could I blame it on the local water? Was there something in it that made me want to get out on a Thursday night and meet a bunch of strangers at a bar? A bunch of male strangers?

I was telling myself that because there was no other excuse. Besides extreme boredom. Fuck, there was nothing to do in this tiny little town. I planned to explore all day and ran out of shit to do by eleven. I started at ten.

My mind was melting. And not in a good way.

So, I was standing in front of O'Kelley's, wondering what was wrong with me and finding I had nothing better to do with my evening than get to know some of the local men.

I opened the door and was more than a little surprised by the volume inside. The place was busy. Pool balls clacked together toward the back, tables were full of customers talking and laughing. And the bar was crowded.

I pulled my hat lower over my face, knowing the risk was high that someone would recognize me. As I made my way to the bar for a drink, I caught a few looks, but no one pointed at me.

The bartender caught my gaze and held it while I walked toward him. He was a big guy, shaved head and full beard. He looked like he could have been the bouncer, but with a guy his size behind the bar, they probably didn't need a bouncer.

"How ya' doing?" he asked when I got close enough to hear him over the noise.

"Good."

"New here?"

I nodded.

"Are you Daniel?"

I was a little taken aback that he would know my name, even if it wasn't the name I'd been going by for nearly two decades. "How do you know that?"

He jerked his head farther down the bar and started walking that way.

I looked at where he was going and spotted a group of men with Gavin in the middle of them. I followed the bartender, unsure how I was supposed to break in to the group without coming across like an asshole.

"Daniel's here," the bartender said, interrupting the conversation without a hint of unease.

All the men, more than half a dozen of them, turned at once to where I stood a few feet away.

Gavin stood and came toward me. "Glad you made it! Come meet everyone."

He shook my hand and clapped me on the back, shoving

me into the middle of the group.

"Ian owns Jameson Custom Boats. Colin owns Jones Family Maple Farm. Ramsey is a business attorney. James and Rowan are MacKellar Cove police officers. Nico's an oncologist. Knox owns Al's Hardware." Gavin pointed to the bartender. "Hudson owns this place."

I looked down the line of men and nodded to each of them. I had to admit I was a little impressed. Business owners, cops, and a doctor? Not who I expected to meet at a small town bar.

"Daniel's renting a unit in Piper's building for the next three months," Gavin told them.

"Nice place. My girlfriend lives in the building," one of the guys said. "You must be in the apartment Sofia was renovating the last week. She got all the supplies from my store."

I nodded. Hardware store guy. "Yep. It's all I need for a few months."

"So, what are you doing here? Taking the summer off?" the bartender, Hudson, asked.

I nodded. My cover for the summer was that I was in between jobs and taking a few months off to figure out my next steps. I decided to tell people I lived in LA and worked in the music industry, but that was as close to the truth as I was willing to get. The full truth was we were heading into the studio in the fall, and I needed to bring some new music with me or we wouldn't have anything to record.

"Yeah. Seemed like a quiet area to get focused on what I want to do next," I told the guys, nodding my head and looking at the bar like I was broken up about it and not wanting to talk much.

The trick worked like a charm. A beer slid under my nose, and the conversation around me picked up again.

"If you need anything, let me know," Hudson said. "First

beer's on the house."

I nodded my thanks to him and wondered if I saw a harder glint in his eyes than a moment ago.

He walked away, checking on other customers, and I told myself I was wrong. Everything was fine.

The men talked about work and women and life. There was a comfort with them that I didn't expect. Especially knowing them for an hour. They included me in their conversations, asking about my history with women and if I was involved with anyone.

"Not right now. I'm not very good at commitment," I admitted. It was the truth. There were too many options out there for me to be willing to settle down. It didn't matter that I sang about finding love or romance, I wasn't made for it. I'd spent too many years on the road. At thirty-seven, I was past the point of wanting to settle down. Wanting one person to spend my life with. It wasn't going to happen, and I was okay with that.

"I never was either," Ian said. "But really, I was lying to myself. I slept around because Blake was involved with someone else and I was in love with her."

"How long did that last?" I asked. Because it was good for a song, not for any other reason.

"Five years, she dated Willie. When they split, it took me another nine months to pull my head out of my ass and get up the nerve to ask her out," Ian admitted.

"Yeah, and you didn't even really do that," Ramsey added. "He started sleeping with her without telling her he was in love with her. Met her on an online dating site and played both sides."

"Online dating? I thought you all grew up here?"

The men all chuckled.

"Don't do it, man," Nico said.

"Someone should warn him," Knox said.

"What are you all talking about?" I asked.

"There's this app. One of our friends made it," Hudson said. "All of us have met our wives and girlfriends through it. My wife and I hated each other, but we started talking there and fell in love. Let us see a different side of each other."

"Why did you match if you hated each other?" I asked.

"The app doesn't let you use names and there are no pictures," James explained. "My wife and I were like Hudson and Anna. She couldn't stand me. But we worked it all out." He smirked.

I couldn't help but return the look. I knew that look. They figured it out in the bedroom.

"For Blake and me, we were friends. She's best friends with my sister. I've been in love with her forever, and she wasn't looking for anything serious when we got together, so I pretended I wasn't either. Almost ruined everything, but we got it right in the end. I know you're only here a few months, but Book Boyfriends Wanted is the best app for meeting people in the area."

"Book Boyfriends Wanted?" I was skeptical of the name.

They all nodded.

"The woman who made it, plus all our women and more, meet up at the bookstore next door and talk about men in books. Always say they're better than real life," Hudson explained. "That's where the name came from. Asks you a bunch of questions about books and who you are and pairs you up based on what you read."

"What if I don't read?" I asked. I didn't take a lot of time to read between international tours and women.

The guys shrugged.

"Then don't worry about it. Maybe it's not for you," Knox said.

I nodded, wondering why I cared. I wasn't looking to meet anyone. Hell, I wasn't even considering sex at the moment. I had a goal, and when I had a goal, that was all that mattered. Getting to know Sofia was the only thing I needed to be thinking about for the next three months.

"Haley said Sofia signed up again. And Chelsea. She and Chelsea have been talking about it at the salon. More and more women are signing up," Knox said.

"Sofia?" I blurted before my brain could stop me.

Knox turned to me with a smirk. "You know Sofia?"

I shook my head and reached for my beer. The glass was empty, leaving me holding absolutely nothing. I set the glass back down and tried not to let my panic show. "I met her yesterday. She was with Piper." I nodded to Gavin to back up my story.

"Sofia's great," Knox said. "Smart and funny and creative. She's pretty quiet, though, so if you're looking to get to know her, the app might be a good option. She doesn't let a lot of people in."

"But don't fuck with her. Sofia's a good person," Hudson said.

"Daniel's not like that, guys," Gavin defended me. "He's here for three months. We all know it. Sofia knows it. Nothing is going to get messed up. Hell, Sofia barely dates, so it's not like he's got a great shot, anyway."

I tried not to be bothered by their protective instincts surrounding her. And I tried not to take offense to their comments about me not having much of a chance.

I was Trey fucking Ryan. I was a damn rockstar. I could have any woman I wanted. And I had any woman I wanted. All I had to do was turn on my rockstar charm, and she'd be putty in my hands.

All the way to the studio.

3

SOFIA

A KNOCK ON THE DOOR PULLED ME AWAY FROM THE KITCHEN. I opened it to find Chelsea in the hallway.

"Hey. Am I the first one here?" Chelsea asked.

I nodded and led the way back to the kitchen. "They should be here soon."

"Haley left before me. I thought she'd be here by now. How was your day?"

I met her gaze and poured myself an extra large margarita, letting that answer her question.

Chelsea laughed. "That good, huh?"

I sighed and poured a drink for her. "I really can't complain. I like my job. But some days are longer than others."

"Same. And at the end of my day, I'm still not able to relax."

I cocked my head at her.

"I live in a nonsmoking building, but I have a neighbor who smokes. I've reported it, but the complex isn't do anything about it. There have been times the mat in front of my unit is flipped around, like someone did it just to mess with me. I think he's angry that I reported him."

"That's kind of scary."

She nodded. "It is. I haven't been happy there for a while and I've been trying to decide what to do, but now it feels like I need to leave."

"Yeah, I would be leaving, too. Do you have any idea where you're going to go?"

She shrugged. "I've been thinking about buying a house."

"That's exciting. Have you started looking yet?"

She shook her head. "I just started thinking about this. I know this is the right time to buy a place because it's when inventory is at the highest, but I'm not sure. I don't want to jump too fast. We've only just barely taken over the salon, and it would be really easy to get in over my head."

"But that you're thinking about that is a good sign. My mom was really frugal. Always lived below our means. She worked two jobs most of the time, but she saved a ton of money. When she died, I didn't need a thing."

"Did your dad help?"

I nodded. "He took care of everything when I went to live with him. He wanted me to go to college and paid for that, even though I never finished. After college, I haven't asked him for a thing."

"I've considered moving back in with my parents. The only thing stopping me is I feel like it would be saying I'm a failure."

"There's no reason for you to think that. Everyone's situation is different, and as long as you all agree to it, there's nothing wrong with living with them. I'd probably live with my mom if she were still alive."

"Really?"

I chuckled. "She was my best friend. If she was still alive, I'd almost definitely still be living with her."

"Wow. I feel a little better."

"Are you close to your parents?" I asked.

Chelsea and I got to know each other some when Haley moved to town. Haley moved into the same building as me and worked with Chelsea and ended up introducing us. I was friends with Chelsea's cousin, Elise, but I'd only known Chelsea in passing until Haley.

Another knock on the door had us both moving to the living room. This time it was both Haley and Piper.

"How did I beat you here?" Chelsea asked Haley.

"I made a pitstop," Haley admitted. Her cheeks turned pink, telling all of us exactly where her pitstop was.

"How's Knox?" Chelsea asked.

"He's good. Said to tell everyone hello."

"How are things going with you two?" Piper asked. Piper wasn't around Haley as much over the last year as I was. She was busy with the Inn and life, but things were slowing down a little and she was trying to spend time with friends more.

Haley nodded. She was a little cautious about everyone. She moved to MacKellar Cove to be closer to her boyfriend without realizing her boyfriend was married. It was a disaster, but Haley found a good guy in Knox, and they were happy. But not everyone in town was thrilled when Haley and Knox got together.

"I'm really happy for you," Piper said. I knew she meant it, and judging by the way Haley's shoulders relaxed, she knew it, too.

"Chelsea was telling me she's thinking of buying a house," I said, changing the subject before Haley got too anxious. She didn't like being the center of attention.

"I am," Chelsea said, going with me on the shift. She wrinkled her nose. "I need to get out of my current apartment and my options are buying a house or moving in with my parents. I like with my parents, and I'm close to them, but I feel like I'm ready to buy my own place. Nothing huge, I don't think, but something where I can invite people over."

"You don't want to rent something else?" Piper asked.

Chelsea shook her head. "I want more control over my space. Plus, I want a dog and a yard and maybe a hot tub."

"I would love a hot tub," Piper said with a groan.

"I'm on my feet so much and would enjoy a place where I can come home and relax. Have friends over. Cook meals and watch TV as loud as I want and not have anyone bother me. I've never had that," Chelsea continued.

"Are you thinking neighborhood or someplace a little farther out with land?" Piper asked. She was an excellent investor and loved talking about money and the best way to spend it. She wasn't always that way, but she'd finally accepted it was a strength of hers and was willing to help when people asked her for advice.

Not that Chelsea was asking, but Chelsea didn't seem to mind.

"Definitely a neighborhood," Chelsea said. "I'd love kids, but I'm not sure that's going to happen. Either way, I want to live somewhere that feels safe. Where neighbors will hear me scream if something happens."

"We live in MacKellar Cove," Haley said. "What could possibly happen here?"

"You never know." Chelsea shivered with imaginary fear just as my phone rang.

"Crap," I muttered, seeing the number for the call center on my phone. "This is Sofia."

"Hey," said the smooth voice. "This is Daniel. I was wondering if I could get your help."

"Of course. What's the problem?"

"Oh, um, there's a light out in my bathroom?"

Was he asking me or telling me? "Which light?"

"Above the sink. It was flickering the other day, when I moved in. I didn't think anything of it, but now it's out."

"Usually something like that I will schedule. Can I come by tomorrow?"

"No!" he blurted. "Sorry. I just meant it would be really good to have it fixed tonight. You know, so I can see myself. In the shower. It's dark."

Was he drunk? What the hell was wrong with him?

It didn't matter. He was a tenant, and I was in charge of maintaining the property. I had to answer.

"Okay. I'll be there in a minute. I'm assuming you're home?"

"Yeah, I'm home. You can just come on in when you get here."

"No, I can't. I have to announce my presence. I will knock when I get to your door."

"Oh. Um, okay. I guess that's fine. See you soon."

"I'm on my way," I told him.

I hung up the phone and met the gazes of my friends.

"That was weird." I met Piper's gaze. "Daniel said there's a light out in the bathroom, but he sounded like he wasn't sure and wants me to look at it immediately."

"Does he think there's an electrical issue or something?" Piper asked.

I shrugged. "No clue. He was being weird."

"What were you guys saying about nothing happening in MacKellar Cove?" Chelsea asked.

Piper rolled her eyes. "He's harmless. Trust me. I think

he might have a crush on Sofia, but unless orgasms are now dangerous, she's fine."

I rolled my eyes. "He does not have a crush on me."

"How do you know? You're a catch," Haley said with a wink.

"Nope. I'm not interested. If he does have a crush, he's on his own. But he doesn't, so it's no big deal."

"But—" Piper started.

I held up my hand. "Nope. I gotta go. I'll be back as soon as I can be. Dip is in the oven. Might be done by now. Margaritas are on the counter. Save me some food. And a drink."

"Are you safe to work?" Piper asked.

I nodded. "I only had one sip. I'm good."

Piper held my gaze for another second, then nodded. I would never put myself in danger. She knows that.

I climbed the steps to Daniel's apartment. Music and the scent of roses drifted from under his door. I knocked loudly, making sure he heard me. I felt bad for making assumptions about him. He had a date over, and I was worried he was being weird. He probably just wanted to impress whoever was there.

The door opened quickly. Daniel stood there in a pair of tight jeans and a black button-down shirt, unbuttoned to show off his chest. Dark chest hair coated tanned skin and drew me in.

It had been a long time since I found myself attracted to a man. I could appreciate some of the men I knew were attractive, but they'd never done much for me. The first time I met Daniel, I was clouded by my embarrassment at missing his arrival, but this time...

I was clouded by something else.

"Hey," he said, his voice deep and husky and just right to

snap me out of my trance.

"Hi. Sorry it took me a minute to get up here. I can check out the light and get out of your way."

He stood back to let me in. "You're not in my way. Take as long as you need to take."

I glanced around, trying to find his date. No one was on the couch, but the bedroom door was slightly closed. His date must already be in there. And I was messing up their night.

"It won't take long. Then you can get back to your evening."

He followed me to the bathroom. I flipped the light switch and nothing happened. None of the lights came on.

Which was weird because it was working fine a few days ago.

I turned the switch off again and reached up to replace the bulbs. Usually they went out one by one and not all at once, especially when they were all brand new, but...

The first one was loose. Not enough to fall, but maybe enough to not come on. So was the second. And the third. I tightened all of them and flipped the switch again.

All three bulbs came on.

"Huh. I apologize for that. I must not have tightened the bulbs all the way when I installed them the other day. I didn't realize, and they were loose."

"Oh. Um. Okay. Well, that was easy. Do you want to stay for dinner?"

I took my time picking up my tool bag, trying to under-stand what was going on. "Um, I have plans tonight, actually."

"Oh, I didn't realize I was keeping you from a date."

"Not a date. Just time with my friends."

"So, you don't have a date. Are you dating anyone?"

"Excuse me?"

"I was just curious if you're dating anyone."

"That's none of your business."

"I wasn't trying to be weird. I just want to know."

"And you think that makes it less weird?"

"No, I just..." He drew a breath and let it out slowly. "I didn't want to overstep when we go out on a date."

"And what makes you think I'm going to go out on a date with you?"

He smirked. "Because I saw the way you looked at me."

I took a step back, making room for his ego. "Wow. Okay. Yes, you are attractive. And yeah, I found myself drawn to you. But that's done now. I'll see myself out. Have a good night."

"Wait!"

I stopped with my hand on the doorknob. I exhaled slowly, knowing I couldn't be a complete bitch to him when we were going to see each other over and over again. "Yes?"

"I'm sorry. I didn't mean to be an ass. I just... I'm going to be here three months, and I wanted to get to know you."

"I understand," I lied. I didn't understand a bit. He was an asshole who thought I would fall all over him because I'm not skinny. Men thought plus size women needed a little help, and at thirty-nine, it was even worse. It was like I had a neon sign over my head saying I was hopeless and helpless when it came to dating and I'd take any scraps offered.

Nope. Not even close. I was single because I chose to be single. Because I was happier being single that being one half of a relationship that was destined to fail.

"Do you?" he asked.

I looked up at him and saw something different in his gaze. A tiny bit of honesty that said there was something else going on. "Sure."

He shook his head. "You don't. But you're letting me off the hook. I'm sorry, Sofia. I'm really not a bad guy."

"I'm sure you're not. Have a good night, Daniel."

He nodded, a tiny wince at my obvious dismissal of him.

I couldn't worry about that. He was a stranger, and a tenant. I wasn't looking to get involved, especially with a man who was temporary.

I let myself back into my apartment. I set my bag down by the door, where I kept it in case I needed to run out to help a tenant. Chelsea, Haley, and Piper were in the kitchen, eating and drinking and talking.

"How was Daniel?" Piper asked.

"Weird. I think he might be into threesomes," I said.

Chelsea choked on her margarita. Haley gawked at me. Piper shook her head.

"Why in the world do you think that?" Piper asked.

I shrugged. "He invited me to stay for dinner."

"And that means he wanted a threesome? Don't you need three people for that?" Chelsea asked.

"The bedroom door was mostly closed. I think someone might have been in there."

"You're not into threesomes, I take it," Haley teased.

I shook my head. "Never tried it. Never had an interest, honestly. I haven't had a lot of sexual partners, and when I've been with someone, I like being able to focus on just one man. I know people make it work, the ones who enjoy it, but it's not for me."

"I don't share well," Piper said. "If Gavin suggested it, I'd be hurt."

"I think it's different when you're in a relationship with one person and want to bring another person into it," Chelsea said.

"True," Piper agreed. "And Daniel inviting you to dinner

doesn't mean he had someone else there. Maybe he just likes you."

I shook my head and picked up my margarita. "It doesn't matter. He said he knew I liked him and wanted to get to know me."

"Why is that a bad thing?" Haley asked.

"It was weird, in a creepy way. I don't know. It just made me feel uncomfortable."

"I'm sorry. Do you want me to throw him out?" Piper asked.

I shook my head. "It'll be fine. I'll just keep my distance from him."

"What if he needs you to fix something else?" Chelsea asked.

"I'll go with you," Haley said. "If he calls, I'll go with you. Make sure you're not alone with him."

I shook my head. "I can't do that. For one thing, you're not allowed into other apartments without the tenant's approval. For another, it's probably all my imagination. Maybe he was just being nice. I read too much into it."

The three of them looked at me closely, none of them believing the lie I was telling, but all of them knowing they wouldn't change my mind.

"All I know is this dip is amazing," Haley said. "You have to give me the recipe."

"Same," Chelsea said.

"We might need to add a Mexican night to the Inn," Piper said. "I think guests would go crazy over something like this. Hell, I'd put this in a taco, too."

"It's super easy, and delicious. I love it. It's my go-to, when I don't go to Just Tacos," I said.

"I love Just Tacos," Chelsea said.

"Me, too," Haley said. "Knox took me there the other

night. I tried their tostadas. Have you ever had those?"

And just that quickly, my concerns about Daniel were forgotten. We talked about food and enjoyed our dinner and drinks, then moved to the living room. We put on a movie that none of us watched as we continued talking until we started falling asleep on the couches. Haley and Chelsea wandered upstairs to her place, and Piper asked if she could crash in her old room.

"When does your dad arrive?" she asked as she fluffed the pillow.

"A week from Sunday."

"That's soon. Are you ready?"

I snorted. "Not even close. But we'll see if he actually shows up."

"Maybe you should start accepting some of those matches on Book Boyfriends Wanted. Give yourself excuses for not being here when he's visiting."

I laughed. "I just might do that." I thought for a minute. "It's bad that, for me, dating random men is better than spending time with my dad."

Piper chuckled. "True. But maybe you'll meet someone great and it'll be a good thing. And maybe your visit with your dad will be good."

"Or maybe he won't show up, and I can just continue on how I always have."

"Or that," Piper said. "I'm sorry I made things worse by adding Daniel as a tenant."

I shook my head and hugged my best friend in the world. "Nothing for you to be sorry about. It'll all be okay. I know it."

"I hope so."

I smiled and said good night, then went to my room. It had to be okay. There was no other option.

4

———

When did men get so disgusting? Ugh. I had clearly been out of the dating game for too long. Or maybe I was just too old. I never felt like that was the case, but at thirty-nine, I had less patience for bullshit than I did a decade or two ago.

I decided to dive into Book Boyfriends Wanted again. I joined forever ago, but I hadn't had much luck, so most of the time I forgot about it. But with my dad's visit getting closer every day, and only two more days before he arrived, I decided it was time to bite the bullet and take Piper's advice.

Holy shit, did I regret that decision.

Two men introduced themselves by describing their dicks. In detail. Then telling me what they wanted to do to me. Ew. I mean, if we were in a relationship and they were telling me that, then hot, but they were strangers.

Shit. I hoped they were strangers. If they weren't, I was never going to be able to look at them again. I really hoped I never found out.

Those men were why I hadn't dated in years. Nate Catalan was why I didn't date much at all, but when I was willing to try, it was the creeps that sent me back to my job and my friends and my quiet life.

I flipped through a few more replies and told myself not all men were disgusting jerks, even though I had very little proof of that. Thankfully, there was a new one who sounded less like an asshole and more like someone I might be able to talk to.

And his name intrigued me.

GIOIOSO

Hi, TalkNerdyToMe. Where do books hide when they're afraid?

Okay, so maybe my screen name invited the weirdos who thought it was meant to be a pun, but it wasn't. I thought it was funny when I came up with it.

Apparently Gioioso got it.

The message was from two days ago, which wasn't too bad for me. I usually forgot all about Book Boyfriends Wanted and the guys who reached out on it.

TALKNERDYTOME

Under the covers?

I chuckled as I typed. I loved that joke. Really, I loved any corny joke, and I loved reading, so combining the two together had me laughing every time.

I went to close the app and saw three bubbles, like he was messaging me back. I debated closing the app really quickly, avoiding getting caught in a conversation with a stranger, but I was curious about what he was going to say.

G

Yep. I do the same thing! LOL

TNTM

Please tell me you're old enough to be on here.

G

I am. I'm probably too old, but sometimes it's nice to get to know someone new.
And you?

TNTM

Don't you know you're not supposed to ask a woman how old she is?

G

Well, I figured since you asked first, it was fair game. And in my defense, I didn't ask for a number.

TNTM

True. I guess I'll let it slide. And yeah, I could have two profiles on here and be legal.

G

LOL. Yep. I'm in my ahem, later, thirties. I had a nineteen-year-old woman message me and I felt like a dirty old man.

TNTM

If it makes you feel better, there are a lot of dirty old men on here who are probably half your age.

G

I'm not sure that makes me feel better!

I laughed out loud. He was funny. And a little charming. Which equated to dangerous.

TNTM

I think the older I get, the less tolerance I have for a lot of things that seemed like no big deal a few years ago.

G

Same. In so many ways.

TNTM

I have to ask about your name. Do you know what it means?

G

I'm guessing you mean my screen name and not my real name. Unless you're a wizard and know my real name.

TNTM

I plead the fifth on being a wizard, but no, I meant your screen name.

G

You might be a valuable person to know! As for my screen name, it means to perform with joy. My piano teacher used to give me that order constantly when I was learning to play.

TNTM

So did mine. Although my teacher was my mom.

G

I think the only thing worse than my piano teacher would have been living with her. How did you handle that?

TNTM

My mom was my best friend. She taught me on her keyboard. We couldn't afford real lessons, so she taught me herself.

G

That's pretty cool. And I'm sorry.

TNTM

Sorry?

G

You said 'was' so I just assumed. Forgive
me if I'm wrong and she's still a part of your
life.

TNTM

She'll always be a part of me, but she
passed years ago. And thank you.

G

It can't be easy.

TNTM

Are your parents still a part of your life?

G

Diving deep! Okay. Yes, they're still alive,
but we're not close. Haven't been in a long
time, if I'm being honest.

TNTM

Sorry. I didn't mean to get too personal.

G

I don't mind. It's part of it, right? Getting to
know each other. Without actually knowing
each other.

TNTM

True. I always wonder if the people I'm
matched with are people I know.

G

That would be weird. I guess that means I
shouldn't tell you who I am until I know if I'm
willing to overlook that we might know each
other.

TNTM

Well, now I really want to know.

G

LOL. Same. But I'm not going to ask. The mystery is a little fun.

TNTM

True. So, what do you like to do in your free time?

G

I work a lot, so I don't have a ton of free time. At least, it never feels like it. Do you have any tattoos?

TNTM

Whoa. That's pretty personal.

G

Only if the answer is yes and you don't want to tell me what it is.

He wasn't wrong. I had one tattoo. The one I got after Nate. To remind myself of exactly who I was.

TNTM

I have one. It's a treble clef and birds.

G

Really? You're into music? Obviously, since you played and knew what my name meant, but that's more than I learned piano as a kid.

TNTM

Music was always very important to me. It's not something I am very involved with these days, but once upon a time, it was.

G

Once upon a time makes it sound like there's a story there.

TNTM

Not one with a happy ending.

G

I'm sorry for that, too.

TNTM

Thank you.

G

My first tattoo was a dare. A friend told me I
was too polished and perfect and that I
would never be the kind of person who got
tattoos.

TNTM

And you showed him?

G

LOL. I sure did. I have twenty now.

TNTM

Wow. That's... a lot.

G

Yeah. But I love it. Each one is an
expression of a piece of me. Something
significant that either happened to me or
meant something.

TNTM

I'm not sure I could put that much of myself
on display.

G

A lot of them aren't visible on a normal day.
Some have only been seen by my artist.

TNTM

That's interesting. A lot of people want to
show them off. Especially when they have
that many.

G

I'm not like a lot of people.

TNTM

Well, that's really good to know.

G

Life's more interesting when you stand in
your own light.

TNTM

That's a good way of looking at things.

The screen went dark, then flashed with an incoming call. It scared me, and I almost dropped my phone. Especially when I saw it was my dad calling.

"Hi, Dad," I said, answering the phone.

"Sofia! Good, you're home."

He always assumed I was home if I answered the phone. "I am, yes."

"Can you come let me in?"

"What? I thought you were going to be here Sunday?"

"I decided to come a little early. I wanted to see you."

I looked around my apartment. I was not ready. Sure, my apartment was clean. It was picked up. I had sheets I could throw on the bed and plenty of food in the kitchen. But I wasn't ready.

"Are you there?" Dad asked, his voice loud like he'd spoken a few times and I'd missed it.

"Yeah. Sorry, Dad. I just... was surprised. I'll be right there."

"Good." He hung up.

I stared at my phone as it returned to the app. A new message was there from Gioioso.

G

We should all be allowed to celebrate what
makes us unique.

I sighed. He sounded like a man who'd never had to face the ugly realities of life. I love the sentiment, but it wasn't always reality.

Like at the moment. My dad was the life of the party. He was outgoing and talkative. He never saw anyone as bad, even when they showed him they were. He only wanted to have fun.

His introverted daughter was a struggle. When I had to join him on tour, he didn't know what to do with me. When I got mad because he didn't kick Nate off the tour, he didn't know what to do with me. He never knew what to do with me.

Which was why we weren't close.

But he was outside. Waiting for me to let him in.

Shit.

TNTM

Sorry, but I need to go. Something came up. Nice talking to you.

I closed the app before he could reply and make me want to ignore my dad and talk to the funny, friendly man I didn't know instead of the one I did know.

I propped my door open and went to the front. I pushed the security door open, letting my dad in with a huff like he was put out for having to stand outside for a few minutes after showing up two days early.

"I couldn't do that all the time. If there's a locked door, there should be a person there to let you inside instead of leaving you out in the elements."

It was seventy-eight and sunny. Not a cloud in the sky.

"Uh huh," I said instead of replying.

"Do you have someone who can get my stuff?"

"I'll get it. Where's your car?"

"Don't you have a person?"

I sighed. He knew I didn't have a person. I was the person. We already went over this. "No, I don't. I can get your stuff if you'll tell me what you drive."

He waved his hand and led the way to a sleek black sedan parked at the curb. The car beeped as he approached, then the trunk lifted on its own. A matching set of luggage was stacked in the trunk. "There's more in the backseat, too."

I swallowed my groan. The man did not pack light.

I lifted the suitcases out of the trunk. God forbid he risked damaging his hands. That was how he made his money. He told me that more times than I could count, and I could count pretty damn high.

When I had everything on the sidewalk, I looked over at him. He had one bag thrown over his shoulder, a briefcase in his hand, and three bags next to the car.

"Can you get some of these?" I asked, grabbing the handles of two of the suitcases.

"I'll wait for you to take those in and come back. I don't want to risk someone walking away with anything." He glanced up and down the vacant street like criminals were waiting for him to look away before they rushed his precious cargo.

I nodded, ignoring the dig on the place I chose to live, and wheeled the first two suitcases inside. I rolled my eyes at the logo on the suitcases and resisted the urge to drag one of them against the wall or let the door close on it.

With the first two in the room he would be staying in, I went back out to the car. He watched a young couple approaching like they were a threat.

I lifted my hand and waved to them. They smiled and waved back, casting a side-eye at my dad.

"You ready to go inside?" I asked him, drawing his attention from the dangerous threat of locals.

"Yeah." He grabbed the handle of one suitcase, leaving me with two more suitcases and a duffle bag. "I don't know how you live here."

I swallowed my retort and led the way to the door. He locked the expensive car, making sure it beeped more than once, then followed me inside the building.

I'd left my apartment door open, and as soon as he saw it, he gasped.

"Someone's in there. We need to call the police. Are there police here?"

"No one's in there. I left it open."

"Why would you do that? Someone could walk right in."

"Things like that don't happen here. It's a secure building, and everyone knows everyone. It's safe."

He cast a skeptical look my way, hanging back while I walked into my apartment. When I didn't cry out in pain from an attack, he followed me.

"Is this the room you have for me?" he asked when he made it to the bedroom I was putting his stuff in.

I nodded. "Yep. It's private. You have your own bathroom. The curtains are blackout so you can sleep whenever you want."

"It's... tiny."

Deep breaths. "Yes, it's small. But it's all I have. You're welcome to stay at the local inn—"

"An Inn?"

"If they have space. The closest hotel with a suite and the accommodations you're used to is two hours from here."

He looked around the room with a pinched expression.

It took everything in me to not apologize. I was a people pleaser. I liked to be liked. And he was my father. Of all the people in the world for me to want the approval of, he was it. He was the one I craved it from.

I hated that I did, but I did. I always had. From the moment I found out he was my father, I wanted him to like me. To be proud of me and think I was a good person.

Not that his standards and mine were the same. I learned that in a hurry. But there was something about wanting your parent to approve of your life choices. I didn't know anyone who didn't feel the same.

"It's not forever. I will deal with it," he finally said.

I released my suspended breath and forced a smile. "Great. I'll leave you to get settled. The dressers and closet are empty. The bathroom has a few things under the sink for when I have guests, but it should be enough space for what you need." I glanced at his luggage and knew my entire apartment wouldn't fit all of his stuff. Not even close.

"I have someone coming to do that for me."

"You what?"

He shrugged. "I hired a personal assistant for when I'm here. Someone who will get my things settled in and make sure I have someplace to eat the kind of food I like."

"Are you kidding me?"

"Why would I joke about that?"

I sighed. He had no idea how the rest of the world worked. "Okay. Well, then, is there anything you want to do?"

"Here?"

Why did I agree to let him stay with me? To let him visit? I didn't know what I was thinking. Five damn minutes and I was ready to choke him.

And I couldn't even say I was surprised by it. He was always a pompous ass who thought the entire world revolved around him.

"If there's somewhere else you'd like to go, you are welcome to do that as well."

"You're not coming with me?"

"Dad, I didn't know you were coming today. You told me Sunday. It's Friday afternoon. I still have work to do today. I have an apartment I need to check in on and some building maintenance to do."

"Oh. You're busy. I didn't realize I was going to be an inconvenience."

I let out a slow breath. I'd forgotten how good he was at taking me on a guilt trip. It was either that or a tour. We never went on any vacations or did anything fun. Just tours and guilt trips.

"I need to get my work done. We can grab something to eat later tonight and you can tell me what's going on. Does that work for you?"

He nodded. "It's going to have to."

"Yes, it is. Good to see you, Dad. I'll be back in a few hours."

"Have fun. I'll just be sitting here."

I was not going to fall for it. I was not going to blow off my day and change my plans just because he changed his without telling me. I would feel sick all day because of it, but he needed to learn to respect me one day.

Even if it killed me to force it.

5

TREY

I TOSSED MY PEN ON THE NOTEBOOK AND FLOPPED BACK ON the couch. Fuck. When I started out, writing was easy. The words came out like they were divine inspiration. Like they would always be there.

Over the years it got harder, but I always found the words eventually. Then one day it was all gone. The words stopped magically appearing anytime I picked up a pen. The last writing session... It couldn't be like that again. Not if I wanted a new contract. Not if I wanted to keep singing my own songs and not have to go to the market to find songs.

I prided myself on never having to do that. Collaboration? Sure. Bring it on. But buying a song from someone else? Their emotions and words?

I'd rather not record. Which was what was going to happen if I didn't get my shit together.

More than a week had passed, and all I'd managed to do was make Sofia think I was a creep. I promised Piper that wasn't the case when she called the morning after I called Sofia for a bogus maintenance call. I felt like such a dick that I'd been avoiding Sofia. But I had to get to know her. My career depended on it.

A sound outside my apartment drew my attention. Maybe it was Sofia. Maybe I could have a chance to talk to her again.

I opened my door and found an older woman struggling with her keys and two paper bags of groceries. One bag tipped sideways, nearly spilling on the ground before she dropped her weight and caught it.

"Well, shoot," she whispered.

"Can I help you?" I asked.

She looked up at me with distrust in her dark brown eyes. "Why? So you can force your way into my apartment?"

I nearly laughed. She was half my size but twice as feisty if the cocked hip and jutted jaw were anything to go on. She reminded me of my mom's best friend from my childhood. Ms. Emily was as quick with her wit as she was with a wooden spoon. She'd make a joke one second and whack me on the backside the next, then go right back to what she was doing as though nothing happened.

"Not at all," I said, backing toward my apartment. "I was just trying to be friendly."

The woman narrowed her eyes at me. "You're the new guy? The one who's here for the summer?"

I nodded, pausing my retreat. "I am. T—Trying to get some R-and-R and decide my next steps. I'm Daniel."

"You a drug dealer, Daniel?"

I coughed a laugh, but she was not joking. "Uh, no, ma'am. I don't do drugs and don't sell them."

"How can you afford to pay rent for the whole summer without a job?"

"I have a job. Had a job. I saved money."

She raised one dark brow. Her brown skin was wrinkled

around her eyes and drooped below her chin. She wore a long dress that fell below her knees and sneakers that were not made for fashion. She had a black purse slung across her body, partially hidden by the grocery bags she still held in a tight grip. "But you're not a drug dealer?"

I shook my head and pressed my lips together. "No. I am not."

"Are you trying to get into my apartment?"

"Only to help you carry your groceries."

She narrowed her eyes at me once more, then nodded and shoved the bags at me.

I barely caught them before she was turning to her door and unlocking it. She led the way inside, not acknowledging me until she made it to the kitchen and slid some mail aside for me to set the bags down.

I stepped back and looked around her apartment. It was a mirror image of mine. Her furniture wasn't as nice as the stuff in my apartment, which made me think not everyone rented furnished apartments.

"I hope you don't expect a tip. These apartments are affordable, but I live here because I know Piper takes care of the place."

I nodded. "I'd never expect a tip. I haven't been in any other apartments besides my own. Just taking in the flip. It's a nice building."

"Usually it is. Sofia makes sure everything is handled. You met Sofia yet?"

I nodded. "When I moved in."

"You better be good to her."

"I wouldn't dream of anything else."

"Good. Now, you need to go. I have groceries to unpack and I didn't buy enough to feed you."

I chuckled and nodded, heading toward the door. "It was

nice to meet you. Feel free to knock on my door if you need anything."

"What do you think I'm going to need?"

I shook my head. "I guess nothing. I'll see you around."

She nodded once to me, then went back to unloading her groceries while I let myself out.

I went back to my apartment and ignored the notebook taunting me on the table. I had to get the hell out of there. Do something different. Maybe meet a woman. Hell, the one I was talking to on that app was interesting, but there was only so much I could handle without real live human contact.

As the thought crossed my mind, I knew I wouldn't do it. Where was the line? When I went from hot rockstar to creepy old man? Had I already crossed it?

I was definitely feeling like I'd crossed it. When teenagers threw their panties on stage and promised they could do things I'd never seen before, and I did the math and realized they could be my daughters, creepy was the dominating feeling.

TalkNerdyToMe hadn't replied to my last message, so I grabbed my keys and headed out.

The water was beautiful. I walked toward it, letting it draw me in. Gavin said one of the guys made boats. Ian, maybe? I didn't go to their guys' night again after making Sofia uncomfortable, but maybe I could go into O'Kelley's and find out where Ian's shop was.

I found myself in the town square, watching the water and caught unaware until I was in the middle of a crowd. Food trucks lined the streets, and a band warmed up under the gazebo at the top of the hill.

"Daniel!" someone shouted from a few feet away.

Ian. The guy I was just thinking about. He was with a

pretty brunette, the server from the breakfast place I went to the other day, if I remembered correctly. He was holding a squirming toddler.

I approached them, reaching out to shake his hand when I got closer. "Ian, right?"

"Good memory. This is my wife, Blake, and our terror, Maddox."

I laughed at his obvious joke. "He's adorable. Do you work at Cracked?"

Blake nodded. "I do. I didn't want to introduce myself the other day because I figured that would be weird."

"You knew who I was?"

"Small town. Everyone knows everything," Ian answered for her.

Blake nodded.

I panicked. Did that mean they knew why I was there? Or that they knew who I was?

"We get a lot of people here for the summer, but they come and go. When Ian said you came to guys' night last week, I was looking for you. Even though you're not here forever, you didn't have the same rushed look of the tourists," Blake explained.

"Tourists look rushed?" I asked, trying to play off my panic.

Blake chuckled and nodded. "Oh, yeah. Trying to catch a ferry or get to a tour or see something before it closes for the day. We have a pretty laidback kind of attitude around here, but the people who are here for a week act like they have to see it all right now."

"Life moves fast," I said.

Maddox gurgled something, drawing the attention of Blake and Ian.

"It definitely does. We're going to grab some food. Are you here for the band?" Ian asked.

"I was just getting a break from sitting around my apartment all day. I was actually going to see if I could find out where your shop was. I was wondering if you rent boats or anything," I told him.

"No, I don't do rentals. But I have a few you can borrow," Ian said. He bounced with the baby to calm the fussiness brewing.

"I couldn't do that. I'd have to pay you."

"Why? If it's just sitting there, it's good for someone to take them out on the water. You're welcome to whatever I have. I'm down Ontario Street. Can't miss it. Come by Monday."

I nodded as they walked away, talking to the baby and trading him between them to keep him entertained. Ian laughed at something Blake said, and that pang hit me square in the chest again.

That's not what I want.

I turned away from the happy family and continued on my way.

People waved as I walked past them, heading toward the activity I'd just walked away from. Families and couples all flocked toward the center of town.

It was like something out of a movie. I'd never lived in a small town, and being there made me feel trapped. Especially after Blake said she knew who I was.

That left me wondering why no one had outed me yet. If they all recognized me, was this small town so lost on the planet they'd never heard of *Broken Record*?

The first beats of our first hit filled the air as the thought drifted through my mind. The kids on stage. They were playing our song. My song. The one I wrote when I was barely old enough to know what it meant to want to be a rockstar. The song I scribbled on the back of a napkin one night. When writing songs used to be easy.

I stopped and sat on a bench in the middle of the sidewalk. I closed my eyes and let the familiar music fill me.

I couldn't remember the last time I enjoyed music. When it wasn't a job. When I could feel it inside me like a physical piece. Like it was an organ that only some people had. Like a musical appendix that a person could live without, but that some people got to keep forever.

It felt like mine had been cut out. Like I was missing that part of me, a part that once felt like the biggest part of me.

But listening to those kids play my song, sing it with their entire souls and belt out the lyrics that once upon a time flowed from my subconscious like they weren't meant for me to contain any longer, I knew I hadn't completely lost that part of me. It was still there. My music organ was fiddling with its instruments. Trying to find its way back to the surface.

The song ended, and the kids rolled into another cover by another band. I opened my eyes and centered myself. I wasn't on stage. I hadn't been the one singing. I was just a guy on a bench.

I kept walking away from the concert, finding my way through the small town streets to where Ian said his shop was. It was a huge metal building right on the water, and yeah, there was no way to miss it.

I turned back toward the center of town, knowing I had to pass through the activity in order to get back to my apartment. I wasn't really excited about that, but it was necessary.

I ended up a block away from the water and kept walking, figuring there was no way to get lost in a town the size of most of the venues we played in. I made it back to my building without running into too much traffic and found myself back on my couch with the pen in my hand.

I closed my eyes and tried to tune back in to the feeling I had listening to my song being played, but everything was once again quiet inside. The moment was gone. Opportunity passed.

Shit.

Sunday afternoon, I went out to grab something to eat. I wasn't used to cooking my meals, but I was going to work on it. Eventually. Until I learned how to not burn water, I was going to try the restaurants in town.

I was almost through them all.

So far, Just Tacos was my favorite, but Will Work For Burgers was a close second. Cracked was excellent for breakfast, but I wasn't a breakfast anytime kind of person and usually grabbed a premade smoothie for breakfast. When I was up before noon.

I'd just picked up some Italian from Gino's and was on my way back inside when the door was yanked from my grip and I was knocked on my ass.

The container of food popped open, spilling my food for the next two days all over the sidewalk and me.

"Oh, my God. I am so sorry. I wasn't paying attention to where I was going. I didn't see you. I didn't... Let me replace your food and pay for your dry cleaning. Or whatever I can do. I really am so sorry."

I looked up at Sofia, the words rushing out of her so fast they were tripping over each other. Her eyes were red, and her cheeks were streaked with tears. Her hands twisted in front of her, even as she reached to help me off the concrete.

"Are you okay?" I asked. I'd learned long ago a woman in tears was a dangerous thing. Ignore it and it could mean disaster. Bring attention to it and it could mean disaster.

Sofia pulled me to my feet and nodded. "I... I should have been paying attention to where I was going."

"Are you safe? You were in a pretty big hurry to get out of the building. Is someone after you?"

She laughed mirthlessly. "Not unless you count a father who's trying to make up for a lifetime of absence all in one summer."

My brows shot up. "Your father's here? I didn't realize."

She looked at me like I was insane. Probably because I sounded like it.

"I just meant I didn't know you lived with him."

"I don't. Not usually. He came to visit. He was supposed to get here today, but he showed up Friday, and nothing I do is good enough for him. It never was, so that's not really a surprise, but I haven't had to deal with that in twenty years." She let out a full breath, then sucked another one back in and let it out.

"Parents can be a challenge. Mine never had much time for me growing up. Treated me more like a burden than a blessing like people say kids are."

"I'm sorry."

I shrugged. "I guess I'm used to it."

"It still sucks, though."

I nodded, knowing she needed a response.

"Anyway, I'm really sorry for running into you. It looks like you were picking up dinner for a date, too. I ruined your whole night."

I looked at the carnage of pasta and sauce on the ground and chuckled. "No date. Just stocking up for a few days. I don't really cook, so I've been trying all the takeout places in town."

"Gino's is so good. I can call them and have them remake your food right now." She was already pulling out her phone.

"You don't have to do that."

"It was my fault."

"It sounds to me it was your dad's fault."

She snorted. "The number of therapists who'd have a field day with that statement."

I laughed with her. She was beautiful when she laughed. And when she cried. And when she was determined.

Fuck, she was just beautiful.

Full, pouty lips and a thick figure. I wish I'd known she was the one who plowed me over. I'd have taken a minute to enjoy the feel of her body against mine.

Instead, I was left wishing I'd get another chance to lean into her curves.

"Hey, hun, this is Sofia. You guys just made up some food for Daniel?"

She paused her side of the conversation and smiled at me. I was so lost in my thoughts I hadn't realized she'd placed a call.

"Yeah, I ruined it all for him. It's on the sidewalk. Can you remake it? Put it on my tab. One of us will be there in twenty minutes."

She raised her brows at me. I nodded, although I wasn't sure what I was agreeing to.

"Thanks." She paused again. "Hey, can you add an order of ravioli in a separate bag for me? Actually, never mind. I think I'm going to eat there. If you have a table for one." She laughed at something. "Thanks. I'll be there soon."

She hung up the phone and stuck it back in her pocket.

"I'll bring your food back whenever you're ready. That way you don't have to go out again."

"Or I could just join you for dinner," I suggested.

I held my breath while she considered her options. When she nodded, I felt like I'd won something.

"Can you give me five minutes to change?"

She smiled. "Of course. I'll wait here."

"You're not going to ditch me?"

She chuckled. "The thought might have crossed my mind, but you know where I live and you know where I'm going, so I'm thinking that would be a waste."

"But you don't really want to go to dinner with me."

She looked up at me. Her blue eyes were bluer than I'd realized before. They had a hint of sadness, maybe loneliness, in them. Something that told me she had secrets. Lots of them.

Ones I wanted to learn more about.

And not just because I wanted to get to her father. There was something about Sofia I was finding hard to resist.

"I don't date a lot. And I know this isn't a date, but—"

"Why isn't it a date?"

She snorted again. "I don't know why you're here, Daniel, but I know it's not because you're thinking about relocating to MacKellar Cove. As for me? I'm not leaving. I've been all over, and I like it here. I like the quiet. I like being able to think. I like a simple life. But I'm willing to be friends."

I smiled at her, letting my smile do what it did.

She sighed heavily, like she was having trouble resisting the charm I was laying on thick.

"We can start with friends," I said, letting my tone drop, letting her hear my desire, letting her know I wasn't interested in being just friends.

And when she shivered, I knew I had her.

But for the first time, it didn't give me a rush to know I'd changed the mind of a woman. It didn't make me feel powerful. It made me feel like an asshole. Because I wasn't being honest with her.

And Sofia... Something told me she wasn't going to be okay with that.

But like she said, relocation wasn't in the plans for me. Three months. That was it. Then I would be gone, and hopefully, I'd be taking a few new hit songs with me.

6

———

SOFIA

WHAT WAS I THINKING? THE DOOR CLOSED BEHIND HIM, AND I stood there, staring at it and wondering what in the world was wrong with me. A hot guy bats his eyelashes at me, and I'm done. I fold without a second thought.

Shit.

I didn't know what it was about him that had me acting like such a fool. It wasn't like he was the first good-looking guy who'd ever paid me any attention. Not that it happened all that often, but once in a while it did. I never fell for it before. So what was it about Daniel?

I shook my head and decided it didn't matter. If nothing else, I owed him dinner. After the stupid argument with my dad, it was nice to get away for a few hours. That was why I went flying out the door in the first place. I needed a break.

Deep breaths. In. Out.

My dad's open-ended plans might kill me. I liked structure and routine. I liked knowing what was going to happen. And I liked my life how I liked it.

Living with my dad was miles different from living with Piper. Or any of my previous roommates. My dad was inconsiderate and messy. And he'd only been there a few days! My apartment was already overflowing with his stuff. I didn't even realize he had so much stuff. And I carried it all inside.

Ugh. I needed to find a way to talk to him. I still hadn't figured out why he was there, so I was tiptoeing around him, trying not to start a fight. He was like a petulant child when he was called out, so I let things go. All the time. And he pushed. Because he knew he could.

The front door opened quickly, startling me out of my thoughts. Daniel looked around like he actually did expect me to leave him there. When his gaze landed on me, a smile lit his eyes and lifted his lips and made me feel like I wasn't just a pity date or making shit up.

He was happy I was still there. I couldn't remember the last time a man was happy to see me.

"Thanks for waiting," he said, like I did him a favor.

"It was the least I could do since I'm the reason you aren't inside enjoying your food right now."

He grinned wider, then turned toward Gino's. I fell into step beside him, the silence between us not entirely comfortable, but not uncomfortable either.

"So, your dad's a pain in the ass, huh?" he asked after a few minutes.

I chuckled, finding myself unable to hold back when a stranger was passing judgement on my relationship. "We've never been close. I don't know what to say to him most of the time, and he's never understood me."

"But he's here for a few days to change that?"

I shrugged. "I don't think it's only a few days. He brought enough luggage to last a few months. Although he's not a light packer, so it could just be a week."

"Some people are like that. My buddy, Seth, he's horrible. Always packs more shit than he needs, then gets pissed when he can't fit it all back in his suitcase after a trip."

I laughed. "I always end up packing too light. I've had to buy things on vacation that I could have brought from home but told myself I didn't need."

"Underwear, right? You ran out of underwear?"

I snorted and nodded. "Yep. Twice. Now, it's the only thing I over pack. I'd rather bring clean underwear home than have to buy new."

"Absolutely." Daniel stopped in front of the restaurant and opened the door for me. He smiled as I walked ahead of him.

I may have added a little sway to my hips as I walked past him. Maybe.

"Hey, Sofia!" Lucy was the owner and usually worked as hostess for the restaurant. Her husband, John, was the chef. Their kids, Amy and Tina, helped run the place. It was a true family restaurant, and they made everyone in town feel like they were part of the extended family.

"Hey, Lucy." I gave the older woman a hug, inhaling the scent of tomato sauce that always seemed to cling to her.

"Your to-go order is ready, and we have your food at a table for you, so you didn't have to wait." Lucy looked past me to where Daniel hadn't spoken. "But we can plate up one of those to-go orders so the two of you can enjoy your meal together."

"Thank you," Daniel said, stepping closer. His hand rested on my back, possessive like he and I were together. Like he had a right to touch me.

I didn't hate it.

Lucy smirked at me, her eyes wide and her smile even wider. I shook my head, but it was useless. Lucy had already decided we were together.

She led us to a table where a steaming plate of ravioli was waiting, with a glass of red wine and a water. The to-go bag wasn't there, but I knew it would be back shortly, with one less meal in it.

"Here you are," Lucy said, waving her hand at the table. "I hope this is okay for you two tonight."

"It's fine, Lucy. Really."

"Perfect," Daniel said. "Thank you so much. Sofia says the food here is amazing. Is that thanks to you?"

Lucy blushed, and holy shit, I realized I wasn't the only woman falling under his spell. What was it about Daniel that had women feeling like they were special?

"No, not me," Lucy said. "My husband is the master in the kitchen. And the bedroom, if I'm being honest." Lucy clapped her hand over her mouth, eyes wide like she couldn't believe she said that.

"Two most important rooms," Daniel said without missing a beat.

"That's what he says!" Lucy laughed, her embarrassment forgotten.

"Smart man."

"And talented."

Daniel chuckled with her, his eyes twinkling with mischief. "Good for you."

Lucy laughed again. "Yes, it really is."

"Here's your dinner," Tina said, saving us from more stories about Lucy and John. "And the rest of the to-go order is in the back where we can keep it warm."

"Thank you, Tina. How are you?" I asked her with a nod to her pregnant belly.

Tina rubbed a hand over the bump and smiled. "Really good. Still two months to go, but I'm feeling good. Thanks, Sofia. You two enjoy." Tina guided her mother away, as though she knew there was a reason to get Lucy away from Daniel.

"Do you come here often?" Daniel asked.

I lifted one brow at him. "Is that a line?"

He barked a laugh and shook his head. "I didn't mean it to be. They both knew you."

I nodded. "Partly small town, and partly great food. I'm a big fan of Italian food, and theirs is exceptional."

"Then I'm really looking forward to this." He lifted a bite of his dinner, shrimp scampi, and held it up like a glass of wine for a toast.

I chuckled and speared a ravioli, tapping my fork to his. Our gazes locked as we both ate our food, the air sizzling between us.

His eyes slid closed, and he groaned. He lowered his fork, it clanging on the side of the plate. "Oh, my God, this is good. How did I wait so long to come here?"

"Well, I would have told you to come here first."

"I wish you had instead of just running out of my place that first night."

My cheeks warmed with the memory. "You were acting weird. It made me uncomfortable."

He sat up straight. "It did? I didn't realize." He tilted his head. "What did I do?"

I shook my head. "It doesn't matter now. I was wrong, and I'm glad we were able to come here tonight."

He held my gaze another minute, then nodded and let the question go.

We ate our food quickly, neither waiting for it to cool much before we were devouring dinner.

"Did you grow up here?" Daniel asked as he scraped the last bite from his plate.

"No. I sort of grew up all over."

"Military?" he asked, looking up at me. His gaze strayed to the plate.

"Are you going to lick your plate?"

One side of his mouth quirked up. "I was trying to figure out how I could without grossing you out. Maybe you should turn away."

"You want me to leave you alone with your dinner plate?"

He looked at me, then back down to the plate, then nodded solemnly. "Yeah, I think I do."

I laughed, shaking my head and trying to remember the last time I enjoyed dinner with a virtual stranger as much. He made me laugh, and he didn't just talk about himself. He asked questions about me. And seemed like he cared what the answers were.

He set his plate down on the table again and smiled at me. "Your laugh is like sunrise after a night of binge drinking."

I started to say thank you until the rest of his sentence sank in. "Binge drinking?" I laughed. "Is that a compliment?"

He ducked his chin and shrugged, like he was embarrassed. "I just meant refreshing."

I nodded, thinking it was poetic in a dark and twisted kind of way. "Then thank you."

"It wasn't very good. Sorry."

I smiled. "It was unique."

His smile was forced and strained. "We should probably head back."

He raised his hand for the check, but I shook my head. "Are you telling me you don't want dessert?"

"They have dessert?" His tone was excited and eager.

I grinned. "Best in town. Cannolis and tiramisu and cakes that'll give you a sugar rush for days."

"I'm not sure which is more dangerous, you or this place."

"Me?" I wasn't used to being offended and complimented in one sentence.

"You're introducing me to all the delights Gino's has to offer. I just ordered shrimp scampi pasta and lasagna. You teased me with ravioli all night and are now tempting me with dessert."

"It's only a temptation if you don't enjoy it. Then it's a pleasure."

"I'll show you pleasure."

My body flushed hot as my mouth fell open.

"Shit, I'm so sorry. I didn't mean to say that."

Daniel Ryan was a mystery. I couldn't help but chuckle at his inappropriate comments and strange compliments. There was something about him that made me curious what would come out of his mouth next.

"Maybe we should start with dessert and go from there."

He opened his mouth to say something. He closed it again and a smirk slowly spread over his lips. The kind of look that said he knew exactly what I was saying, and exactly what I was thinking, and he was in complete agreement with it.

"Dessert tonight?" Tina asked, refilling out waters and propping the pitcher on her belly.

"She talked me into it," Daniel said. "What do you recommend because I kind of want one of each?"

"We do have a sampler dessert menu," Tina said. "It comes with one cannoli, a small slice of chocolate mousse cake, a half size piece of tiramisu, and a small slice of lemon cake."

"Done," Daniel said. He looked over at me. "What are you going to have?"

I laughed, shaking my head. "I think I'll have the same."

Tina tapped her screen to put both orders in, then walked away.

"I have a feeling I'm going to be here every week."

"If I could afford it, I would be, too."

"I have more money than skills, so I have to rely on others to cook for me."

"I can cook for you sometime," I offered before my brain had a chance to stop the words from exiting. "I mean, if you ever want to not go out to eat."

He stared at me for so long I thought he was going to laugh and walk away. I wasn't used to putting myself out there with men. I was the quiet one. The woman no one noticed. The one who worked on your apartment, then left. I wasn't the bombshell every man in the place wanted to have dinner with. I was the best friend, at best.

But the way Daniel looked at me... I couldn't explain it. I couldn't figure it out. There was something in his eyes. Something that said he wasn't just being friendly because I'd be the one answering his calls if he had any issues. He wanted to talk to me.

It was exciting and unnerving and amazing.

"Maybe you should come to my place and cook so you get an escape from your dad."

"Your place was supposed to be my escape," I blurted, again, before thinking my words through. That wasn't like me. I always thought through what I was going to say and do. But Daniel kept short-circuiting my brain.

"What do you mean?" he asked.

Tina delivered our desserts before I had a chance to answer. Daniel moaned softly when he took in the plate of sweetness. "Holy shit. I'm going to gain so much weight being here all summer."

I snorted. "I doubt that. You don't look like anything sticks to you."

He shook his head. "I was definitely blessed with a fast metabolism, but I indulge a little too much a little too often."

"Sometimes we need to indulge. Makes life more pleasurable."

He choked on his tiramisu, inhaling sharply and choking on the powdered chocolate sprinkled on top.

"I'm so sorry!"

He coughed the chocolate from his lungs as his eyes watered. "Totally worth it. Too good to waste."

I stabbed a bite of mine. "It really is." I brought the bite to my lips, pausing when I saw him watching me. "Are you going to try to make me choke?"

He shook his head. "I wouldn't think of it. Just wanted to watch you enjoy that."

The words were innocent enough, but his tone was soaked in desire and temptation. Both had me squirming in my seat and wondering when we could get the check and get out of there.

Daniel enjoyed every one of the desserts, groaning and praising each one as he tasted it. He finished every bite, then lamented how full he was.

Tina brought the check, and Daniel insisted on paying for both of us, even though I was the one who ruined his first attempt at dinner.

"It's worth it to enjoy the company of a beautiful woman," Daniel said, making me blush.

When we left the restaurant, with Daniel's to-go bag loaded down with a few extras, we walked back toward the apartment. The night air was calm and cool, just enough to remind me that I was essentially on a date with a man none of my friends had ever dated. A man no one I knew had dated. A man who wasn't off-limits, or permanent.

Daniel was there for three months. I knew because I made it happen. He was temporary.

But just like my mouth spouting words without my brain processing and approving them, my mouth was ready to do other things without approval from my brain.

Daniel opened the door to the building, holding it for me to walk inside ahead of him. He spun his keys on his finger, like the end of a date when you're stalling for time. We stood at the bottom of the stairs, him going up and me not.

"Thanks for having dinner with me," he said. "And for taunting me with the desserts that I can't get enough of."

"Thank you for treating me, Daniel. Next time I pay."

"We'll see."

He made a move toward me, and I went for it. I tilted my head up and puckered my lips. I closed my eyes just before my lips connected with his.

"Oh," he said.

My lips landed on his jaw. Which he turned to the side when he saw me coming at him, poised and ready for a kiss.

A kiss he obviously didn't want.

"I... Um..."

"Shit. I..." I drew a breath and took a huge step away from the man who was just being nice and not hitting on me. I couldn't look at him. "Have a good night."

"Sofia," he started.

But I didn't wait around to hear what he was going to say. I turned and hurried to my door, thanking God my key slid into the lock without any resistance.

I slammed the door behind me and leaned against it, closing my eyes and pretending I didn't just surprise kiss a man who did not want me kissing him.

"Where were you?" my dad barked.

Great fucking night.

7

TREY

I COLLAPSED ONTO MY COUCH AND STARED AT THE WALL. Meeting women was so much easier when we both knew what we were getting into. When there was an agreement, even if it wasn't spelled out.

Being the lead guitarist for Broken Record meant I could get any woman I wanted. They threw themselves at all of us. I never spent a night alone if I didn't want to.

But with Sofia...

I wanted to kiss her. I wanted to invite her up to my apartment. I wanted to make her scream my name and beg me for more.

But it was all lies. I wasn't who she thought I was. I wasn't Daniel, the guy in town for the summer. I was Trey Ryan. Rockstar in need of a new song. A song I was there to get from her father.

I never expected him to actually be in town. For him to show up. I figured I'd get his location out of her with a little bit of seduction and some good guy behavior.

And then I met her.

I knew a lot of people in the music industry. None of

them were like Sofia. Cutthroat, ruthless, and manipulative would be the first words I'd use to describe anyone involved with music. Sofia had none of those talents. She was sweet, kind, and generous.

Fucking her and walking would be the biggest mistake of my life. I couldn't do it.

Which meant I couldn't kiss her.

She knew I was leaving, but she didn't know anything else. She didn't know there was no chance I'd stick around. I'd met more than a few who thought they could change my mind, who thought they could be the ones to convince me to give up the life I'd built for myself. None of them had done it, and none would.

Including Sofia.

A better man would apologize to her. Would explain the situation. Would try to make amends.

I liked Sofia. I liked being around her. And I knew I could get what I needed.

I just needed to sleep on it and get my head around what I was doing. I could do this. I could get the introduction I needed and get a song and go back to my life far, far away from Sofia Frank and the nosy people of MacKellar Cove.

FAR TOO EARLY O'CLOCK, my phone rang. I'd forgotten to put it on silent when I crashed, and regretted that slip when the shrill tones of the label's ringtone sent me scrambling for the noise to shut it off.

"Yeah?" I barked into the phone. I was less than thrilled and wanted whoever the fuck was calling me so early to know it.

"Do you have a song yet?"

I closed my eyes. The voice on the other end? Not a guy who would give a shit if he woke me up or pissed me off. Robert Miller was the executive in charge of our contract. When he called, shit happened. And if it didn't, the next call was from a lawyer ending the contract.

"Not yet, sir."

"Do you have a location on Jensen Carmack?"

"Yes, I where he is."

"Well, that's why you went there. When do you leave?"

"He's actually in town, sir."

"Carmack is in..." Papers shuffled through the phone. "MacKellar Cove, New York?"

"Yes, sir. He's here visiting his daughter. In the same building where I'm staying."

"Well, I guess I have to admit I'm impressed. When you came up with this idea, I thought for sure it was a bunch of bullshit."

"It worked out in my favor, sir."

"Now that he's there, it should be even easier to get a song done. Have you started something with him yet?"

I sighed. "No, sir. I haven't technically met him yet."

"Then go knock on the damn door. Introduce yourself. He's a has-been. You need to swing your muscle around and show him you're the next big thing, and if he wants a chance at recording more music, he'll help you out."

I nodded, even though he couldn't see me. "Yes, sir."

"Get me something, Trey. Soon."

I opened my mouth to answer, but he'd already hung up on me.

"Shit," I breathed.

The last thing I wanted to do was knock on Sofia's door and introduce myself to her father. But it was why I was there.

It would have been easier to find out where he was and get the hell out of town. To leave her out of it once I knew his location. Him being in town, living with her, complicated things.

Complicated everything.

There was one person who could help. One person who understood what was going on. I scrolled through until I found Seth's number and tapped the screen. It was early for him, but I didn't care. We needed to talk.

"What the fuck, dude? It's like the middle of the damn night," Seth answered.

"Robert Miller just called me," I told him.

"Whoa. Seriously?" Seth sounded more awake with that news.

"Yeah. He wants the song. Now."

"So, give him a song."

"I don't have one. Not yet."

"You don't know where Carmack is, do you? I knew his daughter wouldn't know. They're not close."

"He's living with her right now."

Seth laughed. "You're shitting me, right? Carmack is in that dumpy little town where you went?"

"Living two floors below me."

"Well, fuck, go talk to him. Tell him you want to work on a song together. Tell him anything. Even better, now you don't have to bang his kid to get in with him."

The image of Sofia in my bed flashed through my mind. What would she look like as she came? What would she say? Would she be quiet or loud? Would she talk dirty? Would she want me to?

"Yo!" Seth shouted in my ear.

"What?"

"Did she get hot? I only met her a few times, and she was

always a little on the chubby side for me. Is she hot now? Is that why you're thinking about fucking her anyway?"

"I'm not thinking about fucking her."

"Yeah, you are. No judgement here, man. Whatever it takes to get the job done."

Seth wasn't wrong. Hearing him say it settled a piece of me that'd been jumbled since I met Sofia. This was business. We had a contract to fulfill. Seth wasn't a songwriter, but he was the face of Broken Record. He was the lead singer. He brought me into the business. He made things happen for me.

"Listen, I know what writing our songs means to you. I get it. But if you're all messed up and can't write anything, this is what you have to do. Miller isn't known for giving second chances. If we don't have something soon, we're going to be recording whatever the fuck he wants us to record."

"I know," I growled. "I know. I have to do this. I have to get in with her, and meet Carmack and make this work."

"Do you think he remembers you?" Seth asked the question that had been on my mind since Sofia said her dad was in town.

We'd only met once. I was at a show with Seth and his brother. Seth's brother introduced us, but it was brief. It was only after when Seth and I started Broken Record, and when I learned Jensen Carmack was the one who wrote most of the songs his band sang, I was impressed. It inspired me to start writing my own music.

Music had always been a part of my life. I loved it. My dad was the music minister at church when we were little. He gave it up, but I'd already fallen in love with music. It was in me, a part of me. As much as anything else I'd ever loved.

"I doubt it," I finally answered Seth's question.

"Are you going to tell him who you are?"

"I think it'll be better if I do. It'll piss off his daughter, though."

"She'll get over it. They always do. Sign a few things for her, and she'll be fine."

"Her dad's famous. Do you really think a few signed things will impress her?"

"Maybe if you sign her tits." Seth laughed like it was the best joke he'd ever told. He was crude, but he was my best friend. He was the only one there for me for the last twenty years. Crude was part of the deal, a part I could handle.

I chuckled with him, knowing Sofia wouldn't find the same humor in the joke and wondering how soft her skin was. Maybe I could sign something for her.

I shook my head. Getting in good with Sofia had to be separate from screwing her. It was obvious she was up for that, but I wasn't into leaving a trail of heartbroken women behind me. Never had been.

"You gotta lighten up," Seth said, his laughter dying down. "You need to get laid, too. Maybe you should fuck her. Get it out of your system. Or find someone else. But shit, no sex makes you grumpy."

"Fuck you."

"Yeah, yeah. I'm not the one waking up with my own hand around my dick this morning. I've already got lips on my cock and my fingers in a pussy. What do you have?"

"Fucking hell, dude. I didn't need to know that."

"Then you shouldn't have woken me up."

The soft moans of a woman came through the phone, and I choked a strangled retort. "I'll let you go."

"Keep me posted. Let me know if I need to come up there and take one for the team."

"All good, man. Enjoy your morning."

"Already am. Later, dude."

I hung up, my dick hard and useless without someone there to help me. I couldn't think of the last time I had to jerk-off, but Seth wasn't wrong. I wouldn't survive three months without some kind of action. I was already turning into a grumpy asshole.

I tossed the covers back and stalked naked to the bathroom. The shower was hot, and my hand wrapped around my dick was better than nothing.

Especially when I called up Sofia's image and the light in her eyes when she laughed.

I blew my wad all over the shower wall, then finished my shower and got dressed.

The building was busy when I walked out my door. Neighbors were rushing to work and school and wherever else they spent their time during the day. I locked my door and followed them downstairs, turning toward town and Cracked.

Blake was working again, and she waved and pointed to a table. I headed that way and realized she was pointing to Ian and their son, Maddox.

"Hey, man. You want to come get that boat today?" Ian asked.

I nodded. "Yeah, sure. After breakfast?"

"Sounds good. Blake should be right over. Coffee?"

I nodded again.

Ian flipped over one of the mugs on the table and poured me a full cup of coffee. I ignored the cream and sugar and went for a sip of it black. It was rich and hot and perfect for a morning that started far too early.

"You doing okay?" Ian asked. The baby on his lap held

onto his fingers, chewing on one of them. Ian looked perfectly content with his small town life.

"All good. You lived here your whole life?"

Ian nodded. "Yep. My parents are still in town. My sister and her family are here. I can't imagine being anywhere else." He smiled as Blake walked by. "Where are you heading back to after this?"

"LA," I said without thinking.

Ian whistled. "Swanky. What do you do out there?"

"I'm in the music business. Between things right now but hoping something comes up," I said, hoping I wasn't giving too much away.

"I hope it works out. It's good to do something you love."

"Something I love?"

Ian shrugged. "Sure. Why are you in such a tough industry if you don't love it? I started working with wood when I was in high school. I loved having my hands on every piece. Boats came later, but I always knew I'd do something like that. Blake's an artist. Works here because she likes to talk to people and see everyone in town, but her passion is her art."

"I didn't know that."

"Life here is different than other places. It's slower, so we have a better chance at figuring out what makes us happy. Too many people come here from big cities and are miserable. Spent their whole lives working in a job they hated, only to realize there's another way to live. Another way to be."

"True," I agreed.

"I think we all have something in our lives we're afraid to do. Most people, it's work. They're afraid to give up the security they have with their job, even though they hate what they do. For me, it was taking a chance on love. Telling Blake I wanted her."

"It all worked out, though," I said.

Ian nodded as Blake approached us. "It did. I'm a lucky man."

"What are you two talking about over here?" Blake asked.

"Just telling Daniel how much I love you," Ian said.

Blake leaned down and kissed him. Maddox grabbed the necklace she wore, and Blake laughed before kissing the baby. She pulled his fingers off her necklace and wrapped her arm around Ian's shoulders.

"What can I get you for breakfast, Daniel?"

"Coffee is a good start. How about an omelette?"

"What on it?"

"Mushrooms, onions, peppers, and cheddar."

"I'll put it right in. Theirs might come out first, but I'll ask Earl to put a rush on it."

"No worries, but thanks."

Blake walked away, leaving me with Ian and Maddox again. "How old is he?"

"He'll be two in November. Just before our second is due." Ian's face was full of pride and excitement as he shared his news.

"Congratulations. I had no idea."

Ian nodded. "Thanks. We've only just started telling people. She keeps insisting she's showing and everyone knows, but no one suspected. Or they were nice enough not to say anything."

"I'm learning that's how it is here. People are pretty nice."

Ian chuckled. "Most of the time. There have been a few

situations where the good people of MacKellar Cove weren't too friendly to newcomers."

My brows went up, wondering if he was referring to me for something I wasn't aware of.

"Not you," Ian said. "That one involved a cheating husband, his girlfriend showing up in town, and her sticking around. It all worked out in the end, but it wasn't easy for her."

"This place has some secrets," I said as Blake set down plates in front of Ian and me.

"Are you telling him about Finley and Trent?" Blake asked.

"Who?" I asked.

Blake snorted. "Guess not."

"I was telling him about Valentina, Dawson, and Haley," Ian explained.

"I think there's a Haley in my building," I said.

"She's the girlfriend," Ian said. "Ex-girlfriend, and she had no idea what she was in the middle of."

"Wow. So, who are Finley and Trent?"

"Finley's my sister," Ian said, "and Trent is her husband, but that was another one that didn't start out so great. Come to O'Kelley's Thursday night and we'll tell you all the stories."

"Just don't believe all the stories," Blake teased.

I chuckled with them.

"You guys need anything else?"

"All good, beautiful," Ian said.

"All set," I told her.

She winked at Ian, then went to help other customers.

Ian's gaze lingered on her until Maddox made a noise of frustration.

"Always getting between me and my woman," Ian said with a chuckle. "You have anyone back in LA?"

I shook my head. "No." The word was true, but nothing about my life was simple. Especially lately.

"You sure? You didn't really sound like that was the case."

I shook my head. I wasn't about to spill my whole story to a man I barely knew. I didn't get the feeling he was digging for dirt, but I'd learned the hard way that not everyone could be trusted. Hell, most of the time, no one could be trusted.

"Yeah, I'm single."

"Good. Then you getting together with Sofia won't be a problem."

"Who said I'm getting together with Sofia?"

Ian raised an eyebrow. "You two were on a date last night, and you walked her home. Just putting two and two together. Happens quick around here. Especially when it's someone like Sofia that everyone likes. I'm just making sure you're going to be good to her."

I thought about her trying to kiss me and dodging it. If Ian knew the whole story, he wouldn't even be talking to me.

"I'm gonna do my best."

Ian nodded. "Good enough for me."

8

———

I SPENT THE DAY ON THE WATER. IAN GAVE ME A QUICK LESSON about the boat, with additional instructions on where to stay on the water to avoid getting run over by any barges or other large ships.

It was peaceful. It was gorgeous. It was boring as fuck.

I wasn't used to having so much time on my hands. I wanted to be doing something. To be playing or writing or hanging out with my band. I wanted a woman to lose myself in or a club to throw myself around in.

But I didn't have any of that. I had a sleepy little town on the edge of the Saint Lawrence River with a cove that was ringed with houses and people who all knew each other.

And I was dragging my feet.

That wasn't the whole truth. I was terrified. What if I worked with Jensen and a song still didn't come? What if he refused to collaborate? What if my chances of being a success were gone? If this was the end? If I was a washed up has-been at thirty-seven?

I wasn't sure I was ready to face any of that. Yeah, we could play songs other people wrote. We could make it our own. But when Seth and I started Broken Record, we decided we were going to do it ourselves. Write our own music, make our own choices, do what we wanted to do with the band.

Along the way, we'd lost a lot of those original promises we made to each other. We signed with a label who took control of so many things. But the music was ours. The music was pure. The music was original. No one had ever heard our songs before us because they were our songs. But now...

I couldn't think of another option. I wasn't ready to. Not yet.

But it meant I had to take a risk. It meant I had to get an introduction from Sofia and ask her dad to work with me. And not take no for an answer.

I returned the boat to Ian and thanked him for the relaxation. He grinned like a man who knew his craftsmanship was exceptional. It was a beautiful boat. Something I would have indulged in if I were a local. But I wasn't a local. I wasn't ever going to be a local. I was leaving as soon as I got a song and that spark back.

Back at the apartment I was calling home, I checked my phone, surprised to find a message from TalkNerdyToMe.

TALKNERDYTOME

How do you know if you're reading a guy's signs right?

I thought about it for a minute and started typing.

GIOIOSO

Men suck. Signs are confusing. The only way to know is to ask.

TNTM

Well, that doesn't help.

G

Sorry. It's the truth.

TNTM

Is there ever a time when men don't suck
and aren't confusing?

G

I wish.

TNTM

Why do men do that?

G

Again, men suck. Honestly, I don't think a lot
mean it to be confusing. We're just as
confused.

TNTM

I find that hard to believe. Men are always in
charge.

G

Not as much as you think. I never feel like
I'm in charge when it comes to women.

TNTM

I had a date the other night, and I thought I
was getting all the signs he was interested,
but at the end, nothing. Didn't ask for
another date, try to kiss me, anything.
Dating sucks.

G

Maybe he was trying to be respectful.

TNTM

Maybe, but it didn't seem that way. I think
he just wasn't interested. Sorry to bug you
about this, though.

G

I don't mind. If we ever decide to meet, I'll know not to give you any mixed signals and to make sure I'm clear about what I'm thinking.

TNTM

Well, thank you. Now if you can send that message to the rest of the male population, I'd appreciate it.

G

Getting out my MAN phone now. Sending an alert.

TNTM

LOL! The women of the world appreciate the assistance. I appreciate the laugh. I needed it.

G

Rough day?

TNTM

My day was fine. Still feeling off from my date. I know I shouldn't let things like that get to me, but it felt like I misread everything.

G

Men suck.

TNTM

Yes, they do. I'm sure women aren't much better most of the time, though. If I'm being honest.

G

I don't date a lot. I guess I'm not the best bet when it comes to anything long term.

TNTM

What's your longest relationship?

G

A few months. I move around a lot.

TNTM

That's not easy. Hard to get to know someone if you're only around for a little while.

G

Yep. I like my life, though. I can't complain.

TNTM

I definitely understand that. I'm a homebody. I love being in my home, surrounded by my stuff. I can't imagine moving more than once a decade or so, but I know most people aren't like me.

G

Just the thought of that gives me shivers.

TNTM

LOL. Well, the differences in people is part of what makes life interesting. If we were all the same, it would be really boring. And quiet if everyone was like me.

G

Quiet isn't always bad. I don't prefer it. I've been getting more than my fair share lately. I could go for some noise right now.

TNTM

Not me. I'm on my couch with my glass of wine and a movie on. I'm content.

G

What movie are you watching?

TNTM

Walk The Line

G

Seriously? I love that movie.

TNTM

It's a good one. I can't complain. I'm a
sucker for a good romance.

G

I just like the music.

TNTM

That's good, too.

G

So, I have a question.

TNTM

Okay.

G

How should a guy apologize if he feels like
he messed up?

TNTM

How badly did he mess up? Cheating?
There's no apology. Walk away. Forgot her
birthday? Definitely a gift.

G

What if he gave her some mixed signals?

TNTM

Ugh! Really? Don't tell me you did that to a
woman.

G

Okay, I won't tell you.

TNTM

That's so not cool.

G

Is it redeemable?

TNTM

It depends on the reason.

G

She deserves better than me.

TNTM

You could always try telling her that.

G

Would you believe your date if he said that to you?

TNTM

Um…

G

Exactly what I was afraid of.

TNTM

I guess I would feel like it was a copout.
Like he was saying it to get another chance
without proving to me he's earned it.
Without making me think he's worth risking
my time and heart on him again.

G

Well, damn. I can't argue with that.

She was quiet for a minute. I let her words sink in. The last thing I wanted was for Sofia to think I was not worth the risk, but it was true. I wasn't worth the risk. I was a shitty bet, and a shitty guy because I was willing to get to know her in order to get in with her dad.

TNTM

Sorry, but I need to go. Hopefully you figure
out what to tell her.

G

Thanks. I'll try.

I closed the app just as a loud knock sounded in the hallway. I was out of my seat before I could think twice. Like a creep, I peered through the peephole and saw Sofia going into the apartment across the hall.

The door closed behind her. How weird would it be to happen to walk out when she leaves the apartment?

I shook my head. Super weird. I couldn't do that.

But I wanted to.

I SPENT the next two days trying to figure out Sofia's schedule. If I happened to see her, I could try to talk to her, but I wasn't able to decipher any sort of a routine.

And knocking on her door wasn't a good idea.

I tried out more local restaurants and ended up at Cove Bakery one day. The lady who owned it convinced me to take some extra breakfast home so I would have something to enjoy for a few days. It was the best decision I'd made all week. And the luckiest.

I was on my way back into the building when I spotted Sofia. She was at her door. She locked it and turned toward me. Her gaze hardened when she saw me, but it melted when she saw the pink box in my hands.

"Did you go to Cove Bakery?" she asked, her voice soft and full of praise.

"I did. Harriett talked me into taking home a few extras." I opened the box so Sofia could see everything I had inside. It was more than I'd finish in days, and I was happy to share. "You're welcome to help yourself."

She shook her head and turned away, as though accepting a pastry from me would be crossing a line.

"Please, Sofia. I want to apologize for the other night, too."

"You have nothing to apologize for."

"I do." I stepped closer to her, crowding her so she couldn't get away. I knew it was a shitty thing to do, but I knew the moment she sucked in a breath that she was feeling the same attraction I'd felt since we met. "I wanted to kiss you. So bad. But I'm only here for three months. I would be an ass if I didn't talk to you about that before anything happened."

"I'm aware how long you're here," she said softly.

"Good. But are you okay with that for someone you're seeing?"

She took a step back and looked up at me. Her gaze cleared, and she narrowed her eyes at me. "Is that really why you didn't kiss me?"

"Believe me, Sofia, there was nothing I wanted to do more than kiss you that night. But I've had too many women in my past upset because I wasn't clear. I don't want that to happen with you."

"And if I'm okay with you leaving in three months? Then what? Are you asking me for a summer fling?"

I took a breath and looked at her. She was beautiful and innocent, but she wasn't a child. She was old enough to understand what we were talking about. She was not going to be fooled and feel manipulated. She knew.

Mostly. She knew I was only there for three months. She knew I was leaving. But she didn't know I wanted to get in with her dad. She didn't know I was on the cover of magazines. She didn't know the songs I wrote in the future could be about her.

I wanted the things she knew and the things she didn't to stay separate. One didn't influence the other. We could have a summer fling and I could meet her dad and get my career back on track, and it would all be okay.

"I'm not sure I'd use those words, but yes. I'm attracted to you. I enjoyed having dinner with you. I want to spend more time with you. But I'm not a forever kind of guy. I'm not going to be."

"Ever?" she asked. The look in her eyes was one of sadness, not disappointment. She wasn't hopeful she could be the one to change my mind. She felt sorry for me.

That was a punch to the gut.

"I have never imagined myself with a family. Married with kids, settled down. It's not the life I want. I have the life I want."

"One where you're on the go and only temporary."

I nodded.

"I wouldn't be happy if you asked me to change, so it isn't fair for me to think I could change you."

I inhaled a sharp breath. I'd never met a woman who saw that truth. They always wanted to change me. To make me someone I'm not. To take the rockstar and turn him into the suburban husband.

To know she not only wasn't looking for that, but she wasn't looking to change me was refreshing and sad.

Not that I wanted to change. I loved my life.

And she loved her life.

There was no reason for that to be a bad thing.

"So?" I asked, flashing her my most charming smile.

"My dad is staying with me, so we'll have to go to your place."

"Is that a yes?"

She nodded. "Yes, but first, I need one of those brownies and a croissant and a quiche."

I opened the box again and smiled while she picked out

her treats. She moaned when she bit into the brownie, and my dick hardened at the sound.

"If I'd known all I needed to do was buy you brownies to make you moan, I would have done that the day I moved in."

Her eyes popped open. She looked up at me, shocked and humored both. "Brownies can do magical things."

"I will remember that."

"Good." She pushed the last of the brownie into her mouth, then stuck the croissant between her lips and lifted the quiche in toast. "Thanks," she mumbled, then headed up the stairs ahead of me.

"I could have held that for you."

She shook her head, his hips swaying in front of my face. I wanted to reach out and grab one cheek, feel the weight of it in my hand, but that would definitely be crossing a line.

"I'm used to eating on the run. I can't go into another unit with food in my hands."

She'd already finished the croissant and was starting on the min-quiche.

"I'm glad I could share breakfast with you. Maybe one day we can do that in my apartment."

"Maybe," she said. "If you promise to bring more brownies."

"I'll buy out the store every day," I growled.

She laughed, then stepped off the staircase to go to a unit on the second floor. "I actually believe you might do that."

"I would definitely do that. If you're willing to give me another chance, and you're okay with how this has to be, I will do anything."

She raised one eyebrow. "Anything?"

The gleam in her eyes had me a little worried. "Um, maybe?"

"Either it's anything or it's not."

"Fine. Anything."

She nodded slowly. "That is really good to know."

She started to walk away, but I wasn't ready for our conversation to be over. "You're not going to tell me what you're thinking about?"

"Maybe I will one day. Dinner?"

"Tonight?"

She shook her head. "Tomorrow. Seven o'clock. I'll meet you in front of the building."

"I'll be there."

"Wear something comfortable."

"Why?"

She smirked. "You'll see."

Then she was gone, down the hall and knocking on the door of a unit.

I shook my head and carried my box of treats upstairs. I put it on my counter, knowing I would eat all of it if I kept it near me. I picked up my guitar and sat on the edge of the couch.

My lips curled up as I thought of the way Sofia's hips swung when she walked up the stairs. My fingers ran over the strings, not making a noise, but remembering the feel of the music as it poured through me.

It was there. Like a memory. Just outside my reach, but still there. I could feel its power, its pull. It wasn't gone. For the first time in months, I knew it wasn't gone.

Just sleeping. Dormant.

Almost a year of waiting for it to come back, wondering if I'd ever feel like myself again, and it all changed because of a woman.

A woman who didn't want anything from me.

She was the only person who'd never asked for anything. Who'd never demanded something from me. Everyone wanted something. A song, a tour, an appearance.

Child support.

Not Sofia. She had no agenda. No demands.

How was I ever going to resist that?

9

SOFIA

I was dressed and ready for our date. I wasn't sure Daniel was going to be on board with it, but I had plans, and I figured this was a good test. And a good way to make him regret all the mixed signals.

"I'm heading out for the night." My dad was in the living room when I walked out of my room. "Don't wait up for me."

"Where are you going?"

"I told you I volunteer at the Community Center, helping once a month to fix things up."

"Oh, right. And that's tonight?"

"It is."

"We've barely spent any time together."

"Dad, I told you I would be working. I can talk some time off, but whenever I ask you—"

"No, no. I'd never ask you to take time off. I'll find something to do. Is there any food leftover? Something I can eat for dinner?"

I swallowed my groan. He'd been staying with me for a full week, and I learned he was even more useless than I thought. He didn't know how to cook and could barely heat up food on his own. The first day he used the microwave, he left a fork on the plate. Thankfully, I saw it before he started the timer, but he got annoyed with me.

And he still hadn't told me why he was there or how long he was staying. I was not going to survive the summer. Which was why Daniel was a good distraction.

"There's food in the fridge you can heat up. No metal in the microwave."

"I'm not stupid, Sofia," he snapped.

I rolled my lips in. The man was sixty-six years old and didn't know you couldn't put metal in a microwave. He was intelligent, but he was definitely not smart sometimes.

"I know, Dad. I just wanted to remind you."

"It only happened once and nothing even happened."

"I know, Dad. But I need to go."

"So, I came all this way to visit and you're not going to spend an evening with me?"

"I committed to this a long time ago. How about we spend tomorrow evening together?"

He pouted, twisting his lips and scowling. "Fine."

I nodded. "Sounds good. Think of what you want to do, Dad. Whatever you want, tomorrow night is for us."

"I don't really know anything to do in this minuscule town, but I'll try."

"Thanks, Dad. I'll try to be quiet when I get home so I don't wake you up. Have a good night."

He waved dismissively, annoyed at me for leaving. It had been the constant attitude since he arrived. He barely left the apartment, claiming he'd get mobbed by fans if he went out in public. His assistant, a college student home for the summer and looking to make some money, was bringing him food and groceries and taking care of things around the apartment. Erika was nice enough, but there were times I saw the exhaustion in her eyes. The fear that she wasn't going to be able to do all the things she was asked to do and would end up losing the job she probably thought was easy and cushy for the summer.

I couldn't afford to keep paying her if he went back on it. He'd only grumbled a few times about her, usually at night when I was going out and he was bored.

But I couldn't stop living my life. He never stopped living his for me, and I wasn't willing to stop living mine for him.

Daniel was waiting for me outside the building when I walked out. He turned as I stepped out, smiling when he saw me. His gaze landed on my tool bag, and he frowned. "Should I be worried you're going to chop me up into little pieces and dispose of my body?"

"Did you do something that would warrant that action?"

"Not that I know of, but the night's still early."

I laughed, enjoying the easy flow we had. Sebastian, who was like a brother to me, was one of the only men I'd found the same level of familiarity with, and I'd never felt any attraction toward my friend.

Daniel was a different story.

"So, what's with the tools?" Daniel asked as I turned toward to walk down the street to where I'd parked. He fell into step with me.

"We're going to help out at the Community Center. Minor repairs and fixing up things for the kids. A lot of kids use the Community Center on a regular basis, and once a month, there's an organized night out where whoever is available and either handy or willing to help comes to do whatever can be done."

He held up his hands. "I'm not overly handy. I've never been."

"That's okay. There will be something you can help with. There's always a few smaller projects for the kids who come with their parents or the people who want to give back but don't have the skills."

He looked anxious. Like he was going to be sick. "Um, I'm not so sure this is something I'm going to be any good at."

I stopped just before we reached my SUV and faced him. "You don't have to come. I already had these plans, and I thought it would be fun for us to do something together. But if you're not up for it, we can catch up some other time."

He stared at me. He knew it was a test. He knew I was waiting to see what he was going to do. If he left, I wasn't sure I'd see him again. Not for a date. He was the one who avoided my kiss and made me feel like an ass. I needed to know I could trust him not to do it again.

"Are you sure there will be things that don't require skills?"

I nodded. "There always are."

"Okay. I'll do my best. But don't expect much."

I fought my grin. He passed the first test. Not that it was really intended to be a test, but he was willing to go outside his comfort zone and do something new. And help a community he wasn't a part of.

I nodded to my SUV, going around the back to put my bag in before climbing in behind the wheel.

"I hope I don't disappoint you," he said.

"I'm sure you won't. The Community Center is always looking for some help. A friend of mine volunteers there every week, helping the kids with craft projects. Her husband's mom actually runs the place. A lot of the local kids go there for anything from afterschool care to sports practices and games. It's a good place for the younger kids in town to be active and have fun."

"We had a place like there where I grew up. My brother and I used to go when we were in elementary school."

"I didn't know you have a brother."

He nodded. "He, uh, he died when I was in high school."

"Oh, Daniel, I'm so sorry. I can't imagine losing a sibling when you were so young. I lost my mom when I was fourteen. It's different, though."

"I think no matter what, it's hard to get over that kind of loss."

I nodded. I could say I still wasn't over my mom. Losing her the way I did, having the one and only person who'd always been there for me taken away in a blink. It was devastating. And then for my dad to have been such a broken part of my story. Someone who wasn't there for so long and who argued if I was even his for so many years of my life... Building a relationship with him was not easy. Even after all that time.

"They say time heals all wounds, but I think some can never heal all the way."

"That's been my experience, too."

We shared a sad smile in the quiet of the vehicle. People who knew loss were bonded in a way others weren't. And we'd just found a new bond.

Voices outside the vehicle brought me back to the evening, and I opened the door to join the others there to help with the repairs. I grabbed my bag from the back and walked inside with Daniel.

"Daniel!" a voice shouted almost as soon as we walked in.

He waved to James. "I should go say hi."

I nodded. "His mom runs this place. He's the one I mentioned."

"Oh. Good to know. Thanks."

He took off, and I went in search of Amelia, only to find her with Sebastian.

"Hi!" I said, surprised and happy to see Sebastian. Ever since he and Zoey, the love of his life, got together, they'd been busy. Zoey had two kids, and she got pregnant with a third shortly after she moved back to town. Sebastian was a great father. He loved his family and was happier than I'd ever seen him.

"Hi!" Sebastian gave me a warm hug. "How are you?"

"I'm good. How are you? How are Zoey and the kids?"

"Everyone's doing well. The kids are ready for summer, but I think Zoey would rather they could stay in school a little longer. She's already trying to come up with things they can all do together."

"I'm sure there will be some options here," I said, bringing Amelia into the conversation.

"That's what I was just telling Sebastian. The older ones will have more options, but the baby will still be able to get out a few mornings. Give your wife a break sometimes."

Sebastian nodded. "She's going to need it. Summer is busy for me. I will be around as much as possible, but it's mostly on Zoey."

"I'm sure there will be other parents in the same position. Maybe it's an opportunity for us to start a new program. The new summer camp is opening up this year, but I know Zoey doesn't want them in every single week."

Sebastian was shaking his head as Amelia spoke. "She just needs a few days a week."

Amelia thought about it for a second. "Maybe I'll get in touch with Natalie and see what we can figure out. See if there's an option for us to work together to help out the parents in town."

"That would be amazing," Sebastian said.

"Well, what do you need help with today to get things done for right now?" I asked Amelia.

"The list is on the wall," she replied with a laugh. "There are a few things I might ask the two of you to work on together. Having you both here is a huge boost. If you don't mind."

"Not at all," I said, smiling at Sebastian.

"Ahem."

I jumped, the voice right behind me. I spun, finding Daniel over my shoulder. "Oh. Hey."

"Hey," he said, his tone a little icy. He stuck out his hand to Sebastian. "I'm Daniel."

"Nice to meet you. Gavin mentioned you'd moved to town. I'm Sebastian."

"Nice to meet you," Daniel growled. "You know Gavin?"

I rolled my eyes. I wasn't interested in shows of possession and jealousy. I'd seen it enough growing up.

"Gavin's my brother-in-law."

Daniel looked more closely at Sebastian, noting the ring on his left hand, then shook his head. "Sorry, man. I was a jerk."

"No worries. Sofia's a great woman. I don't blame you for being a little protective."

"I'm right here, guys." I exhaled heavily.

"She is a great woman. And I already have one strike against me, so I should be more careful than to piss her off," Daniel confessed.

Sebastian laughed. "I know how that goes. My wife is a bit hot-tempered, too."

"Hey!" I shouted.

Both men turned to me with raised brows and matching grins.

I sighed and turned away, stomping my way across the gym toward the board with all the tasks on it.

Amelia followed me, chuckling as she trailed behind. "Who was that?"

"Daniel. He's living in my building for the next few months."

"And you're dating?"

"No. Yes. Sort of, I guess. We went out last week, but he wanted to make sure I knew he was leaving. He's only here for three months."

"He's cute. What does he do?"

I thought about it and realized I'd never asked. "I don't know, actually."

"Well, whatever it is, he likes you. He's been watching you since we walked over here, and he was glaring at Sebastian from the moment you walked over and hugged him."

"He was talking to James. I'm surprised James didn't tell him who Sebastian was."

"Do you know my son?" Amelia asked, with a note of teasing in her voice.

"Ha! True. James probably enjoyed watching Daniel get angry."

"Exactly."

I shook my head. "Well, I didn't come here to worry about men. I came here to work. What do you want me doing?"

"Are you sure you're okay working with Sebastian? Daniel isn't going to get mad?"

"Daniel isn't here forever. And Sebastian is happily married. There's no reason for me to worry about Daniel's feelings. Whatever we might be will be temporary."

"Okay. If you're sure, then I'm going to ask you two to replace a few sections of the flooring. It's not bad when you've got shoes on, but if the kids fall, they're going to end up with splinters."

"That would not be good," I agreed.

"Nope. Let me show you."

I followed Amelia to the spots on the floor where it was damaged. It could have been some water damage from a while ago, or it could have been something else more recently, but whatever it was, the boards needed to come out.

"Do you have replacement pieces?"

Amelia nodded.

I grabbed the pieces and by the time I was back, Sebastian was standing over one of the rough sections of the floor. He kicked the edge of it with his toe, flaking off a small chunk of wood.

"This is what we're doing?" Sebastian asked.

Amelia nodded. "If you're willing."

"Works for me."

"Thank you both. I really appreciate it. If you need any other help, let me know and I'll find someone who can be your gopher."

Sebastian and I exchanged a glance and shook our heads. "We should be good."

"Sounds good. Thank you, guys." Amelia squeezed our hands and walked off, leaving us to our work.

Sebastian and I worked together easily. He chipped out one piece, and I fitted a new plank to the opening. One-by-one we worked to replace the sections of the floor. We got through about half of them when Sebastian stopped and glanced around, then looked up at me.

"So, what's the deal with you and Daniel?"

"There is no deal," I spat. I adored Sebastian and thought of him as one of my closest friends. But I didn't like being questioned about things that I myself didn't quite understand.

Sebastian chuckled. "Do you remember what you told me when things with Zoey were getting started?"

I shook my head. We had many conversations about Zoey. I wasn't sure which one he was referring to.

"You showed up at my place one night. Got it out of me that we were together but not telling anyone. I was still convinced what Zoey and I had was temporary. I wasn't ready to consider she might stay. You said I was making a mistake."

"Daniel is different," I said.

"I know you believe that. But I saw the way he looked at you. I think he was going to try to break my hand. He squeezed pretty tight. He might be telling himself he's temporary, but he's not acting like you and him are temporary."

I sighed. I couldn't go there. We hadn't even kissed yet. We'd been on one date. Thinking of something more than three months wasn't on my radar.

Not that I was going to admit, anyway.

"I know now why you got so mad at me that night," I said.

Sebastian laughed. But he didn't push. He knew not to.

We worked a few more minutes. I rocked back and looked at him. "It's been a long time since I've dated."

"And that means you can't have hope?"

I exhaled a laugh. "It means I don't know how to have hope. Did you have any?"

He chuckled. "You know I didn't. You and me... we've

always been able to see each other. I know how you feel right now."

"Do you?"

He nodded. "You're scared because you want to believe it's possible, but you don't think it is. It's the world's worst paradox. Because it's your heart."

"My heart was shattered a long time ago. I'm not sure I ever figured out how to patch it back up."

"Your mom?" he asked.

I shook my head. "She was only the beginning of it."

"Do you trust him?"

I sucked in a breath. "That's always the question, isn't it?"

He smiled. He got it. He knew what I was saying, and what I wasn't. He'd been there. He'd lived through it. He understood.

He reached over and hooked his hand around the back of my neck and pulled me in close. Our foreheads touched. We shared air for a minute.

Everything outside faded. It was just me and my friend, sharing a moment.

And I knew he'd always be there for me. If things didn't work out for me with Daniel, I'd still have Sebastian and Piper and Haley and all my other friends.

Maybe it was okay to take a risk. On Daniel. On my heart. On love.

10

─────────

"WANT TO GRAB SOMETHING TO EAT?" DANIEL ASKED AS WE headed outside after the Community Center clean-up.

"Yeah, I'm open to that."

"Good. Of course, I have to ask you to decide where to go."

I chuckled. "What do you think of tacos?"

"One of the best foods ever invented."

I laughed. "My thoughts exactly. Have you been to Just Tacos?"

He groaned. "I think they know my order by now because I'm there so often."

"Same. But it's worth it."

"I agree."

I pulled out of the lot with all the others who worked to fix up the gym and other areas of the Community Center. I was happy with the work Sebastian and I did. We replaced all the sections of flooring that were coming apart and noted a few more that would need to be replaced soon. Amelia had plenty of supplies, and Sebastian and I agreed we'd be back next month to get ahead of the next sections.

"You and Sebastian looked like you're close," Daniel said once I was on the road back toward town.

"We are. He's like a brother to me."

"Didn't look like it," Daniel muttered.

"What was that?" I asked, even though I heard him.

He sighed. "I've never seen anyone that affectionate with a sibling. Or with anyone who isn't a significant other."

I shook my head, trying to figure out how to explain my relationship with Sebastian. Then I decided I didn't have to. It was my relationship. And if Daniel didn't like it, he didn't have to stick around.

"You don't need to understand it. And you don't get to judge us. His wife is a friend of mine, and Seb and I have been close for years. I love him like a brother, and he feels the same about me. It's no different than how I feel about Piper or Gavin or Knox or Haley. You are only here for three months. I'm not going to change relationships I've had for years because you're uncomfortable with them."

He was quiet for the rest of the drive to Just Tacos. I almost went to our apartment building instead, but I was hungry. If he didn't want to eat with me, he could sit at another table, but I wasn't going to skip dinner because he didn't have friends like I did.

"You're right," he said before I opened my door. "If he was female, I wouldn't think twice, but that's narrow-minded and wrong. I was jealous, and that's shitty. I'm not used to feeling that way."

I glared at him. "You need to get over that. Sebastian is a good friend. A lot of people in this town are close friends of mine."

"And I have no right to tell you how to behave around them. I apologize for trying to do that." He reached for my hand, holding it firmly in his.

"Thank you." My breath caught in my throat. He looked at me with an intensity I rarely saw directed my way.

"Sofia," he whispered. He leaned toward me. He paused halfway, letting me decide if I wanted to kiss him.

I did. More than I cared to admit. I leaned forward, keeping my eyes open. I stopped with a few inches between us. I wasn't going to be the one who went in for the kiss again. Not after the epic failure last time.

He reached up, his hand brushing my neck. His fingertips teased the fine hairs that didn't get caught up in my ponytail. He curled his fingers, tugging me forward with pressure on the back of my neck.

I leaned in, testing out trusting him again. He met me in the middle, his soft lips touching mine. I sucked in a breath, shock and joy and relief melding.

His lips moved against mine, retreating only to press to mine again. His tongue darted out, teasing my lips and making me sigh with contentment.

He licked his way into my mouth, with absolutely no resistance on my end. I slid my tongue alongside his, moaning softly at the tentative teasing of him. His fingers tightened on the back of my neck and pulled me closer as he shifted in his seat.

"Sofia," he whispered.

"Yeah?"

"I've been wanting to do that since the day we met."

I chuckled. "I doubt that. I slept through our first meeting."

His face was close, our lips still brushing as we spoke. His eyes were open, searching mine. "When I saw you on the sidewalk, I thought you were stunning."

I snorted and pulled back. "I'm happy with how I look, but mostly because I'm happy to be alone. I don't need a relationship to feel like I'm doing okay. My mom taught me that."

He was quiet for a minute. I missed the feel of his hand on the back of my neck, his lips against mine. But I was the one who retreated.

"I have always wanted the approval of others. Part of that seems to be being involved with someone. I don't do well in relationships. I always mess things up."

"Maybe that's because you ask a woman on a date, then refuse to kiss her because you think she forgot you were only here for three months."

His grin was one-sided and full of self-deprecating humor. "For example, right?"

"Yeah, just a random example of what might have happened."

He chuckled. "Maybe one day I'll figure women out."

"Doubtful. We're confusing and frustrating, just like men are."

"That's for sure."

We laughed together, then climbed out of my SUV. Daniel insisted on paying for our food again, even though I said I was going to pay this time. He waved away my attempt and handed over enough cash to cover our food and that of the family in line behind us.

"That was a nice thing you did," I whispered when we sat down.

He shrugged. "It's good to give back. Families are always a good target because most of them are struggling. Even if they're not, they have a harder life than I do."

"That's really kind of you."

"Thanks. So, how did you get involved with the Community Center?"

I sipped my water and tried to remember the first time I

went there. "It's been a while. James's wife, Trinity, started working there when she moved to town. I didn't know her, but I knew James a little. Piper started hanging out with that group and dragged me along."

"You make it sound like you didn't want to."

I shook my head. "Not really. I don't do well in big groups. I have an easier time when I'm with a few people. Piper used to be a server at O'Kelley's. She's really friendly and talkative, and she always served them when they went in. They invited her to hang out with them one weekend, and she kept going back. I'm better with them now, but at first, I resisted going."

"It's nice to have friends to spend time with."

"Yeah. A lot of them are married to or dating the guys you met at O'Kelley's."

"How do you know I met the guys at O'Kelley's?"

"Small town. And I assumed it was either that or James arrested you, but I figured he probably wouldn't call across the room to someone he arrested."

Daniel laughed. "Good deductive reasoning."

"I thought so."

"Sofia!" Maria called from the counter.

"I'll grab it," Daniel said.

I watched him walk up to the counter. He said something to Maria. She smiled at him and laughed at whatever he said. She looked my way and waved. I waved back, laughing when Daniel turned back to me and Maria swooned behind the counter.

"What are you laughing at?" Daniel asked as he set our tray on the table.

"Nothing," I lied.

He pursed his lips to stop his smile and shook his head but didn't push for me to tell him.

We divvied up the food, each grabbing our chosen tacos. I unwrapped my first one and took a bite, groaning the same time as Daniel.

Our gazes met, and we both chuckled.

"So good," he said.

I nodded. "Always. Good choice."

"You picked it."

I smiled. Some men would take the credit, but Daniel was willing to admit it was my idea. Something I didn't think about until after he said that.

We ate our tacos quickly, devouring the food and scraping up what fell with chips. Daniel asked about the Community Center and the kids they help there, and asked about going back next month.

"I don't know how helpful I really was, but it was fun. I don't get a chance to do a lot of things like that."

"What do you do?" I asked, realizing I didn't know much about his life.

"I work in the music industry."

I froze. What were the odds? My dad was there for the summer and so was Daniel. Did he know my dad? Did he somehow find out my dad was going to be staying with me and decide to come? Was there a reason for him to be there?

"Really?" I asked. "Not a lot of people in this area have anything to do with the music industry."

He laughed. "I know. It's refreshing."

"What did you say you were here for?"

"I needed a break. A few months off to get away from the toxic environment I'm always in."

"That's for sure," I mumbled.

"What was that?"

"Nothing. I've heard it's not overly positive. What do you do in the industry?"

"Nothing right now. I'm kind of between things," he said, looking down at his wrapper and picking up one tiny piece of shredded cheese. He put it in his mouth, then smiled at me. "Are you ready to go?"

The subject change made me wonder if he was hiding something. I'd never gotten a weird vibe from him or felt like he was trying to get to my dad, but I'd been fooled before.

We threw away the trash and set the tray on top of the bin. Daniel held the door for me and followed me to the SUV. I started it up and paused.

"I used to know someone in the music industry," I admitted. "We dated for a while."

His face betrayed his shock, even as he quickly schooled his expression.

"I have a high level of distaste for anyone involved in it."

"Even me?" he asked.

"I don't know you well enough to determine that exactly."

"Wow." He leaned back in his seat, his smile fading. "I don't know a lot of women who have that feeling. Most want to get into bed with me in hopes I can change their lives. And not just while we're in bed."

I laughed at his assessment, knowing it was the full truth. I'd seen it more times than I could count. Women who wanted to screw a rockstar and would settle for a sound guy or roadie if it meant they got into a place where the general population wasn't allowed.

"I told myself I would never get involved with anyone in the music industry again."

"I was not expecting that."

I drew a breath. When I made a decision, I never went back on it. Ever. But I'd never made two decisions that contradicted each other. I chose to get involved with Daniel before I learned what he did. Maybe it was foolish to not ask more questions before I decided I was willing to spend the next few months with him, but maybe the more foolish thing was to decide not to get involved with anyone in the music industry just because of Nate.

There were shitty men in all walks of life. Men who were willing to do whatever it took to get ahead. Men who saw women as pawns and possessions to manipulate and use as they saw fit.

If Daniel was like that, it wouldn't matter what his job was, I wouldn't want to be with him. But I didn't think that was him. I couldn't say I completely trusted him, but I was attracted to him. And it had been a long time since I'd found myself drawn to a man, any man. Dating was a frustrating exercise, like all exercise, and I hadn't enjoyed it in years.

But I enjoyed spending time with Daniel. And that kiss? I was still tingling in parts that hadn't tingled in a long time.

I didn't have a good reason for denying myself time with him. He might change my life, but I was only looking for the life-changing in bed stuff. Not the real world stuff. I had no interest in getting involved with the music industry ever again. And when Daniel left in three months, I'd happily wave and watch him go back to that life.

Before I could talk myself out of the decision I made, I leaned across the center console and grabbed his shirt. The surprised look on his face was enough to tell me he didn't expect me to change my mind, but the way he gripped my hip and tried to pull me over the console told me he was completely on board with what I was doing.

Our mouths met with tongues leading the way, lips a secondary thought. He tasted vaguely of tacos, but I was sure I did, too. I just wanted to feel him, to prove to myself I made the right decision.

And the moans and sighs coming from me said I did.

"Your place," I breathed, pulling back. I shifted into drive and turned toward our building.

His hand seared my thigh through my jeans. I wanted him to move it higher, but I knew that would be a very bad idea. His fingertips tensed on my thigh, then released and smoothed over the skin he squeezed.

I parked a block away from our building, groaning when all the spots close by were taken. I turned off the vehicle and reached to get out, but he stopped me.

"One more," he whispered as he pulled me in for another kiss.

His hand went to my neck, tugging me close and holding me where he wanted me while he devoured my lips. His tongue thrust into my mouth, teasing and tasting me. His hand kept me still, not that I had any intention of retreating.

I let my hands wander, wanting to feel his solidness beneath my fingers. It had been far too long since I'd felt like I could let go. Sex was a release, but it was so infrequent for me that I'd forgotten it could be something that captivated me in so many ways. That the feel of his five-o'clock-shadow could send whiskers of anticipation through my body. That his breath on my cheek could send whispers of excitement through me. That his firm muscles and soft grunts could make me desperate to get his clothes off and his body on mine.

"Inside," I begged, shamelessly needing more from him. My decision was made, and he let me make it without influencing my choices. I wasn't going to go back on it, and now that we were at the moment of it, I was more than ready to let go and enjoy the rest of my night.

We pulled apart, both of us reluctant and going back in for another kiss before finally getting out of the vehicle. He waited for me on the sidewalk, reaching for my hand and hurrying me toward the building as the last light of the night slipped away.

The door to the building suddenly had the world's trickiest lock, and I fumbled my keys three times before I managed to unlock the door and let us in. It had nothing to do with the kisses he left on the back of my neck or the way his hands splayed wide across my belly and teased the top of my jeans. It had to have been the door.

Inside, we stopped in the entryway, but I pulled away before I lost myself. I didn't want any neighbors to see me making out with anyone in our building. I dragged Daniel up the stairs and hissed at him to be quiet when we made it to his door.

"No one's going to care," he assured me.

"Mrs. Watson will definitely care," I said, nodding to the apartment across from his.

"She likes me. It's all good."

"She likes you?" I blurted. Mrs. Watson didn't like anyone.

"Yeah. I helped her carry in groceries one day. We talked."

"That doesn't mean she likes you."

He shrugged and slid the key into the lock, twisting to unlock the deadbolt, and finally let us into his apartment. "Doesn't mean she doesn't like me."

I started to argue, but he closed the door and immediately pressed me against it. His keys fell to the floor and his entire body covered mine, including one long, thick, hard appendage that I couldn't wait to get my hands on.

Yes, both.

11

TREY

MY BRAIN SAID TO SLOW DOWN, BUT MY BODY TOLD IT TO SIT down and shut up. God, this woman. She had no agenda. No added desire to meet the next guy up the ladder. She wanted me.

I couldn't think of the last time a woman wanted me for me. I honestly wasn't sure it had ever happened. The first woman I was with was one Seth's brother introduced me to. One he said would take good care of me. She was a groupie, but she liked the younger guys. She was my eighteenth birthday gift from Seth, who'd turned eighteen a few months before me and knew Valerie would be a very good gift.

She was, not even laughing when I came against her leg the first time before I even got inside her, then let me try again and rolled with it when I only lasted two minutes. She instructed me on how to make it worthwhile for her, then let me try again. I lasted five minutes that time and felt like a king.

After Valerie, I jumped in with both feet, using my tentative connections, then my actual ones, then my own fame to get women into bed. Panties were tossed on stage with phone numbers written in them. Scraps of paper shoved into pockets. Numbers on napkins. And then there were the women delivered to us by the managers and executives. Women who paid extra to meet the band. Who got the bonus of fucking one of us sometimes.

To each and every one of them, I was Trey Ryan. Daniel didn't exist. No one knew the name Daniel, my middle name, and none of them ever would. It was the name I shared with my dad and my brother. A family tradition passed down from my great-grandfather.

But Sofia called me Daniel. She whispered the name as my hands wrapped around her hips and cupped her backside. I tugged her to me, letting her feel the way she affected me.

I wanted her. More than I'd ever wanted a woman in my life. Because she was a prize. She wasn't handed to me. I had to work to get her into my apartment. I couldn't flash my rockstar status and get her to drop her panties. She did that because she actually wanted me.

"Bedroom," she whispered, her voice as desperate as the blood pulsing through me.

I forced myself away from her and tugged at her top, lifting it up and over her head. She wore the least sexy sports bra I'd ever seen in my life, and yet it made me ever harder to find her full breasts wrapped in it.

"I was clearly not planning for this tonight."

"Neither was I, but that makes it better, right?"

She nodded. "Turnabout's fair play." She reached for my shirt, grabbing the edge as a smile lifted her lips.

I reached back and helped her pull it off.

She gasped, the sound going straight to my dick. A flush crept up her neck, and fuck me, I was going to lose it. This woman was so honest and pure.

"You're... hot as fuck," she whispered.

I chuckled, surprised by her words. "I could say the same for you."

She glanced down at her body. "I know."

I laughed as she shifted her hips and let her belly jiggle. She was stunning. I couldn't see bones through her skin. I couldn't count her ribs. Her collarbones didn't stick out. She was nothing like most of the women I'd slept with. She was so much better.

We came back together, hands meeting bare skin and mouths fused. We stumbled in the direction of the bedroom, me realizing halfway there that Sofia knew my place as well as I did. Maybe better.

We shoved the door open and turned on the lights. Sofia pulled back from me, but I shook my head.

"I want to see you. I need to see you."

She nibbled her lip but didn't argue or reach to turn the lights off.

I took her hand and led her to the bed. We sat on the edge, our hands linked. "I know we've talked about this, but I don't want to hurt you, Sofia. I like you. If things were different... I'm leaving at the end of my lease. And I'm not saying that to hurt you."

"Is this your way of backing out? Or do you think you're that amazing that there's no way I'll spend three months with you and not fall in love with you?"

I laughed at her honest assessment. "You don't hold anything back, do you?"

"We've talked about this. More than once. If you want

me to go, I will. No questions asked. But if we've gotten to this point and you're backing out again, I won't give you a third chance. Even two is pushing it for me."

"I'm not backing out. I'm barely hanging on right now. It's taking everything in me to not strip you and watch you ride me."

"I'm not the one slowing things down here."

I tucked her hair behind her ear and smiled. She was right. I kept waiting for her to be like all the other women I'd ever known, but she wasn't. Every step of the way she'd shown me she was different. I was the one who was having a problem with it.

No more. I wanted her. The fact that she was also Jensen Carmack's daughter was irrelevant. We were two consenting adults who were good together. That was all that mattered.

I slid back on the bed, leaving my feet on the ground, and tugged her to me. I reached for her hip, encouraging her to crawl over me.

She did, but she stopped before she kissed me. Her gaze met mine, searching for something, before she slowly leaned forward.

It was game fucking on.

The woman was a threat to my sanity. She rocked her hips as she kissed me, dragging her jeans-clad body over my dick and making the greedy fucker beg for more.

I was halfway to losing my fucking mind in my damn pants when she pushed me back.

"If I'm going to ride you, I hope you have some condoms because I'm not going to my apartment right now."

"Bathroom," I breathed.

"Get naked. I'll be right back."

She turned to walk into the bathroom, extracting herself

from her sports bra on the way. She let it fall to the floor before she reached for the front of her jeans, then she disappeared into the tiny space that connected to both the bedroom and the living room.

I snapped out of my trance and unbuttoned my jeans, shoving the zipper down before I stood and pushed my jeans and boxer briefs down my legs. I bent over to get my socks off and kicked all of it to the side, standing as a completely naked Sofia walked back into my room with a strip of condoms.

"I figured it's better to be prepared," she said, tearing one off and tossing the rest of the nightstand.

"Holy fuck, you're beautiful," I whispered.

Her belly was full and round. Her breasts rested on top of her belly, with pink nipples standing upright. The curls between her thighs were darker than I expected and thick like the rest of her. She wasn't a woman who primped and polished her body for a man. She was a natural woman who took my breath away and made me want to worship her curves forever.

No. Not forever. For three months. That was it.

"I'm a sure thing, Daniel. You don't have to sweet-talk me."

I shook my head. "Definitely not sweet-talking you. Just being honest."

"Well, then thank you."

"Come here," I whispered. I wanted to feel all of her pressed against my body. Her warmth and her softness and her curves.

It was even better than I told myself it would be. I let my hands glide all over her back, belly, and breasts. I tweaked her nipples and toyed with her bellybutton. I cupped her ass and pulled her tight to me.

She moaned and gasped and grunted. Her hands wandered as much as mine did, her nails scratching down my spine and her fingers twisting my nipples.

I'd never explored a woman like that. I never took the time to find out what she liked. And I'd never had one discover what I liked. Fuck, I didn't even know I liked nails on my spine or the whisper of breath on my face.

One hand drifted between us, nudging her thighs apart. She didn't protest or hesitate to let me in, spreading her thighs wide for my hand to slide through her curls and to her folds.

She moaned when I first brushed over her clit. I kept going, wanting to test how wet she was. Her folds were soaked, and come leaked from her, coating my fingers before I pressed one inside her.

"You're so fucking wet," I groaned.

"It's been a while."

"Thank you for choosing me."

She grunted. "I think I'm the one who should be saying thank you right now."

Her fingers dug into my shoulders to support herself, but she didn't make a move for the bed. I added a second finger to her channel before dragging both back up to stroke her clit. One finger on each side had her hips rocking with me and her panting.

"Oh, fuck," she whispered.

"You feel so damn good," I told her.

"Uh huh." She grunted, her thighs shaking as I stroked faster and her orgasm crashed over her.

I held her up with my free hand, supporting her weight as her knees buckled. She bit down hard on my shoulder, her hips slamming against my fingers.

"Yes, yes, yes." She moaned and whimpered, her whispered pleas barely audible with my shoulder in her mouth.

"More, Sofia," I demanded, plunging three fingers into her and pressing her clit with my thumb. "Again."

She whimpered but didn't pull away. Her hips kept going, begging me for exactly what I was giving her. Her mouth was open, her eyes were closed, and she looked like she was in heaven.

I was hooked. Fuck, I wanted more. I could watch her all night. I didn't even need to come myself, just watching her lose her mind was enough.

I'd never seen anything more beautiful.

"Daniel," she breathed, turning her lips to my neck. She licked where my neck and shoulder met.

My dick twitched, refuting the idea of not getting in on the action.

"Come for me, Sofia." I curled my fingers inside her, rubbing her g-spot, and she stopped breathing. Her hips stopped rocking.

Then she exploded. She moaned long and loud, unable to hold back. Her body shook. Her hips moved toward my hand, then away once I made contact with her clit. Her face twisted, like she was in pain. She clutched my neck, pressing her face to it again, opening her mouth and locking her teeth around the tendon running to my shoulder.

"Fuck," I hissed. The pain brought a shock of pleasure, and I wasn't sure I'd last until I was inside her.

"Yes, let's do that," she said, pulling back from me and reaching for a condom. "Now."

She held the condom in her teeth and pushed me to the bed. She stroked me with both hands, working opposite and making my eyes roll back in my head.

"Holy fuck, Sofia. I'm... You need to stop that."

She smirked at me. The minx knew exactly what she was doing. But I wasn't the only one about to lose my mind. Her hands shook as she tore the condom wrapper. She reached for me, rolling it on slowly and stroking back up once it was in place.

My eyes rolled back in my head and stayed there. Until I felt her crawl onto the bed and straddle me.

I watched her spread her thighs wide over my body. She was wet and plump and perfect. I wanted to taste her. To lick her until she came hard and begged me for more.

Next time.

"Guide yourself into me," she said, her voice a strangled whisper.

I held my cock in one hand and put the other on her thigh. She watched me as I watched myself slide into her. She took half of me in before she lifted up and stroked back down, spreading her thighs to take more of me. Three strokes and her body met mine.

I was too fucking close already. Just that little bit of her tight channel on me had me ready to go. I wanted to fuck her hard, but if I did, it would be over in a few seconds.

"Fuck me, Daniel," she whispered.

My gaze snapped to hers. Her heavily lidded, lust-filled, fuck-me gaze. I had no answer for her. No rebuttal. No argument.

Just my greedy dick and the sexiest woman I'd ever had in my bed who were both on team hard and fast.

My hands went to her thighs. She lifted at the same moment, her muscles flexing and showing me how strong she was. I surged up into her as she came back down, and we both moaned.

Our rhythm was easy, the slapping sound of wet bodies a steady beat neither of us could resist following. Her pants and my grunts added depth to the music we made. Her rock hard thighs and her soft core worked together, pumping me and begging me to take her where she needed to go.

"Daniel," she whispered. Her rhythm faltered.

I pressed on her clit, and her rhythm synced with mine again. Her breasts bounced, her belly rippled, her entire body moved with the rhythm of us fucking.

It was a beautiful song, erotic and passionate. My hands tingled, my dick twitched, my balls ached.

And then Sofia came.

She shouted her orgasm out, the vocals to our carnal song. Her core pulsed and rippled around me. She fell forward onto her hands, her nails digging into my chest.

All of it sent me right over with her, my orgasm catching me off-guard as I watched the stunning display of Sofia.

"Oh, fuck," I moaned. The eruption made my vision go dark and my fingers curl. The one on her clit sent her into another orgasm, milking my dick as I throbbed inside her.

"Oh!" she cried.

A second later, she collapsed onto me, her energy completely spent.

One hand was trapped between us. The other held her thigh. My dick refused to soften, wanting another go at her.

For once, my brain and dick were in agreement.

A melody played in my mind. One I didn't know. One I knew was my muse teasing me again.

Our breath was the only sound outside the tune in my mind. I closed my eyes and tried to hold on to the rhythm, but it was fleeting. By the time Sofia pushed herself off of me, the song was gone.

"Wow," Sofia said.

I chuckled. "Yeah."

"I don't really know what to say. That was amazing."

I shook my head and pulled her back to me. With my hand free, I could hold her with both hands. "There are no words for that. I don't think they've been invented yet."

She laughed, her breath on my chest as she rested her head on me.

She didn't try to move off me or rush to the bathroom. She just laid there, as content as I was to stay in the moment a little longer.

The tune came back, with Sofia's head on my chest. Too soft for me to hum along, but there. For the first time in months, there was music in my mind.

"It's good to know my cotton sports bra wasn't a turnoff," she said, pushing herself up again and climbing off me.

My dick sagged but didn't sink. I was still hard-half and ready to go with a little encouragement. I sat up and watched as Sofia left the room.

I heard her use the bathroom, the open door revealing a new level of intimacy for me. The toilet flushed, and the water ran. Then she was back.

"We probably need a new one before next time." She nodded to my dick as she spoke.

I looked down, wondering what was wrong with it before I realized she meant a new condom. "You scared me for a minute," I admitted.

She laughed. "Definitely not a new dick. That one is addicting."

I stood, my body right in her personal space. "So's your pussy."

She gasped at the crass word, but a slow smile lifted her lips. "Then I think we need a minute to refuel before we succumb to our addiction again."

"I'll succumb to that addiction as much as you're willing," I whispered.

I kissed her hard and cupped between her thighs, loving that she moaned and spread for me. I pressed one finger into her, finding her still soaked.

"I'm definitely not done with you for tonight."

She smirked. "Good."

12

SOFIA

MY ALARM WENT OFF FAR TOO EARLY THE NEXT MORNING. I really intended to go back to my apartment, but Daniel was very, very persuasive and talked me into sharing his bed all night long.

"What time is it?" he asked, his voice rough with the morning.

Shivers raced up my spine. His hand circled my waist and pulled me back under the warm covers and against my other favorite thing about the morning.

And to think I was never a morning person.

He kissed my cheek and teased one far-too-awake nipple before sliding his hand down over my belly.

"It's time for me to go," I answered him, as I made absolutely no move to get out of his bed.

"Already?"

"It's seven. I start my day at eight."

"Good Lord, why? Isn't it Saturday?"

I chuckled. "It is, but I have things I need to check on every day of the week. Besides, most people have to work to be able to afford their rent. Unlike you."

"I work," he grumbled, sounding more offended than I expected him to be.

I rolled over to face him, finding a scowl and a look of guilt. "I shouldn't have said that. I'm sorry. I made assumptions based on you being here for three months. It was snarky and nasty."

He drew a breath and visibly shook off the mood that settled over him. "It's fine. I just... My parents have a tendency to tell me the same. That I don't really work. That my job isn't important."

"That's shitty of them. Music brings people joy. It makes people happy. My issues with the music industry have nothing to do with the end result. I know the importance of it. I know the way a song can change your day or, in some cases, your life."

He nodded, his gaze going soft with a memory. "The first time I felt like that, I cried. My dad was a music minister at our church, so music was always around me, but there was one day, shortly after my brother was diagnosed with throat cancer, that I heard this song. It felt like I wasn't alone. My parents were completely focused on Michael, and most of the time, I was alone. But in that moment, I wasn't."

I gawked at him, shocked and sad and understanding. He'd mentioned his brother died when Daniel was in high school, but cancer? "I'm so sorry, Daniel."

He shrugged. "I'll always miss him. He actually beat it and was doing well, but it came back. The second time, it was farther along before he told my parents about it. He wanted a chance to be himself. They pushed him into treatment, but it wasn't enough."

"Wow. I have no idea what to say."

He hugged me to him. "It's okay. I don't really know why I'm telling you all this. I never talked about Michael."

I wrapped my arm around his waist and burrowed into him, not caring about my alarm or running late or anything besides a few more stolen moments with this man.

"I write music," I whispered.

"You what?" he blurted.

"I've never told anyone, but I've written a few songs. Usually just the lyrics, but I've tried a few with the music."

"That's amazing. And not easy to do."

"I grew up with music, too. I know that feeling you're describing. I felt it when I was a teenager. Where it sinks into your bones and becomes a part of you. I've fought it a lot of my life, but music is always there. Songs and melodies and dancing... It's a part of me."

Daniel nodded. "Me, too." He was quiet for a minute, then he whispered, "Will you play one of your songs for me?"

I inhaled quick and sharp. I'd never shared my songs with anyone. I'd never even considered it. Piper had no idea, no one did. The songs weren't for anyone else. They were for me.

But I found myself saying, "Yes."

"Thank you."

Daniel leaned forward and kissed me. It was soft, like the moment we were in. There was no rushing, no timeline. We were just two people who had all the time in the world and were choosing to spend that time together.

He rolled on top of me, his erection sliding between my legs. The rough nest of hair at the base brushed my clit and made me tremble. He shifted, bringing his cock between us and rubbing my clit with the crown.

"Oh, fuck," I moaned.

He stroked against my clit, using his dick to bring me to a fast and overwhelming orgasm. By the time he reached for a condom on the nightstand and slammed inside me, I was breathless and begging.

"So good," I whispered.

"Yes," he grunted in agreement.

He thrust in hard, the never-ending time ahead of us shrinking as the clock continued to advance. He hovered above me, his eyes searching mine as he shifted his angle and made my eyes slam shut.

"Come, Sofia."

"Yes," I said, reaching for the edge. It was right there.

He pounded into me, chasing me toward pleasure. I opened my eyes and watched him, his face twisting in agony as he waited for me.

I reached between us, the back of my hand rubbing his stomach. His eyes snapped open. Realization lit his gaze before lust filled it.

He propped himself up, rising to his knees and letting the covers fall behind him. His gaze landed on my fingers, lightly stroking my clit.

"Fuck me," he grunted, slamming back into me as he stared at my hand. "Holy fuck, Sofia."

My fingers went faster, the rough intensity of his voice pushing me closer. He swelled inside me, and I pressed down hard on my clit, rubbing the little nub hard enough to send me flying and carry him with me.

"Oh, fuck. God, yes. Sofia," he grunted, his words louder with each syllable.

I moaned through my orgasm, shaking with the intensity of it.

"How does it keep getting better?" Daniel whispered as he collapsed next to me. He rolled me toward him and slid his arm around my waist, threading his fingers with mine. He kissed my shoulder.

"Makes you wonder how much better it can actually get," I teased.

"I'm willing to sacrifice the rest of my time here finding out."

I laughed. "I bet you are. But I need to get to work. I'm already running late, and I should really go home and change instead of working all day smelling like I spent all night having really good sex."

He inhaled my neck and licked behind my ear. "I never got to taste you, but that part tastes really good."

I pushed away from him and scrambled out of his bed. "You are dangerous. If I let you do that, you're going to end up talking me into spending the entire day in bed. And I can't afford that, no matter how much Piper loves me."

He snickered and followed me out of bed. "Then maybe I can talk you into coming back here tonight. I can order a mean takeout."

I walked out of his room and right back into the bathroom to give myself a minute to think without staring at his beautiful body. He was tantalizing and thought-destroying. I needed clarity.

"I told my dad I'd spend the evening with him. I haven't seen him much. I'm still not sure why he's here."

"Doesn't he visit often?"

I snorted. "This is the first time he's ever visited me."

"Wow. I assumed it was a regular thing since he's staying with you."

I flushed the toilet and washed my hands, walking back to his bedroom where my clothes were. "Nope. We're not close."

"So you think there's a reason he's here?"

I nodded. "There has to be."

"What do you think it is?" Daniel took his turn in the

bathroom, meeting me in the bedroom where I fixed my bra and pulled on my panties, with Daniel's eyes tracking my movements.

I shrugged. I hadn't let myself think much about what the reason could be. "I don't know. I'm trying not to worry about it. He's not perfect, but he's the only family I have."

"I get that," Daniel said softly.

"Are you close to your parents?" I tugged my jeans on, and Daniel followed suit, foregoing boxer briefs to slide jeans over his naked hips.

He shook his head. "No. They got divorced after Michael died. They were too broken. I get it, but it's hard. Michael was... he was great. He held us together at the end, and without him, we all fell apart."

"You seem like you're figuring it out."

He breathed a laugh. "I'm doing my best."

"That's all any of us can do."

"Very true." He followed me to his door and stopped me before I opened it. "When can I see you again?"

I tried to think through my schedule, but I knew it was busy. "Text me tonight and I'll check."

"One problem."

I raised an eyebrow, my hand on the doorknob. "What's that?"

"I don't have your number."

"What? Really?" I thought back and realized he was right. We'd talked and ran into each other, but I didn't know how to contact him without knocking on his door. "You're right. Here." I handed him my phone so he could put his number in.

He typed something, then deleted it and retyped it.

"What was that?"

He shook his head. "Nothing. Just being funny, but I

realized you might not be able to find my number if I put my name as Best Sex Ever."

I accepted my phone back and smirked. "You're right. I already have that name saved for two other guys."

He gasped and clutched his chest. "You're killing me."

I laughed. "I'll change their names later."

He laughed with me, pulling me close and laying a kiss on me that would have me clearing my schedule to make time for him. I moaned against his lips, hitching my leg around his hips and honestly debating playing hooky for the day.

Then he pulled back and opened the door. "I'll see you soon."

I smiled at his dismissal, and promise, and walked out his door.

With a smile that lasted all the way downstairs until I opened my apartment door.

"Where have you been? You didn't come home last night. I called the police!" my dad shouted.

"You did what?"

My dad paced and glared at me. "You always come home. You're rational and reasonable. You don't do things that I have to worry about. But you didn't come home. Where were you?"

A knock on the door interrupted me before I could speak. I turned around and opened it, knowing who I'd find on the other side.

"Hey, James," I said as I opened the door.

"You're home," he said, looking past me to my father.

I stepped back to let James in. "I'm home. I just got here. I'm sorry he bothered you."

"It's no bother. Rowan's out looking at your SUV. Everything okay?" James asked.

"No! It's not okay. My daughter was out all night long. Anything could have happened to her."

James looked closely at me and smirked. "You want me to stick around?"

I pushed him toward the door, knowing he knew exactly why I was out all night and knowing I did not need a witness to the conversation I was about to have with my father. "We're all good, James. Thanks for checking up on me. Hi to Trinity."

James let me shove him out the door. I closed it to the sound of him chuckling as he walked toward the exit.

I turned to face my dad, anger boiling inside me until I saw the look on his face.

"I thought something happened to you," he breathed.

"I'm sorry, Dad. I never thought you'd be worried."

"You're my daughter. Why would I not be worried?"

I laughed mirthlessly. I didn't have time to get into it with him. Not when I was already running late to start my day.

I tried to walk past him, but he stopped me. "I've never been a good father, and I'm sorry for that."

And there it was. The one thing I'd been wanting my entire life. An apology. Or maybe it was the admission. Something.

But I was no longer sure I needed it. His words didn't have the effect I expected them to have. It didn't sink in and heal all the broken pieces of me. All the chips and cracks I'd lived with since I was old enough to understand my father claimed I wasn't his.

I turned to face him. He looked older than I remembered him being. It had been years since we'd seen each other, and since he came to stay with me, I'd been avoiding him. Avoiding the conversation he was starting right now when I had to go. When I would be the one walking away.

"Can we have dinner tonight like we planned? Talk?"

He nodded, looking partly relieved and partly fearful.

I started to walk away again, needing to take a quick shower and change before I started my day.

"I have a lot of regrets, Sofia. You have always been my biggest one."

Holy... ouch. The words every girl wants to hear from her father. Wow. That one broke off a whole new chunk, a chunk I didn't realize was so fragile and could break so easily. "Thanks, Dad." I didn't turn to face him, not wanting to show him the tears in my eyes. I just retreated to my room, stripping off the pain with the clothes Daniel had stripped from me less than twelve hours earlier.

The water was hot but did nothing to soothe the pain I felt. I let my tears fall, needing to get them out before I faced him again. I reached up for my shampoo and grasped nothing.

"What the hell?" I pried my eyes open and looked at the shelf where my shampoo usually was. It was empty. I know I didn't use the last of it the day before, so what the fuck?

I groaned. I knew what the fuck. My father. The man who thought the world belonged to him and everyone else could go fuck themselves.

I shook my head and squeezed a dollop of body wash into my hand. I washed my hair, cringing at the harsh feel of it before I added extra conditioner. Thank God he hadn't stolen that, too. I washed my body and rinsed everything off, then climbed out, crossing my fingers I still had a towel.

I dried off and wrapped my hair in the towel while I went to find clothes. My anger served as a good layer of protection over the hurt.

My mother used to tell me she didn't blame him for not claiming me. I looked like her, not him, and it was a one-night stand with a rockstar. She was sure lots of women tried to trick him or trap him or get money from him by claiming they were pregnant with his kid. The fact that she actually was didn't really matter.

But it wasn't easy. My mom was the best person I knew. She was the most honest and good person. She made me who I was. She never stopped fighting to get him to claim me as his, but she never went public. She never brought the media into it. She let him continue to deny everything.

Then one day, he asked for a paternity test. When it proved he was my father, he sent her a check. She put it in an account and never touched it. She never touched any of his money. She said it wasn't about that for her.

Every penny of that money was there when she died. It was there when I went to college. It was there when I decided college wasn't for me and moved to MacKellar Cove. It was there for me my entire life.

And now the man who gave me that money, the man who was my only living parent, the man who denied my existence for years, said I was his biggest regret.

For not the first time, I wished I could talk to my mom. I wished I could call her and get advice. But for the first time, I wished he'd been the one who died instead of her. All he'd ever given me was money. But money didn't matter as much to me as telling people you care about how you feel. And he just shared how he really felt about me.

Fuck him.

13

———

I DIDN'T GO BACK TO MY APARTMENT FOR LUNCH. I COULDN'T face him. I needed a break, so I walked down the street to Serenity Salon to see Haley and Chelsea and have lunch with them.

When I walked in, Chelsea was showing off something on her phone. They both turned to see who'd entered and grinned when they saw me. It was so damn nice to know I was wanted by my friends. That they didn't see me as a mistake, a regret.

So damn nice I burst into tears.

"Oh, my God, what's wrong?" Chelsea asked, rushing to me.

"Is it your dad?" Haley asked, coming to my other side.

One of them locked the door, protecting my privacy without knowing why I needed it. They led me to the back, away from prying eyes and nosy neighbors, and eased me onto the new couch they'd added when they took over the place.

I sobbed while they stared at me, waiting for me to get the tears out so the words could follow. "I love you guys."

They both hugged me, giving me exactly what I needed without even knowing why I needed it. It didn't matter to them. They were my friends, and they loved me, and they were there for me.

"We love you, too," they said together, chuckling at their jinx moment.

The three of us sat there for a long moment, me trying to stop the rush of emotion that wasn't like me and the two of them letting me be me.

I finally took a deep breath and sat up. They removed their heads from my shoulders, but neither of them released the hand they gripped in theirs.

"Are you okay?" Chelsea asked.

I shook my head. "Not really. My dad... He called the cops this morning because I didn't come home last night. I told him I didn't realize he would be worried. He was offended by that, I guess. But then he told me he regretted having me."

"He said what?" Haley barked. Her body went rigid with fury. She squeezed my hand tighter, her anger combining with mine.

Justified. I wasn't alone. And I wasn't crazy for feeling that way.

"What an asshole," Chelsea breathed. "I'm so sorry."

I nodded. "Thanks. I..." I exhaled a long, slow breath. "I asked him if we could have dinner tonight and talk, since I sort of felt bad about not being around a ton since he's been here. He agreed, then he told me that, and I just... I have been trying to hold it together since he said that. I cried in the shower, then I left. I couldn't bring myself to go home for lunch and face him."

"I don't blame you. We have food coming, and there's

always enough for you to join us," Haley said. "Wow, though. What a shitty thing to say."

I nodded, my anger fading. I was still angry, but the hurt was flowing in. "I walked in and saw you guys, and you both smiled, and it just felt so good. You two looked happy to see me, and knowing my only living relative regrets my existence... Sorry. I didn't mean to come here and cry all over you guys."

"You never have to apologize for being you with us. We love you, Sofia," Chelsea said, hugging me to her side.

"What were you guys looking at? I need a distraction. Anything good?" I asked.

"I'm buying a house," Chelsea said.

"You found one? Congratulations!"

Chelsea beamed with excitement. "Thank you! It's not a done deal yet, but I saw it yesterday afternoon and love it. I know you're not supposed to get emotional when it comes to buying a house, but it's exactly what I've been looking for. Quiet neighborhood, not too far from my parents but far enough that they aren't likely to stop by at all hours. Three bedrooms, which I don't need, but it has a fenced-in yard so I can finally get a dog. I'm really excited."

"Can I see?" I asked.

Chelsea dug her phone out as someone knocked on the front door.

"I'll grab the food," Haley said, leaving me to look at Chelsea's hopeful new home.

I flipped through the pictures and smiled. "It looks like it would suit you. The hardwood floors are stunning. Ooh, look at that fireplace."

"I know. It works, too. The deck isn't huge, but the patio is nice. It'll be perfect for having people over. The trees are big and offer lots of shade."

"There's a hammock," I groaned. I'd always wanted a hammock under a big tree so I could read a book, fresh air and the warmth of summer. I closed my eyes and dreamed of borrowing Chelsea's hammock a few days.

"You can share," she said, nudging my shoulder.

Haley came back to the back with bags of food that smelled amazing.

"You weren't kidding about having enough food," I teased them.

"This is what happens when we order food when we're distracted and hungry," Haley joked.

"I'm happy to benefit. How much do I owe you?" I stood with Chelsea, following Haley and the food to the small dining table far from anywhere they performed services.

"Not a thing," Haley said.

"Nothing," Chelsea said at the same time.

We all chuckled. "How about drinks at O'Kelley's one night? I need to get the hell out of my apartment."

"Sounds like you did last night," Haley said.

My cheeks warmed. They looked at me with matching expressions of curiosity.

"No comment," I said.

"Oh, come on. You have to tell us. Where did you sleep?" Haley asked. She opened one of the bags of food and pulled out containers.

"Or where did you not sleep?" Chelsea opened another bag.

We all laughed.

"A little of both," I confessed. I opened the third bag. It was a ton of food.

"Yes! Good for you," Haley said. "Daniel?"

I nodded, unable to stop my smile from growing.

"Who's Daniel?" Chelsea asked. "Oh, wait! Is that the creepy neighbor? Do we like him now?"

Haley nodded. "He's really nice."

"How do you know?" I asked. Demanded more like. Jealousy might have spiked when I heard Haley praising him. Which was dumb, because Haley loved Knox and would never even consider cheating, let alone ending things with Knox, but jealousy isn't rational.

"Calm down," Haley said. "I ran into him getting mail one day. He asked me how I liked the building and MacKellar Cove."

"I'm sorry," I said, knowing I was a jerk.

Haley grinned. "All good. Just nice to know you're there."

"I'm where? I'm not anywhere."

Haley and Chelsea exchanged a look and laughed.

They took a break from harassing me about Daniel while we filled plates with food. We all took seats and started eating before the interrogation resumed.

"So, things are going well with Daniel?" Haley asked.

I nodded. "We're having fun. He's only here for a few months, so I'm not getting attached, but we click, you know? I feel like I can be myself with him. Like I can be with you guys and Piper and Sebastian. He's not judging me. Or if he is, I don't care because he's leaving soon and I'll probably never see him again."

"And you're okay with that?" Haley asked softly.

"Yeah. I'm not looking for what you and Knox have. I wouldn't pass it up, but I'm not looking for it. I know I'm not going to find it with Daniel because he's not sticking around, and I'm not willing to leave."

"Dating in this town is not easy," Chelsea said.

I laughed at the frustrated tone of her voice. "No, it's not. Are you on Book Boyfriends Wanted?"

Chelsea nodded. "I've had a few matches, but none who really stuck. So many of the guys I talk to there are immature and annoying."

"You want an older man," Haley teased.

Chelsea shrugged. "I want a man who's not a child. Someone who understands what it's like to have responsibility and goals. More than which bar am I going to next weekend."

We laughed with her. Chelsea and Haley were both thirty-one, but I definitely felt like they were closer to my age. Knox was thirty-eight, and it never felt like there was a gap between him and Haley, even when they first met. When I was their age, I was the same as them. I always felt like I was out of place and older than the number my license said I was.

"Did you select an age range?" I asked her.

Chelsea nodded. "I did, but I think I need to change it. I don't think I have tolerance for people my age anymore. Not men. Not dating."

"Maybe someone will surprise you," Haley said.

Chelsea snorted. "With how many shots they can do in one night without falling over drunk? Yeah, my last date tried that."

"No, he didn't," Haley said, sounding as horrified as I was.

"Let's just say I was not surprised, and I was not impressed. Even less when he tried to tell me he could still rock my world. He could barely say 'rock your world' let alone actually pull it off."

Haley and I laughed so hard tears rolled down our cheeks. Chelsea smiled, joining in our laughter.

"I tell you, I know how to pick them," Chelsea said.

"I could have given you a run for your money before Knox," Haley said.

"Yeah, her track record was pretty bad," I agreed with Haley. The man she dated before Knox was married but never told Haley or his wife until Haley showed up on his doorstep, ready to surprise him that she moved to town so they could be together. The surprise did not go over well.

"Any of these guys could have been married. I didn't stick around long enough to find out, or care. If they are, I feel bad for their wives. For so many reasons," Chelsea said.

I ate my lunch and thought about that. "I don't get why people cheat."

"Same," Haley said. "I still want to ask Dawson why he did it. My guess is there's some kind of victory in the idea of doing something you shouldn't be doing. But it's just shitty."

"Agreed. But I will say I'm happy it brought you here, and it got Valentina and Brantley together. Dawson is a jerk, but everyone is better off without him around," Chelsea said.

"Except his girls," Haley said softly. "I feel bad for Bianca and Samantha. They were caught in the middle."

"It sounds like they're doing well, though," I said. Valentina's oldest daughter was making plans for her future. She was going to be a high school senior in the fall and was a bright girl. Her younger daughter was a year behind her sister, but she was just as bright and just as focused on her future. Valentina made it sound like both girls were thriving with Brantley, their new step-dad, in their lives and aside from the hurt of their dad not being around, they were happy.

"That's good. Dawson is still an asshole, though," Chelsea said.

We laughed, nodding and agreeing with her assessment.

We talked about less serious things as we finished our lunch. Chelsea promised to keep me posted about the house news, and I assured her I'd help with any repairs she needed to have done and would be willing to walk through it with her during the inspection. She was grateful.

I left Serenity Salon feeling better. I didn't need my dad to be happy I existed. I knew who I was. I had friends who were like family, and they'd been there for me through more than my dad ever had. I'd be lying if I said I didn't care what he thought, but I refused to let it ruin my life. Because I had a pretty good life.

I went through the motions the rest of my day, setting things up for the following week and working on some of the projects I had lingering around the building. I made a plan to replant all the exterior landscaping and scheduled a meeting with the nursery to select new plants that would blend well with what I wanted to keep. I didn't intend to work all day on a Saturday, but it wasn't like I wanted to do anything else.

When I couldn't delay any longer, I returned to my apartment. My dad was kicked back on my couch, feet up on the coffee table, watching the show I'd been planning to binge the next day.

"This is a really good show," he said as a greeting. "I can't believe the boyfriend was behind the whole thing."

My breath froze in my throat. My entire body went rigid. I'd been waiting all season to find out what happened. I'd avoided all the blogs and spoilers all over every site online. And my dad ruined it with one sentence.

"Guess I don't need to watch it."

"Oh, you should. It's fantastic. So many twists. Like that one." He pointed to the main character's best friend on the screen. "She's in on it with the boyfriend. The two of them have been sleeping together and planned the whole thing. It was his idea, but she added to it. I never saw that coming."

I gawked at him. He had no clue he'd just ruined the entire thing for me. That or he didn't care. Maybe both. "Really, Dad? Really?"

"What?" he asked, his gaze flipping between me and the screen, which still played the show.

"Never mind," I breathed. I walked past him to my room, pausing when I got inside to return. I needed shampoo. "Where's my shampoo?"

He glanced over his shoulder. "I borrowed it."

"And you didn't think I would need it back?"

"I figured you'd get more."

"If I knew I needed more, I would have, but I didn't know my shampoo wasn't in my shower. I need it back."

"Jeez, okay. Sorry. I didn't realize you weren't okay with sharing." He paused the show and went to his room. His head twitched like he was having a conversation with someone.

I rolled my eyes. He was being petty and mean. He took my stuff, and I was the bad guy.

He came back with the bottle in his hand, dripping water all over the floor. He thrust it toward me. "Here."

"Thanks," I said, letting my sarcasm flow. I was a little beyond placating him. He didn't want me to exist, so why was I going to make myself nuts trying to be nice to him?

I stomped to my room and closed the door a little harder than necessary. I set the shampoo on my bathroom counter and tossed my clothes in the hamper. I showered quickly, then changed into something comfortable. Dinner didn't have to be fancy. Especially when he was just going to tell me what a disappointment I was.

The show was just ending when I walked back into the

living room. "Wow, that was good. I can't believe you haven't seen that show yet. When I saw all those episodes, I figured you'd already watched them all, but then it said they were new."

"I was waiting until all of them were out to watch the whole season."

"It was worth it. Well done. You'll like the part where—"

"Stop!" I shouted.

"Whoa. What's wrong?"

"I was saving that show, Dad. You already ruined most of it for me. Please don't tell me anything else. I don't want to know all the best parts of the show. I'd rather be able to watch it and enjoy it myself."

He held his hands up like I was threatening him. "Sorry. I didn't realize you were so touchy about it."

I drew a deep breath, counted to ten, and let it out. I still wanted to strangle him, so I counted to ten again.

"What are you doing?"

"I'm trying to convince myself that you just don't know any better and that you being such a jerk is because you've never had anyone tell you that you are."

"That wasn't very nice."

"Neither was telling me you regretted having me!" I blurted.

"What? When did I say that?"

"This morning, Dad. When you said I was your biggest regret."

He inhaled, then sighed heavily. His shoulders sagged. "That wasn't how I meant it, Sofia."

"Then how did you mean it? That you wished you'd never acknowledged me? That you wished you'd let me go into foster care when Mom died?"

"No! No. None of that, Sofia. I meant not being a part of

your life from the beginning was my biggest regret. Not doing more to have a relationship with you." He let out a shaky breath. "I know I was never a good parent. Your mom was. She was amazing. I didn't really know her well, but she would reach out every few weeks to let me know how you were doing. She was always sending me updates and pictures and doing what she could to keep me in touch, even though I wasn't. She wanted me to feel like I knew you."

"She never told me," I breathed.

"I know. She knew I wasn't any good. She knew the most I could do for you was send you money. When she... when she died, I was terrified. I had no idea what to do with you. We were in the middle of a tour, so I had to bring you along, but I didn't know you. It didn't matter how many updates she sent me, I was still a stranger to you."

"I didn't want you to be," I confessed.

He smiled sadly. "Neither did I. But I felt like it was too late. I tried. It didn't seem like it, but I tried. When Nate joined the tour... All of that was my fault. I asked him to look out for you. He was closer to your age, and I thought it would be good for you to have someone your age to talk to."

"You set us up?" I asked.

Dad shook his head. "No. Not like that. I never encouraged a relationship beyond friendship. I didn't think he would... that everything that happened would happen like that."

I closed my eyes and brought back those memories. I hated my father when he chose Nate over me. When he decided the band and the tour were more important.

"You still chose him," I whispered. "You still sided with Nate."

Dad shook his head. "I didn't side with Nate. He had a

contract. A contract I had no say in. I couldn't get him kicked off the tour. He didn't work for us."

I scoffed. "You could have done something."

"I tried," he admitted. "When you left, I didn't know the extent of the whole situation. I didn't know you'd been involved for as long as you'd been. I tried to have him arrested, but since there was only a year age difference between you two, no one would press charges. It wasn't illegal for you to be together."

"You did what?"

"I wanted you to come back to the tour. I wanted you around. If I'd paid better attention or been a better father, you might not have gotten involved with him. I know it was all my fault, but I promise, I didn't know he was going to do what he did."

"It's fine, Dad. It was a long time ago."

"He's still an asshole."

I snorted. "Piper said the same thing when I told her about him."

"I always knew I liked her."

I laughed. "You haven't even met her yet."

"Well, maybe we should change that. Maybe I should meet some of your friends. Get a look at the life you have here. Make sure my favorite daughter is being taken care of."

"I'm your only daughter," I said with a roll of my eyes.

He shrugged. "As far as we know."

I snickered because it was true. "How about we go to O'Kelley's for dinner next weekend? I'll tell all my friends to meet us there on Friday night."

Dad nodded. "Sounds good to me."

"Me, too."

14

———

Introducing my famous dad to my small town friends was definitely cause for panic. What was I thinking? There was a reason I moved to MacKellar Cove. I knew no one would care who my dad was. But that didn't mean I wanted them to know.

But it was too late to go back on that. I had to trust that my friends wouldn't care. They would understand I'm the same person I've always been. But I had no idea who else would be at O'Kelley's on a Friday night, and it could be bad.

"Are you ready to go?" my dad called through my bedroom door. He'd been a different person in the week since our talk. Happier. More talkative. And kind of more of a pain in my ass.

He was getting ready to be Jensen Carmack instead of my dad.

"I'll be right out!" I called in response. There was nothing else I needed to do, but I was anxious. I didn't love Jensen Carmack, rockstar. I loved my dad, but the rockstar version of him was kind of a dick.

And I'd invited that guy in.

"It's going to be fine," I told my reflection. I hoped I was right. I walked out of my room, ready for the night.

"Is that what you're wearing?" my dad asked, sneering as he took in my outfit.

I looked down at the clothes I'd chosen. Jean shorts that were worn and comfortable and almost as soft as pajamas. A pink tee that was almost too small but I hadn't been able to bring myself to give it up yet. It was a big shirt, so no one else could tell it was small. I added a pair of small hoop earrings and a touch of lipgloss and tied my hair up into a knot, the only style that captured the short layers that framed my face.

"What's wrong with it?" I asked, wondering if I'd popped a button or torn a seam or something. I couldn't see or feel anything out of place.

My dad was dressed like a rocker. He wore black jeans and his favorite stage shoes. Ones he always said were comfortable enough to spend hours on his feet but stylish enough that he wouldn't risk being called out by the media for his appearance. He added a black button down with silver buttons and bright blue stitching. He left it untucked and rolled the sleeves up to show off the tattoos on his fore-arms. His hair was styled back, the not-daring-to-recede hairline he was so proud of on full display.

He could have been going to play a show. I could have been going to work.

But I knew he'd be the best dressed person in O'Kelley's. By far. Even Trent, who was likely the only person I knew who had more money than my father, would be in jeans and a tee and casual for a night out.

Not Jensen Carmack.

He assessed me with a gaze that said he was looking for a way to tell me to change without telling me to change.

"Let's go, Dad. The place is casual, and I'm not changing."

He huffed and followed me out the door.

I opted to drive since I knew he wouldn't tolerate walking to the bar. The coolest people drove in his world. The fact that I wasn't cool, and had never cared about it, was just one more thing we would never agree on.

Parking in front of O'Kelley's was nonexistent on a Friday evening, even though it was early. I drove past the bar and turned up a side street, looking for a spot.

When I slowed down, my dad spoke up. "Are you going to park here?"

"I was planning to," I said, putting on my blinker to parallel park.

"Can't you just drop me off in front?"

I sent him a glare. "Really? You're going to make your favorite daughter walk alone? You don't know who my friends are."

"I'll figure it out."

A horn behind me told me someone else wanted the spot if I wasn't going to claim it. I sighed and pulled away, knowing I'd be dealing with an even more obnoxious pain in the ass if I made him walk.

I circled the block and hit my flashers when I made it to O'Kelley's again. Dad opened the door and waved with a *thanks, hun* before he skipped up onto the sidewalk and flashed a grin for the random couple walking toward him.

I rolled my eyes and pulled away, finding parking down the street. I made it to the sidewalk just as Trinity and James were walking out of their apartment building.

"Hey," Trinity said brightly. She stepped away from James to hug me. "How are you? Where's your dad?"

"I'm good." I hugged her back, reminding myself these were my people. I hugged James, then nodded toward O'Kelley's. "I dropped him off in front."

"He let you do that? Why wouldn't he walk with you?" James asked.

I shrugged. "It's a safe town. I'm not worried."

"Sure, but that's kind of a dick move," Trinity said. She looped her arms with mine and James's, then started walking toward O'Kelley's.

"He's eccentric. He doesn't think about things like that."

"Like not demanding the police department search for his daughter immediately because he's rich and famous and someone could have kidnapped you to get to him," James said, leaning in front of Trinity to raise an eyebrow at me.

She gasped, and I dropped my head.

"He said that?" I asked.

"Yep. Doesn't matter to me. There are plenty of rich people around here. You don't buy an island in the river without having some serious cash to throw around. But is he really a famous rockstar?" James wasn't judging, as far as I could tell. He was curious.

I nodded. "He was the lead singer of Four on the Floor."

"Wow. That's pretty cool. I had no idea," Trinity said. She stiffened.

I laughed mirthlessly. "No one knew. Not even Piper until my dad decided to visit."

"Wait, seriously? You never told anyone your dad was famous?"

I shook my head. "Remember when Trent started hanging around? Or when we all figured out who he was? Or Nico? People can be weird when money's involved."

"True, but it's us. None of us care," Trinity said.

I nodded. "I know. I haven't had a lot of contact with my dad. At first, I didn't want anyone to know. I didn't have a great relationship with him and I needed a break from his lifestyle. Once I started getting to know people in town, it wasn't a big deal because we weren't close. My dad and I. Then once I got closer with everyone here, even though I still hadn't spoken to my dad much, it felt weird to be like, so hey, my dad's famous."

Trinity and James laughed with me.

"I understand that," James said. "I didn't tell a lot of people about my past. Different end of the spectrum financially, but I hid that part from anyone who didn't already know about it."

"That's what I did. Except I moved to a town where no one knew," I admitted.

They laughed with me. James stepped forward to open the door to O'Kelley's for Trinity and me. I thanked him as I walked ahead, searching the inside for my father.

A chorus of laughter rang from a table, and I found him in the middle of the noise. I looked at the people he was sitting with and didn't recognize any of them.

"Is that him? Who's he with?" Trinity asked.

"His adoring fans," I said sarcastically. That was Jensen. He couldn't be bothered to find my friends. He just found the closest group of people who wanted to listen to him talk.

"Don't worry about him right now. Come on. Ian and Ramsey are getting drinks. I see Blake and Finley and the others," Trinity said. She guided me from my father's display. "Did you invite Daniel?"

I nodded. "I figured it's a group thing and not a big deal. If he shows, then good, but if not—"

"He's here. He's talking to James."

I sucked in a breath. I wasn't sure if I felt better or worse that Daniel was going to witness my father in all his glory, but too late to back out now.

"Who's the blowhard in the corner?" Rowan asked, nodding to the table where my father sat.

James whacked Rowan on the back of the head. Trinity tried to flash him a look.

Rowan turned on James. "Ow! What the hell?"

James nodded to me. Rowan turned and mouthed, "Oh." He pursed his lips and pressed them into a smile. "Sorry, Sofia."

"It's okay. You're not wrong. He is a blowhard. But we don't get to choose our parents."

"That's for sure," Rowan said, nodding in understanding.

"She needs a drink," Trinity told the group.

A pitcher of something red and fruity was poured into a glass, which was then shoved into my hand. I took a healthy drink from it, letting the alcohol soak into my brain before I remembered I drove there.

"Shit," I said, setting the drink down.

"What's wrong?" Blake asked.

"I drove," I told her.

Blake waved her hand. "We'll get you home. There will be plenty of sober people here. No reason for you to be one of them."

I chuckled and thanked her, then picked my drink back up.

Collectively, they sucked in a breath, and I knew my father was making his approach.

"Sofia! I thought that was your group of friends!" my dad said, his voice carrying over the noise of the crowd.

I shook my head. "Nope." I looked at the table he'd left

behind. All men that were at least fifteen years younger than me. Not one I knew.

"You should have told me." He turned his charm on for my table of friends. "It's nice to meet all of you! I'm Jensen, Jensen Carmack. Sofia's dad. How are ya?"

Dad made his way around the table, introducing himself to everyone at the table. He took a minute with each of them, or each couple when it was obvious they were together. By the time he made it back to me, everyone was smiling and looking at him like the rockstar he was.

He had a gift. Every single one of my friends felt special after a minute with him. He didn't rush through his introductions. He said hello and asked something about them. And even more impressive, I knew he remembered what they all told him.

I didn't know how he did it, but it always impressed the shit out of me to witness it. I clearly wasn't the only one.

"Drinks!" Ian and Ramsey announced, joining the rest of us and setting two pitchers on the table each. "Hudson's bringing more."

Ian narrowed in on my dad and reached out to shake his hand. "Mr. Carmack, nice to meet you. I'm Ian Jameson." He put his hand on Blake's shoulder. "Her lesser half."

My dad laughed heartily at Ian's joke. "I think we all should feel that way, Ian. Blake's a beautiful woman, and I hear you have a second one on the way. Congratulations."

"Thank you, sir."

"None of that, now. Just call me Jensen."

"I will do that," Ian said.

My dad turned to Ramsey, who was talking to his wife, Melody. "And you must be Melody's other half?"

"I am. Ramsey Holland. Nice to meet you."

"You as well. Hopefully I can meet Amber while I'm here. She sounds like a pistol," Dad said.

Ramsey laughed, clearly taken with my dad already. "That she is. And she's as beautiful as her mother."

"My girl's the same," Dad said, catching my gaze and flashing me a genuine smile. "There's nothing quite like being a father. Although, I'm sure Sofia can tell you I have a lot to live up to."

I shook my head, not looking to air anything in public. Not that any of it mattered that much, anyway. The past was gone, and I got the feeling my dad was trying.

"I think we all have things to live up to," Ramsey said. "No parent is perfect, but the best ones keep trying to do their best."

"Well said," Dad told him. "I understand why you're such a well-respected member of the community. And so successful."

"Thank you," Ramsey said, looking a little shocked and touched by my dad's words.

It was the Jensen effect. I definitely didn't get that gene.

My dad gathered everyone around, encouraging them all to take seats. He stood when Hudson joined us and took a minute to speak to him. Even hard-ass Hudson left with a grin and a nod toward me.

Everyone was laughing at one of his stories when my phone buzzed in my pocket. I pulled it out, smiling when I saw Daniel's name on the screen.

I looked up and found him watching me. He grinned.

I smiled back, then looked down to unlock my phone.

DANIEL

Your dad's a character.

ME

Yeah, he likes to tell stories.

DANIEL

Any about you I should ask him to share?

ME

Nope. I only spent a few years with him when I was growing up. They weren't great years.

DANIEL

Sorry.

ME

Long time ago

DANIEL

Is he where you get your songwriting skills from?

ME

How do you know I have skills? My songs could be horrible.

DANIEL

I can't imagine anything you do is horrible. Especially if you put even a tiny piece of yourself into it.

ME

Thank you

DANIEL

Maybe you can share one of your songs with me this weekend

ME

I could probably be talked into that

DANIEL

Like if I nibbled on that lip you keep biting?

I sucked in a breath, catching my father's attention. He looked over at me. "You okay?"

I nodded. "All good." I shoved my phone in my pocket and tried to focus on my dad again, but my gaze kept drifting toward Daniel.

When I stopped resisting, I found Daniel watching me. A smile lifted his cheeks.

His eyes went wide, and I realized I'd pulled my lip between my teeth. I laughed soundlessly, and he shook his head.

I dragged my attention back to the story my dad was telling. Something about a tour he was on a few years ago. It wasn't a story I knew, so I listened and sipped my red drink.

"He's not so bad," Piper whispered in my ear.

I nodded. "Every so often."

She chuckled and leaned her head on my shoulder. "I'm glad you brought him out to meet everyone. He's really good with people."

"Too bad I didn't get that talent."

"We love you just the way you are. I don't think you and I would have clicked if you were like him."

"Thanks," I whispered. I understood exactly what she meant. Connections mattered. Finding my people.

And I'd found them. Piper and Haley and Sebastian and Chelsea. I looked around the table and knew all the people sitting there, and the ones who couldn't make it, were my people. They were the ones I'd chosen, who'd chosen me.

It wasn't always to see that, but I was lucky as hell to have them. They weren't sitting there to listen to Jensen Carmack. They were there to listen to my father.

And there was a difference. A big difference. And I could feel it.

And it felt damn good.

15

TREY

Watching Sofia blush when she saw my text was better than I expected. When she pulled that lip between her teeth, I would have sworn she was doing it on purpose to tease me, but the look on her face was priceless.

I was in trouble.

And not the kind of trouble I half expected to be in when she invited me to meet her dad with the rest of her friends. I was sure he would recognize me and completely blow my cover and my chances with Sofia.

But Jensen shook my hand and accepted the name I shared and rolled with it. He asked me how I was liking MacKellar Cove when James mentioned I was in town for the summer. I think James was trying to help. In his way. Which meant he was laughing at me and helping me at the same time.

Is that what friendship meant?

It kind of felt like it. Especially when James did the same thing to Rowan and again to Hudson when he came to refresh the pitchers.

With Seth, there wasn't time for relaxation. Downtime

meant finding a woman and screwing her until you were tired enough to crash for a few days. We didn't hang out and drink beer unless there were at least a dozen people around and there was a reason for getting together.

Being with Sofia and her group reminded me of life before Michael got sick. Movie nights with my family, school events, church. All things that went away when we started spending all our time in hospitals and clinics and at fundraisers.

The only time I felt like myself after Michael got sick was when we would sing together. In his hospital room when it was just the two of us. Mom and Dad would cry if they heard us, but when it was just us, Michael and I would sing. The smile on his face made me think he would get better. That life would be normal again.

But it never was.

"You okay?" Sofia asked.

I hadn't noticed her stand or her walk over to where I was. I pasted on a smile and nodded. "Yeah. Your dad's a character."

She looked back at him. He was regaling everyone with one of his many stories from life on the road. I didn't have the same level of interest as the others since I was living his life, but I could appreciate the way he told a story. It was the same as how he crafted a song. Pause at the right moment, crescendo to pull in the audience, and a bridge that tied it all together and had the crowd swaying along like they were on the road with you. It was beautiful to watch.

But not nearly as beautiful as the woman standing next to me.

"He knows how to tell a story and how to make people love him," she said after a minute.

I nodded, sensing there was something she wasn't

saying. Something important that she wasn't ready to admit, or admit to me.

"You were staring off. I just wanted to check on you."

"Come to my place tonight," I whispered. It was an impulse. A desperate desire I couldn't hold back. I wanted to touch her, to pull her into my arms and kiss her, to feel her body wrapped around mine like the other couples near us. I wanted to claim her as mine.

But she wasn't mine. I would leave once I got what I wanted, what I needed. I would never see her again. She would hate me.

"Okay," she whispered. "After he goes to bed, though."

I nodded as though I understood her need to sneak out of her own place so her father didn't know she was going somewhere else. It didn't matter. She said yes. That was all I was after.

Sofia went toward the bathrooms, and Piper and Haley followed quickly behind her. Knox and Gavin both winked at me. Jensen was into another story and didn't notice.

Maybe Sofia sneaking out was a good idea.

After a few hours, some of the couples with kids started to leave. Sofia mentioned needing someone to drive them back to her apartment.

"We'll drive you home," Blake assured her before I could say anything. "Maddox is with my mom for the night, so we can take you. No problem."

"Absolutely," Ian said, lifting his glass of water. He'd switched from beer after his first drink, like I had.

"You can tell me more about these boats you build," Jensen said to Ian. "I've never owned a boat, but maybe it's something I should do now that I'm retired."

"You're retired?" Sofia blurted.

Jensen shrugged. "I'm not going out on tour anymore. I

still write music here and there, but even those contracts have dried up, mostly. I'm just an old rockstar reliving his glory days now."

"But you're okay? I mean, you're not sick?"

Jensen shook his head. "All good. Just figuring out the next part of my life."

"Do you two want to head out?" Blake asked, reading the room and understanding the lightness and fun of the evening had passed.

"Yeah, I think we should," Sofia said softly.

Everyone filed out of O'Kelley's, hugging and shaking hands on the sidewalk before heading toward their vehicles and homes. I considered catching a ride with Ian and Jensen, or with Sofia and Blake, but I already felt like a third wheel in the middle of the entire group.

I let my thoughts wander as I walked the few blocks toward the apartment building. Sofia's question made me think Jensen's visit wasn't as innocent as he wanted her to believe. Something was going on. But I was as in the dark about it as she was.

The building was quiet when I let myself in. I tried not to make any noise as I climbed the stairs and unlocked my door. I locked it behind me and dropped my keys onto the table next to the door.

I went to the fridge and grabbed a beer, twisting the top off and taking a long pull. I dug out my phone and started searching.

There was no news online about Jensen Carmack from the last few months. Nothing leaking a mystery diagnosis or a secret visit to a doctor.

On a hunch, I searched Carson Beck, the lead guitarist from Four on the Floor. He and Jensen were like Seth and me. The two of them, along with Ricardo Waters and

Andrew Oscar, formed Four on the Floor. The story I heard was the band name was a play on their names all having the word *car* in them and the first vehicle they toured in when they were getting started. I assumed the well-earned stereotype that most rockstars woke up on the floor was a second meaning for the name. Either way, the name stuck when a promoter heard it and declared it catchy and good for marketing.

Search results for Carson Beck loaded just as a soft knock sounded on my door. I locked my phone and set it on the table with my keys and opened the door.

Sofia had her hands twisted together, her lip between her teeth, and a worried look on her face. "Hey," she whispered.

I stepped back to let her in and closed the door behind her. "Are you okay?"

She shrugged and headed for the couch. She tucked her feet under her and sat, looking small and scared.

"What's going on? Your dad?"

She nodded. "His visit always felt off. Like something happened."

"Is it?"

"I don't know!" she blurted. "Sorry. I just... He's not perfect, but he's the only family I have left. We've never been close. He's never visited me, anywhere I've lived."

"And you think him being here now means there's more to it than fatherly affection?"

She snorted. "He's never shown me any affection. When I was a kid..." She drew a breath and studied her hands. "He wasn't in my life for a long time. When he finally... started trying to get to know me, it was mostly through cards he sent and other gifts. He didn't visit. He invited me on tour with him a few times, but my mom never let me."

"I can't say I blame her. His stories were... interesting."

She laughed and shook her head. "Every man's dream, right? Freedom and lots of willing women."

"Maybe not every man's," I said, thinking sitting on the couch with her was pretty damn nice at the moment.

She blushed. "Anyway, I always wanted to be closer to him. After a while, I stopped trying."

"And now he's trying."

She nodded slowly, trying to figure out what reason her father had for reaching out.

It sucked, but I understood what she was thinking. I hadn't spoken to either of my parents in months. Neither of them knew where I was or what I was doing on a regular basis. When Michael died, our entire family imploded, leaving me without either of my parents on top of losing my brother. My parents were so deep in their grief they seemed to forget about me.

Every so often, one of them would reach out, but it always felt like it was out of obligation instead of a desire to hear from me. If either of them showed up and tried to act like things were good, I'd have a hard time with it, too.

"I know you didn't sign up for this," Sofia said. "Maybe I should go."

I grabbed her hand before she could stand. "You don't have to go."

"I'm not sure I'm going to be good company tonight."

"Then maybe you're just here. Maybe I'm the one who's good company tonight."

She looked at me closely, trying to figure out my ulterior motives.

I wish I knew what they were because spending the evening, maybe the night, with a woman who wasn't interested in sex used to mean an end to the night for Trey Ryan.

No questions asked, no thought behind it. If Trey Ryan was in the presence of a woman, it meant we were going to have sex.

As Daniel, I couldn't muster the same distant, dickhead behavior with Sofia. I wanted to listen to her talk. I wanted to sit on the couch and watch a movie with her. I wanted to hold her hand and help her to feel better.

It was a weird feeling. But good.

"Are you sure?" she asked, sounding hopeful and anxious at the same time.

"Absolutely. Why don't we find a movie? Comedy or drama?"

"Comedy. I've had enough drama for a while."

"Sounds good."

We settled on the couch, a movie on the screen. I tried to be good and keep my hands to myself. I focused on the movie, and I must have done an okay job because Sofia fell asleep.

I watched the rest of the movie alone, smiling when her head slid to my shoulder and she snored softly. I eased her head to my lap and ran my fingers through her hair, which she'd taken out of the knot that held it up while we were out.

She looked peaceful and beautiful. Her lashes rested on her plump cheeks. Her hip lifted off the couch. Her legs were tucked under a blanket, one I had no doubt she'd selected when setting up the apartment for me.

I let another movie start and felt myself fading. When it was over, I needed to wake Sofia up and let her decide if she wanted to stay the night or go back to her apartment. Just one more movie.

A bite of pain woke me up with a start. It took me a second to realize where I was. I looked down at my lap and found Sofia watching me. Her hand was beneath my shirt, her fingernails digging into my nipple.

"It seems you like having your nipples played with, too," she whispered. Her voice was husky and soft, like she was afraid to be too loud but was already turned on.

"Is that an invitation?" I asked, reaching for the hem of her tee.

She shifted so I could ease her shirt up and nodded.

I pulled her shirt up and her bra down, exposing her breasts to the cool air-conditioned air. She sucked in a breath when I brushed my fingers over her nipple.

"I want to suck all your carbon dioxide," I whispered.

Her lips curled up. "Like a tree? Or like a vampire? A vampire tree?"

My cheeks warmed. I could blame my half-awake-all-hard state, but the reality was I'd never been very good at talking to women. I'd never needed to be. They didn't care what I had to say as long as I fucked them.

"Both?" I said, not knowing if there was a good answer.

She chuckled and rolled her body, ending up on her knees. She crawled to me on the couch and straddled me with her thick thighs. "Vampires are pretty hot, and I am definitely a fan of saving our planet."

I cupped her ass and brought her body into contact with mine. "I think you should stop me from saying anything else stupid and let me fuck you until we're both unable to speak."

"That was definitely not stupid," she whispered.

I thrust my hand into her hair and dragged her mouth down to mine. She met me with her lips parted and her tongue seeking mine.

I groaned and dove into her. Tongues wrapped around

each other, hands grappled for bare skin. Breath rushed out of us in hurried pants.

She shifted her hips and rubbed herself against my erection. My eyes rolled back in my head, and I urged her to do it again.

"Fuck," I hissed, dragging my lips from hers.

"Yes," she moaned in response.

"Condom," I growled.

"Now." She stood and dropped her shorts and panties to the floor.

I was momentarily stunned, lost in the perfect woman standing half-naked in front of me.

"Condom, Daniel," she said with a laugh in her voice.

I snapped out of my daze and lifted my hips. My wallet was in my back pocket and I'd shoved a condom in it earlier, for no other reason than pure blind hope.

I loved that hopeful fucker right now.

Sofia took the condom from my hand and helped me drag my jeans and boxer briefs off. She sank to her knees in front of me, shoving the coffee table back so she had room.

I watched as she opened the condom, then as she looked at it and my dick, a few inches from her face.

She looked up at me with a devilish smile. I didn't have time to protest before she leaned forward and sucked my dick to the back of her throat.

"Holy fuck. Jesus, Sofia. Dammit."

She withdrew enough to meet my gaze, then licked my cock and deep-throated me again.

"Fucking hell."

She chuckled, the sound going straight to my balls and making me buck against her. She moaned, and fuck, I nearly lost it.

"Sofia, I'm about five seconds from coming in your

throat. While I'd love that, I really want to fuck you until you come first. So, what do you say you come on up here and ride my dick while I play with your clit?"

She shivered and nodded as she released me. "Never let me tell you you're not good with words again."

"You like dirty talk?"

She shrugged. "Apparently I do."

I took the condom from her hand, knowing I'd waste it if I let her roll it on. She hovered over me, waiting not so patiently for me to have the condom in place. As soon as it was, she lowered herself onto me.

"You feel so good," she whispered.

"Same," I hissed, the feel of her tight channel even better than her mouth.

"You on the edge?"

"Hanging on by my fingernails," I admitted.

She chuckled, then lifted and sank back down. "Better?"

I grunted a laugh and shook my head. "Is that a challenge? Who can get the other to come first?"

She raised one eyebrow and smiled. "I like that thought."

I surged up into her on her next stroke, and the cocky look on her face slipped.

"I like that, too," she whispered.

I lifted her shirt to expose her breasts again. Her nipples were still above her bra. I brought my mouth to one, biting down onto it while she rode me.

Her rhythm faltered, and I smiled around her nipple. I let her bra hold her breast up and moved my hand between her thighs, finding her plump nub. One stroke, and she cried out.

"I don't think this is a fair challenge."

"I think it's the best one ever," I said around her nipple.

She kept going, not wanting to miss out on a minute of pleasure. I raced with her, fingers, tongue, and cock all working together to wring out every drop of pleasure I could get from her.

"Daniel," she breathed.

"Come for me, Sofia. You win. All I want is to see your beautiful face as you come all over my dick."

As soon as I said she won, her channel rippled around my dick. The flutters of her orgasm spread through her body, everything releasing at once and triggering the same reaction in me.

I held her tight to me as I came hard. I groaned into her neck, knowing I wasn't completely done. It wouldn't be long before I'd want to be inside her again.

She sat on my lap, holding me as tightly as I held her. "I'm sorry. I didn't mean to take advantage of you like that."

"You can take advantage of me like that any time you want. But just so you know, I was a willing participant for that. Very willing."

She pulled back and looked at me. "You were sleeping."

"I was very much awake for that, Sofia. And I meant what I said. I'll gladly lose to you on the race to an orgasm if it means I get to watch you come."

She blushed and ducked her chin. "You make me feel half my age."

"I don't want that Sofia. I want the beautiful, confident, curvy woman you are right now. You're stunning. And I'm lucky to know you."

"For a few months," she said. "Then you're going to have to find another beautiful, confident, curvy woman to ride you on your couch."

Her words were delivered with a teasing tone and a laugh, but they hit me deep. I didn't want to find another woman like her. But I knew I couldn't keep her in my life. She didn't want to be a part of it.

But I had her for now. And I would enjoy every minute I got with her.

"I'm going to use your bathroom. Then maybe we can move to the bed?"

"Wherever you want me," I teased.

She smiled and leaned down for a quick kiss before she walked away with her beautiful ass bare to my gaze.

I was going to miss that view when I went back to my penthouse overlooking the water. Nothing could compare to Sofia.

16

SOFIA

MY ALARM WENT OFF, DRAGGING ME OUT OF A DEEP SLEEP that I did not want to come out of. But if I didn't, my dad would call the police again, and no one wanted that replay.

I kissed Daniel softly, enough to wake him up and tell him I was leaving.

"Do you have to?" he grumbled, sounding adorable in his petulant begging tone.

"I don't want the cops at my door again because my dad panicked. But maybe I can come by a little later?"

He nodded against the pillow and reached for me. I put my hand in his and he squeezed, tugging me down for another kiss before snuggling back into the covers. I think he was back to sleep before I even left his room.

I found my clothes in the glow of the light over the stove and the nightlight on the vent fan in the bathroom. I was pretty sure my underwear was inside out, but all it had to do was get me back to my apartment.

I locked his door and snuck out, closing the door as quietly as possible. I glanced at Mrs. Watson's door, holding my breath. It didn't open, and I was able to sneak away without anyone seeing me there.

My apartment was still quiet when I let myself in. I started the coffee and went to my room to change into pajamas.

Dad was in the kitchen when I got back in there, filling a cup of coffee and adding the last of my caramel syrup. He tossed the container in the trash, not the recycling, and stirred the concoction in his mug.

"Good morning," Dad said, turning and scanning me with a careful gaze. "I thought I heard you come in just now."

I considered lying to him for a second, but what was the point? I was an adult, and he had no say in my life. "I did."

"Were you with Daniel?"

I nodded.

"You two are seeing each other?"

"We are. He's only here for a few months, so it's very casual."

Dad nodded thoughtfully. "Spending the night with him doesn't seem casual."

I shrugged. It didn't feel casual either, but I didn't know how to explain that to my father. I knew there was an end date with Daniel. I knew he was going to go back to his life and we'd probably never see each other again. I was okay with that. Was being the key there.

But I wasn't going to be one of those women who fell in love and changed the rules. We laid it all out ahead of time. I knew when we started seeing each other that he was leaving. I refused to get upset with him for doing exactly what he told me he was going to do.

"You're in love with him, aren't you?" Dad asked.

I shook my head and moved to pour myself a cup of

coffee. "I can't be. He's leaving, and I know he's leaving. He's going back to his life."

"That doesn't mean you can't be in love with him."

"Falling for him would be the dumbest thing I could do."

Dad snorted. "Who ever told you love was smart and rational and came at the right time?"

I laughed with him. "Touché."

"What are you going to do?"

I looked at my dad. We'd never talked like that. About feelings and emotions and other people in our lives. "Have you ever been in love?"

He looked startled by the question, but he didn't hide from it. He considered it after his shock faded and he nodded. "A few times. My life... I never made space for love in my life. Your mother..."

"Please don't lie to me and say you were in love with her."

He shook his head and sat at the table in my small dining area. "I wasn't going to. You know I was barely good enough to her to be allowed to say her name. She was far better than I ever deserved."

I nodded and joined him, with my cream and sugar coffee instead of caramel. My mother never spoke badly about my father, but I also knew she never loved him. She was sad he didn't acknowledge me when I was little, and when he finally did, she was grateful, but she'd built a life for us that didn't need him or his money. But he was my father, and she thought it was important that I had a relationship with him, and she never wanted to influence that.

"I wish I'd gotten to know her. I know from the little I know of you that your mother was an amazing woman. When she got pregnant with you, I wasn't equipped to handle anything. It took me a long time to figure out that I could have changed who I was, but by then she was gone and you'd left and the band stopped touring and I was alone."

"Is that why you're here? Because you don't want to be alone?"

He shook his head. "I'm here because I should have been here for you years ago. You don't need me now, but I know I made a lot of mistakes with you. I will never be able to fix them, but maybe I can get to know you and not make the same mistakes with you going forward."

"You're not sick or dying or in a twelve-step program?"

He chuckled. "None of that." He sobered and his smile turned sad. "But Andrew is sick. Carson called me a few months ago and told me."

"Oh, no. Dad, I'm so sorry."

He nodded. "Thanks. I went to see him. We all did. He's not likely to make it to the end of the year. We had talked about doing a reunion tour or something, but with Andrew sick... I'm a selfish prick."

"Why?"

"Because that was my first thought when Carson called me. That we won't be able to do the tour."

"You've always been a little bit..."

"Self-centered?" he provided.

I shrugged and didn't argue.

He laughed. "I know. I'm working on that, I guess. I've been going to a therapist."

"No," I said, trying to hold back my laugh.

"I know. Hard to believe. Like I said, not being a part of your life earlier is my biggest regret. I have a lot of things to work through. And this therapist is used to dealing with people like me."

"Narcissistic rockstars with a Me First complex?" I

teased.

He snorted. "Don't hold back on me."

I laughed with him.

"I fell in love with a woman about a year ago. I thought I was finally going to get married. Bought her a ring and everything."

"Really?"

He nodded and sipped his coffee. This wasn't the performer. This was a heartbroken man taking a moment to collect himself before he finished his story. "She'd been married before. Said she loved me, but there were too many things about me that reminded her of her ex. That she wasn't willing to get into another marriage with another man who was more worried about himself than another person."

"I'm sorry, Dad."

He shrugged, but the pain in his eyes wasn't fooling me. "She's not wrong. When I had to choose between what she wanted to do and going out and being the center of attention, I always chose the attention. I never put her first. I never showed her how I felt about her."

"Can you now?"

He shook his head. "It's too late. She's probably moved on."

"But you don't know that."

"Why would she want to be with a washed up old rockstar?"

"Maybe she wouldn't. But she might want to be with a man who loves her."

Dad froze at my words. He opened his mouth to protest, but closed it again. He looked up at me with the most vulnerable look I'd ever seen from him. "I have nothing to offer her."

"Let me tell you a secret, Dad. The women who want to screw a rockstar are not the same as the women who want to settle down with a man they love. Not every woman wants to use you to get ahead or to boost herself up or to go on to the next guy. When I was with Nate, I didn't see him as Nate Catalan. I saw him as the man I hoped to spend my life with. I was young and foolish and I'm sure it wouldn't have worked out anyway, but he was just a man to me. I was still grieving from losing Mom, and I wasn't ready to be an adult. But I thought I was. I didn't care that he was on tour or that he had potential to be famous. I cared that he liked me."

Dad was quiet for a long minute. He contemplated my words with the last of his coffee. When he spoke again, he sounded more hopeful. "I've never thought of myself as someone worthy of a person like Monica. She's kind and caring and she gives all of herself to others. She works with underprivileged youth and is always giving back to the community."

"She sounds very sweet."

"She is. So much better than me."

"She obviously didn't think so when you met."

He chuckled at a memory he didn't share. "No, she didn't."

"So, what are you going to do?"

"What do you mean?" He was honestly confused by the question.

"How are you going to get her back?"

"I don't—"

"Dad, you're a rockstar with a dying friend. Are you really going to tell me you're not going to go after the woman you love and tell her how you feel and convince her you mean it?"

I watched as his chest puffed up and his confident stance returned. "You're right."

"Of course I am."

"Thank you, Sofia. I really appreciate the vote of confidence."

"You're welcome."

"Do I have to leave right now?"

I laughed. "No, Dad. You can leave when you're ready. But before you go, you might want to start thinking about others. Paying more attention to what the people in your life need."

"What do you mean?"

I raised my brows and laughed. He had no idea. "Well, you used the last of my caramel creamer and never bothered to tell me you were using it at all so I could add it to my list."

"Sorry. I... yeah, I should have done that."

"Same with my shampoo. And you left a bag of chips in the pantry that was only crumbs. Without closing it so when I grabbed it all the crumbs dumped all over the place. And—"

"Maybe I can start with one thing at a time?"

I shook my head and exhaled a laugh. "Probably a good idea."

He smiled at me. "Thanks, Sofia. For letting me stay here and for giving me hope."

"We should always have hope, Dad. No matter what."

"I think you're right."

"Back again?" Mrs. Watson asked.

I hadn't noticed her when I walked up the stairs to

Daniel's apartment after lunch, but she was there, in her open doorway, watching me.

"Good afternoon, Mrs. Watson. How are you?"

"I saw you leave his apartment this morning. Before then, I thought you were fixing things, but that doesn't seem to be the case."

"Is there something I can do for you, Mrs. Watson?" I didn't want to be rude to the woman, but I also didn't owe her an explanation.

She shook her head. "He's a nice man, Sofia. Helps me with my groceries and talks to me like a person. Doesn't judge."

I was taken aback. Daniel said she liked him, but I didn't believe him. It was nice to be wrong about the cranky woman who barely tolerated others. "I think he's nice, too."

"It's nice to see you with a smile on your face. I've worried you'll end up a lonely, bitter old woman like me one day."

"I'm not sure those are the words I'd use to describe you, Mrs. Watson."

She snickered. "That's why I like you, Sofia. You're nice. But you know those words are truth. I have more than my share of regrets. Don't let your pride hold you back from going after what you want."

I wasn't sure how to respond to her and by the time I recovered from my shock, she'd closed her door.

I took a minute to process her words. They were laced with regret and pain, with a touch of perspective that allowed the past to be negative. We all had our moments, but to look back and be so frustrated that you isolated yourself from everyone else was a step I'd never imagined.

Daniel's door opened before I knocked. He looked surprised to see me standing there. "Hey. Are you okay?"

I nodded. "Yeah. Just talking to Mrs. Watson."

"I thought I heard her. Is she okay?"

I nodded again and stepped inside. He closed and locked the door behind me. "She saw me leaving this morning. Told me not to let my pride stop me from going after what I want."

"Really? That's cryptic. Unless you were having a deep and meaningful conversation in the hallway just now?"

I shook my head. "No. She said she had regrets. It was sad. Like those songs that talk about missing out on what could have been the best thing in your life."

"Those are the songs that touch people the deepest. We all have those moments."

I nodded. "I've been thinking about that all morning." I held up the notebook I brought with me. "Want to hear my latest song?"

"Really? Hell yes."

He followed me to the couch. I was nervous to share my music with someone, but if I was going to share it with anyone, Daniel was the one.

I opened the page to where I'd been scribbling words all morning. Between my dad talking about Monica and my rampant thoughts about Daniel leaving, a song had started to play in my head.

Regret Pain Love

Nothing to share
Nothing to give
No reason to make you stay

From the first kiss
It all felt different

Electric, magnetic
Push and pull, spark and arc

"It's not much. It's not really anything. But it's what came out today," I said, reaching for the notebook as Daniel studied my words.

He pulled the notebook out of my reach and set it on the coffee table. He grabbed his guitar and started to play.

He changed keys and started again. The tone was haunting and melodic. It tingled through my body and made me sad immediately.

"Wow," I breathed.

He looked up at me and smiled. "Yeah?"

I patted my chest. "That hits me hard."

He nodded. "Same with your words. I heard this before, in my head, but I couldn't reach it until just now when I saw your words."

"Really?"

He turned his attention back to the guitar. "Do you think it'll work together?"

"Absolutely."

He studied my notebook again and played the same notes. He started singing my words, his voice soft and smooth. It hit me in a way I'd never felt before.

"Holy crap," I breathed as he played the last note.

"Was that okay?"

I swallowed around the thickness in my throat. "I've never heard one of my songs out loud before. No one's ever sung one of them."

He set his guitar on the floor against the accent chair and leaned toward me. "Shit. I shouldn't have—"

"No, it was... amazing," I breathed. "I... obviously my

dad is famous. I don't talk about it much because a lot of people want something from him or me. But we aren't close because he accused my mom of lying when she got pregnant with me. Said she was just trying to get his money."

"Oh, shit," Daniel breathed, paling.

I nodded. "Yeah. My mom said that wasn't what she was after, but it never mattered. I was in middle school before I met him. He finally decided he needed to find out for sure and did a paternity test. He paid child support and all that, but my mom never used the money. When she died, I went on the road with my dad. We were basically strangers, and it wasn't a great situation, but it was all I had."

"I'm sorry," Daniel whispered.

"Thanks. It was hard. But that's where I fell in love with music. Where I first heard a song that gave me chills and made me feel like I wasn't so alone. One of the opening acts had a song that resonated with me on such a personal level that I ended up dating a backup singer. It was a bit of a disaster and didn't last, but my love for music did. I stayed *far* from the music industry since then, so hearing one of my songs was never something I imagined would happen. Ever. But I'm happy. That was better than I could have ever hoped it would be."

Daniel sucked in a breath. "I'm sorry for everything you went through."

I shook my head. "I'm not. I mean, I wish my mom was here, but the rest of it is just part of life. Not everyone is who they seem to be, but we all have pain and regret and heartbreak in our pasts. That's what music does. It takes the biggest pieces of our lives and gives us all a connection for three minutes. We all share the same thing. The same pain or joy. Music connects us. You reminded me of that today. Thank you for that."

"You're welcome," he whispered.

"Will you sing it again? Maybe help me write more of it? And if you're feeling really adventurous, I can show you some of my other songs."

Daniel nodded slowly. "Of course, Sofia. Whatever you want."

I smiled and leaned back while he picked up his guitar. He played his tune and sang my words, and I closed my eyes and pretended I was at my very own concert.

It was magical.

17

TREY

I sang her words, and I played my music, and I hated that it felt right. Fuck, so right. More right than anything I'd ever created.

It had been far too long since I felt that tingle of excitement. That deep knowing that the song was good. The vibration that made me trust the process and enjoy the process.

But it was clouded with the lies hanging over me. Not just why I was there in the first place, but that I was no different than her father. No better.

I'd done the same thing as Jensen. Denied a woman who claimed I was the father of her unborn baby. It was more than a year ago. We were on tour, and the label handled it. Without talking to me. I wouldn't have known a thing except Seth made a comment about it. He thought I knew.

When I asked, the label told me it was handled and I wouldn't hear from Avery Power again. Said she'd been paid to keep her mouth shut. They didn't think the kid was even mine, but it didn't matter. They made sure she wasn't going to be an issue.

But it did matter. I threw myself into the end of the tour and tried to pretend there wasn't a woman out there pregnant with a baby who could be mine. I told myself she didn't matter. That she was just after my money and fame and whatever piece of me she could get. I always, always wore a condom. But condoms could fail.

Still. She was lying. She had to be lying.

I told myself the same story so many times I thought I believed it. Even when I looked her up online and studied the lines of the baby's face to see if it was familiar. I told myself she was lying.

Jensen probably told himself the same. But Sofia's mom wasn't lying. She wasn't after his money. She wasn't after anything from him.

Hearing Sofia's story made me realize that was the turning point for me. I hadn't felt that tingle, that unsung melody in my mind, since I found out about the baby.

Since I refused to consider that I fucked up. Since I let someone else make a decision about my life. A decision that made me the same as Sofia's dad. Someone who would abandon his kid.

"What do you think?" Sofia asked, turning her notebook toward me.

She'd written another verse of her song. While I was thinking about the woman who claimed I'd gotten her pregnant, Sofia was pouring herself into a song, giving me what I'd come to MacKellar Cove for.

I pushed Avery Power from my mind and focused on Sofia. I wanted to ask her who the song was about. Who she'd had to watch walk away. But I didn't have the guts, and I didn't have the right. We were temporary, and I'd already overstepped enough. Even if she didn't know it.

"What if we switch these two lines?" I suggested,

pointing to the ones I thought worked better flipped.

She mouthed the words and nodded. "Yeah, I like that." She scribbled the changes and set the notebook on the table again. "I've never written a song with anyone. Are you going to shop this around when you get back to LA? Am I going to hear my music one day being sung by some random person?"

The lead truth of my presence there sat in my gut like a brick. I shook my head and forced a smile. "I'd never do that to you."

She chuckled and nudged my shoulder. "I was just kidding. I know you wouldn't."

I laughed with her, hoping my laugh didn't sound as hollow as it felt. It would crush her when she figured out who I was. And I couldn't even say I was sorry. The song she was writing was good. It would be a hit. And if I could bring myself to put it out there, it would bring flocks of fans to Broken Record. We'd get a new contract and a new tour and win awards for the song. I could feel it.

But I couldn't say it. I couldn't tell her what was going on. If I did, she'd walk out. The song would never be finished. I'd lose everything I'd worked so hard for since Michael died. I'd be nothing and no one.

I had to keep going.

We took a break just before dinner, and she jumped up when she saw what time it was. "I'm so sorry to run out on you, but I was supposed to help Chelsea pack tonight."

"Is she moving?"

Sofia nodded. "She's buying a new house. The whole process is moving really fast. She saw it earlier this week and has her inspection next week, and if the house looks good, she should close in a month or so."

"And she's already packing?"

Sofia chuckled. "She's manifesting her success, she says. She's ready to get out of the apartment she's in. The house is perfect for her, and she's worried someone else is going to jump in and steal it away, so she's putting it out to the universe that it is meant to be hers."

"Good for her."

Sofia stopped at the door and kissed me hard. She wrapped her arms around my neck and pulled me down for a kiss that made me forget what an asshole I was and made me want to be a better man for her.

"Bye. And thank you."

"Bye," I said, letting her walk out and believe I was a decent man.

I was an asshole.

"What happened with Sofia and your brother?" I demanded an hour later when I called Seth. The way she mentioned dating a backup singer, the emotion behind those few words, told me there was a lot more to the story than Seth had ever told me.

Seth laughed. "What do you mean?"

"You told me they dated. What happened?"

"You know how Nate is."

Which meant Nate fucked around on her. As a teenager, I thought Nate was a badass. I looked up to him and wanted to be him. But now? "He cheated on her," I said.

Seth sighed heavily. "Is it cheating if you're not serious? I mean, come on, dude, you know how things are. No one's serious when you're on tour."

"Did she know that?"

"Why do you fucking care?" Seth barked. "Is her pussy

magical or something? Fat chick got your balls in a sling and now you forgot where you came from? I gave you your career. Me and Nate. Without us, none of what you have would exist."

"Last I checked, the music I write is what put us on top of the charts."

"And how do you think we got a shot in the first place?" Seth growled. "Did you really think some dumb fuck kid with a dead brother was good enough to get a contract? Fuck no. The label didn't give a shit about you or your brother. All they care about is selling music."

The reminder of how we started hit deep. I sucked in a sharp breath. The man on the other end of the phone wasn't the one I'd spent almost half my life counting on.

Seth never said things like that to me before. Never made it seem as though I was lucky instead of good. Or that Michael was inconsequential.

"Nate talked to the label," Seth continued. "He got our single in front of the right people. And he only did that because I'm his brother. You could have been anyone."

"Our songs, our music," I stammered. It had been our mantra, our commitment to each other.

"You're the one who's so hellbent on only singing songs we write. I never cared. Told the label so when I met with them. Nate got me an audition before you came in, but they didn't want Nate's little brother. They wanted a band. After Nate went solo, I wasn't enough alone. I pitched them on the two of us. Said you had music."

"You sold me out."

"I gave you everything!" Seth shouted. "The women and the music and the money. It's all because of me. Because I made it happen. Don't you dare act all hurt now. You selfish prick."

"Fuck you, Seth."

"No, fuck you, Trey. You go to that dinky fucking town and get your dick wet in that fat fucking chick, and you think you're all better than me. You're nothing. You're no one. You're having some existential crisis and think you should be better, leave me the fuck out of it. I didn't force you to do anything. I didn't tell you to go there and weasel your way into her world. I didn't tell you to fuck her. I didn't tell you to do a damn thing. You're the one who refused to listen to the music the label brought us."

"It's not us."

"No, it's not you," Seth growled. "But it's good."

"You listened to it?"

"Yeah, I listened to it. And I'm thinking of recording some of it."

"On your own?"

Seth exhaled. "I don't know. What I do know is I'm done playing second place to you. I'm done having the label wait for you before our next album comes out. I'm better than you. I always have been. And I don't need you around to show that to the label, or anyone else."

He hung up before I could respond. I stared at my phone and wondered what in the fuck just happened.

My oldest friend, the person I thought I could count on, admitted he'd barely tolerated me for the last twenty years, and only because of his career.

I unlocked my phone again to call Sofia, but I couldn't. Not only was she with her friends, but she didn't know the whole story. She couldn't.

I swiped over to the only other option I had. It was sad when the only other person I trusted was someone I'd never met.

GIOIOSO

I just found out my oldest friendship was a lie. I'm unsure how to function right now.

TALKNERDYTOME

I'm so sorry. That's not easy to learn.

G

Yeah, I'm reeling. He told me we were only friends because of work.

TNTM

What an ass. Even if it's true, you'd think after a while there'd be more to a friendship than convenience.

G

We met at a time when my life was kind of falling apart. But I talked to him about everything. It's really messing with me.

TNTM

I can only imagine. What do you call a cow in an earthquake?

G

Um, what?

TNTM

What do you call a cow in an earthquake?

I'm trying to take your mind off your friend. Make you laugh.

Take a guess.

G

Uh, bouncy beef?

TNTM

LOL! That's not bad, but no. It's a milkshake!

I snorted a laugh and shook my head.

G

> That was good. Thank you.

TNTM

> You're welcome. Are you okay?

G

> No, but I will be. Sorry to interrupt your night.

TNTM

> All good. I'm just helping a friend pack.

I nearly dropped my phone. It wasn't possible. Was Talk-NerdyToMe Sofia?

TNTM

> I should probably get back, but I'll check in on you tomorrow if that's okay.

G

> Yeah, sounds good. Good luck packing. And good luck to your friend on the move.

TNTM

> She said thanks. She's manifesting her house, so no news on when she'll be moving yet, but she's hopeful it'll be soon. Have a good night!

Fuck. Fuck, fuck, fuck. Either TalkNerdyToMe was Sofia, or it was one of her friends who was also helping her other friend pack.

I don't know why I didn't think that was possible. I joined the stupid app to meet her, and when I started chatting with the woman, I forgot that it was part of my plan.

And then I started falling for Sofia.

"Fuck!" I shouted into the empty apartment. What the

hell was I going to do? I couldn't tell her who I was. But I couldn't keep even more things from her.

I never should have started any of this. I never should have told the label I knew where to find Jensen Carmack's daughter or that I would get a song by the end of summer. I never should have done any of it.

First thing Monday, I was going to get a few things straight with them. And then I was going to come clean with Sofia.

"No," Robert Miller said.

No explanation, no detail, just no.

"But, sir—"

"Did I fucking stutter? You went there to do a job, Trey. You didn't go there to fall in love or grow a conscience or whatever the fuck you think you're doing there. This is a business. And I'm in the business of making music. Creating a connection for fans. You're the one who volunteered for this mission. It was your idea. I was perfectly content to throw you some music from other artists."

"I know, but—"

"No, you don't know, Trey. You have no idea. Broken Record is one of our most successful bands, but sales have been down lately. The last few years, your concerts are taking longer to sellout. Songs are hitting the charts lower and lower, or not at all. We're not getting requests for you guys to do events."

"It's all about the money."

"This is a business, Mr. Ryan. This isn't a charity. So, yeah, it's all about the money. It's about what's hitting with listeners. It's about who's being asked to be a guest judge or a host on TV. It's about making more money so we can create more music."

I seethed silently while he panted into the phone.

"Listen, if you grew a conscience and all of a sudden don't want to get this song from Carmack's daughter, I'll send someone else to do it."

"No!" I barked.

"Then I suggest you get it done. You're under contract with us, Mr. Ryan. You have a job to do. It's up to you how it's done, but if you even think about taking the song you're working on with her to another label, you will be so buried in legal fees and courtrooms you'll wish you'd had the balls to shove a contract in her face and get her to sign over the rights to the song."

"I'm going to do a paternity test," I said, knowing it would stop him from ending the call before I said all I needed to say.

"I would not advise that."

"Yeah, well, I can't live with myself knowing there could be a child out there who shared my DNA that I've been denying."

"Is this Carmack's daughter talking again?"

"You know about that?"

Robert Miller sighed. "The mother has been paid off. We learned our lesson. If she breathes a word of paternity to anyone, she'll lose her house. Leave it be, Mr. Ryan."

"I can't do that. I can't sit here and pretend that child doesn't exist."

"I would advise you to do just that. Forget you ever heard anything about that woman or the baby and get a song for me."

"But—"

He slammed the phone down, the old style handset

ringing in my ear from the slam. I pulled my phone away from my ear and sighed.

I never should have admitted I'd been working on something with Sofia, but he sniffed it out. That or he'd already spoken to Seth. I was leaning toward the second option.

Which meant Sofia's song was going to be on the radio. The label would buy it and they would play it everywhere and she would know I was the one who manipulated her.

I didn't know how to fix this. Even if I told her, it wouldn't make things better. She'd still be angry and hurt.

There had to be a way out of this. If I could write a song without her, if I could deliver a song to the label, they'd leave her alone. She'd never know.

But it meant finding that spark that only seemed to light up when she was around.

Even knowing I lost the spark when I found out about the baby didn't mean I'd find it again once I learned the truth. If the baby was mine, I owed the mother child support. If the child wasn't, I could move on. But either way, I needed answers.

More than *don't worry about it* and *it's been taken care of.*

I heard someone in the hallway outside my apartment and snuck to the door to check. Sofia was speaking to Mrs. Watson. Both of them looked at my door, and I ducked.

Because that was rational.

I peeked through the peephole again and saw Sofia go into Mrs. Watson's apartment.

I couldn't face her. I needed to get away. Figure out what I was going to do next. There was too much going on.

I grabbed my keys, wallet, and phone and let myself out of the apartment. I locked the door as quietly as I could, then hurried toward the stairs before Sofia could catch me.

18

SOFIA

"How are things going with my neighbor?" Mrs. Watson asked.

I was grateful for my position under her sink so she didn't see the blush I knew was staining my heated cheeks. "Things are good."

"That's good to hear. The last person who lived in that unit was a horrible neighbor. Up all hours and rude. He would brush by me on the stairs and nearly knocked me over one day trying to get out the door."

I made a noncommittal sound of agreement. I didn't have a lot of interaction with Wellington, but Mrs. Watson wasn't the first person to tell me he was an obnoxious jerk.

"I think he got worse when his girlfriend moved out. She was the only thing that kept him from being a complete ass. Of course, she obviously knew that was the case and finally got away from him."

Marci left two months before Wellington did, and I knew it wasn't an amicable breakup. They were both in their twenties and worked out of town in opposite directions. They lived in MacKellar Cove since it was in the middle, but neither of them got involved in the town or made friends with the other locals.

"I didn't know either of them well."

"You weren't missing out. I'm hoping if things keep going well with you and Daniel that he'll stick around." The question was not subtle, but it was effective. Dammit.

"Daniel's not staying here for long, Mrs. Watson. He's only here for three months."

"I figured you'd change his mind."

I chuckled and wiggled my way out from under the sink. Her ring was in my hand, and the P-trap was back in place. "You might want to wash this before you put it back on, but it's out of the drain."

"And you're avoiding my question," she said, far too observant for me.

I sighed. "I wouldn't want to change his mind anymore than I'd want him to change my mind about staying here. I love this town. I chose to be here. He didn't."

"He did, since he's here right now. And if he's rich enough that he can be here for three months without working, then I think he can stay here for good."

"I don't know anything about that, Mrs. Watson. And it's not my business."

"You're sleeping with the man. It's definitely your business."

I snorted at her sassy retort. "That doesn't give me the right to all his personal information. People sleep together knowing far less about each other than I know about Daniel."

She grumbled, knowing I was right.

"Is there anything else you need me to do, Mrs. Watson?" I asked, pasting a polite smile on my face.

She scowled at me and shook her head. "I still think you

should ask him to stay. Let him choose instead of making the decision for him."

"He chose when he signed a three-month lease."

She grumbled as I packed up my things and made my way to the door. I paused long enough to look back at her.

"I know you're trying to help, Mrs. Watson. I heard you when you told me not to let my pride get in the way. This isn't pride. This is me understanding that not everyone is waiting for their life to start. He's here as a pause, not a change. He will go back to his life, and I would resent it if he asked me to change my life to go with him. I would never ask him to uproot his life to stay here with me, no matter how I feel about him."

She nodded, seeming to understand what I wasn't ready to voice yet. What I might not ever be ready to voice.

I let myself out of her apartment and heard her lock the door behind me. I drew a breath and stared at Daniel's door.

What we had was light and easy. It was fun. I'd never had a relationship like it. What I wasn't sure of was if it was different because I loved him or if it was different because I knew it wouldn't last.

There was freedom in temporary. I wasn't worrying if we would have to argue about where to spend holidays or what our next vacation would be. I didn't have to consider if I was spending enough time with him or too much and ignoring my friends. We got together when we could and let it go when we couldn't.

I didn't know what he did all day, but retrieving Mrs. Watson's ring took less time than I expected, so I had a few minutes to see if Daniel was home. I stepped across the hall and knocked on his door.

My lips curled up into a smile as I imagined him

opening the door and sweeping me inside to kiss the hell out of me before I had to turn around and leave again.

The smile faded as the door stayed closed. I knocked again, pressing my ear to the door to see if I could hear anything.

The apartment was silent.

Oh, well. I thought about sending him a text to say I'd stopped by, but I wasn't going to bother him. Besides, I had a job to do. Like Mrs. Watson said, most of us couldn't take three months off.

MY PHONE BUZZED as I pulled up in front of the house Chelsea was hoping to buy. I put my SUV into park and grabbed my phone in case it was Chelsea with a change to the plan.

DANIEL

What about this next:

You said I wasn't in it

I didn't love you

I chose everything but you

I smiled at his words. We'd been trading texts all week about the song we were working on. It was fun. More than I ever thought it could be. Daniel was creative and inspiring and loved music the same way I did. Like it was a part of him.

ME

I love it. I can feel the pain in that. Fits perfectly.

I waited for him to reply, but I didn't get any indication he was going to. A car door closed not far from me, and I looked up to find Chelsea parked behind me.

I tucked my phone away and got out to meet her. She looked adorable in a red top that hugged her curves in a way that was modest but sensual and a pair of jeans that ended at her calves. Her endless brown waves were pulled back into an artful ponytail that would have taken me three tutorials and an hour of finessing to look that good.

"Hey!" Chelsea said when she saw me approaching. "Thank you so much for doing this."

"I'm happy to help. Who's meeting us here?"

"The home inspector and both realtors."

"Good. Hopefully it goes quickly. It's a really cute house."

"I know, right?" Chelsea looked at the little home and beamed with excitement. The house wasn't huge from the front, but it extended back quite a bit. Fifteen-hundred square-feet was plenty for Chelsea, and the house was in a great area and listed for a really good price.

"Can we get closer?" I asked her. We were the only two there, so I didn't want to overstep, but I wanted to get a good look at the cedar shake siding that covered the entire house.

She shrugged and walked up the cracked concrete driveway. "I do wish there was a garage, but I'm thinking I might put up one of those cover things. Eventually, I might try to build a one-car garage right here where the driveway ends at the fence, but I don't think I'm going to have the money for that."

"That could get expensive. Not a bad idea, though. You could also build the garage in the backyard more if you wanted more driveway and less yard."

Chelsea shook her head. "I love the yard. I have been resisting going to look at dogs because I know I'll fall in love with one and it'll be adopted before I'm ready to bring it home."

I laughed with her. "Yeah, probably better to wait on that. And makes sense to put the garage here if you want to keep as much yard as possible. I wish we had covered parking at the apartment building. Parking on the street isn't bad most of the time, but you have to think about it when it snows."

Chelsea laughed. "Exactly. I'm outside now at my apartment, but eventually I'll want something. Aside from that, everything is perfect for me. But I'm in love with it and see nothing wrong, so you need to be honest with me if you think this house is going to be a drain on me for any reason."

I got up close to the siding next to the side door. It was the place most likely to show wear and damage in my experience. "So far, it looks like it was really well maintained. I'm not seeing any water damage or cause for concern."

She sighed heavily. "Oh, thank God. I was so worried you were going to tell me the place is falling apart."

I chuckled. "We haven't gone inside yet, but from the outside, it looks good so far."

"Phew. Good."

More car doors slammed, and we looked up to find two women and a man walking toward us, all waving to each other from where they parked.

"Hi, Chelsea," the man said. "Good to see you again."

"Hey, Mark." Chelsea shook his hand. "This is my friend, Sofia. Mark is my realtor."

"Nice to meet you," I told him, shaking his hand.

"You, too," Mark said. "This is Nicole, the realtor for the seller."

Chelsea and I both shook hands with Nicole.

"And this is Stephanie, the home inspector."

Again, we all shook hands and introduced ourselves.

"Is everyone ready to get started?" Stephanie asked.

The others all nodded, and I followed their lead.

Nicole unlocked the house and let us all inside. Stephanie started in the kitchen, running through her checklist quickly. The appliances were all in good working order. There were no visible leaks or issues. The cabinets looked like they were as old as I was, but all the doors closed tightly. They'd been well maintained, and if Chelsea was happy with the way they looked, I was not going to judge her. Hell, I would have been happy with them if they were in the house I was buying.

The floorboards creaked in a few spots, but they seemed to be level, telling me there wasn't an issue with the support system, but I made a mental note to look at it when we walked down to the basement.

Stephanie led the way upstairs and checked out the one full bathroom in the house. The GFCI outlet tripped when she pressed the switch and reset without any issue. She checked the power coming to it and nodded before she recorded her numbers.

The stoppers held in the sink and tub and both drained as designed once released. The toilet flushed and filled back up quickly. She crawled on the ground to make sure there wasn't any water coming from around the fixtures, then moved to the bedrooms.

Bedrooms were quick and easy with a quick check all rooms had locks on the doors and working lights and outlets. She peeked in the closets and climbed up to inspect the attic.

"The insulation up there is a little light, but it still meets the standard. I'd recommend sucking out the old and replacing it at some point in time, maybe in the next five years," Stephanie told Chelsea when she came back down from the attic.

Chelsea nodded and looked at me.

"It's more messy than anything else, but it'll improve the energy efficiency and require less work to heat and cool the house," I explained to her.

"Oh! Makes sense. Is that something you can do?"

I shook my head. "You're going to want a professional team for that, but we can ask Knox and Teddy for a recommendation."

"I apologize," Stephanie said. "I didn't realize you were buying the house together."

Chelsea and I shook our heads.

"We're not," I told Stephanie, "but I am the maintenance manager for an apartment building in town. Chelsea asked me to tag along and help her understand what she needs to do now, what she should do, and what isn't a big deal."

"That's smart," Stephanie said. "I will include everything I find in my report, but if you don't understand something, it's hard to know what needs to be done."

"When my wife and I bought our house, the electrical panel was outdated. She freaked out and thought it meant the whole house needed to be rewired," Nicole explained to us with a laugh.

"That's so common around here. Building codes change all the time," Stephanie said.

Nicole nodded. "I explained that to her, but she didn't

take my word for it. Insisted on bringing in an electrician to look at it before she would go ahead with the purchase."

"But it all worked out?" Chelsea asked.

Nicole smiled. "It did. But it's definitely easier when someone understands the recommendations. Even a good report will have suggestions. It can make you very anxious."

"But we'll look at everything," Mark said. "It sounds like you have contacts that can help, and I have some people who might be able to help if you need anyone else. So far, it seems like this house is in really good shape. And don't tell Nicole, but I think this is a really good deal."

Everyone laughed with Mark. He was old enough to be Nicole's father and was being respectful and kind. He was knowledgeable but didn't mansplain things to the four women he was walking through the house with.

"The sellers are moving to Florida and really want the house to go to someone who's going to love it. They raised their three kids in this house, and they love MacKellar Cove. They had a potential buyer in the spring who wanted to tear the house down and build something super modern. Their list price was attractive to people who wanted the land more than the house. The sellers backed out of the deal before any paperwork was signed."

"I love this house," Chelsea said. "The only thing I want to change is I want a garage."

Nicole chuckled. "The wife told me that was the one thing the husband always said he wished they'd done."

"That's good to hear, that they won't be disappointed if I do that. Can I ask you about the neighborhood?"

Nicole talked about the family friendly area with a few single people sprinkled in throughout. Stephanie finished her inspection upstairs and started back down. She went through the rest of the first floor, then down to the basement.

The basement had the electrical panel, and Stephanie laughed when she opened it.

"Needs an upgrade?" Nicole asked.

Stephanie nodded. "Yep. It's all here, and it's acceptable, but it's not to current code." She turned to Chelsea. "That means nothing is required to be done. It's safe, but things have changed and an upgrade is possible. But it's not cheap, so it's not something I would recommend. But it's something I have to note."

Chelsea nodded and turned to me with a worried look in her eyes.

I shook my head in response, letting her know it was all okay.

She exhaled her relief.

Stephanie finished her inspection while I looked at the support structure for the first floor. It looked good, with no cause for concern to explain the squeaky floors. Stephanie told Nicole she'd have the report done in twenty-four hours, then shook hands with all of us. Nicole locked the house while Mark said goodbye to Chelsea and me.

"Lunch?" Chelsea asked me.

"Sure. Where do you want to go?"

"Will Work For Burgers?"

"Yum. I'll follow you," I told her.

Chelsea got into her car and pulled ahead of me. I eased out onto the street and followed her into town.

We parked in the lot next to Burgers and met next to our cars.

"So, what did you really think?" Chelsea asked.

"I think it's adorable," I assured her. "It's perfect for you. I can totally see why you fell in love with it."

"Yeah?"

I nodded. "Absolutely."

Chelsea let out a heavy sigh and looped her arm through mine. She insisted on paying for my lunch as a thank you for helping her out, and we grabbed a table near the back to talk more about the house.

"I didn't see anything that really concerned me. Obviously, there are things you can't see. If there's a leak behind a wall, no inspection is going to find that. But I think it's a good house. And the neighborhood is perfect."

"I agree. I wanted something that felt cozy. I don't have a family yet, but I still hope I might one day. I'd love to have a place where I could start a family."

"I think that's smart. Part of your manifesting?"

Chelsea nodded. "It's silly to some people, but I've seen it. There's power in believing. It doesn't matter what you call it, whether it's manifesting or prayer or faith or even working your ass off to get what you want, it's all the same to me. It all means believing in the possibilities around you and making it happen."

"That's pretty inspiring," I told her.

Chelsea smiled and sipped her drink. "If only I could manifest a man."

I snickered. "Right?"

"You have a man," she argued.

I shrugged. "Daniel's temporary. He's leaving soon. He's been here a month already. In two more, he'll be gone."

"And you're not going to see him ever again?"

I sighed. "I don't know. I know I don't want to move, and I know he has no intention of moving here for good."

"What does he do?"

"He works in the music industry."

"Oh, like your dad? Did they know each other?"

I shook my head slowly. "I don't think so. Neither of them said anything."

"Huh. I guess it's a bigger industry than I realized. They say LA is huge, so I shouldn't be surprised."

I nodded. "Yeah, it's pretty big."

Chelsea was quiet for a minute while I replayed the one interaction my dad and Daniel had. Neither of them looked like they knew the other. They couldn't. They would have said something.

"Are you happy?" Chelsea asked.

I looked at her, a little taken aback by the question. "Um, yeah. Why?"

She shook her head. "Debby said something to me the last day she was at the salon. We were talking about work, and I said I love my job and I can't see ever walking away. She said there's more to life than a job, and that I should leap at every opportunity I have, even ones that scare me."

"Is that why you're buying a house?"

Chelsea nodded. "That's part of it. But it also made me realize I'd been throwing myself into work a lot. I was working longer hours and taking on more clients and exhausted every day. I was quickly working myself to death, and I didn't even see it."

"Did something happen?"

"No. I'm good. But I wouldn't have been if I'd kept going like that. My inconsiderate neighbor and all-around lack of privacy have been part of that. I need my own space. I want a dog. And I want to start having regular get-togethers. A chance for us, whoever that is, to hang out and have fun."

"You need to come to book club more."

Chelsea laughed. I'd been trying to convince her to come for months. She'd been a few times, but she wasn't a regular yet. "I know. I'll come on Sunday. Will you be there?"

I nodded. "I will be. And I'm open to whatever else you're thinking. I don't spend enough time with friends."

"Good. I think it'll be fun. I need some time with another single woman, too. Haley still has stars in her eyes."

I laughed with her. "I have a feeling that's not going to change anytime soon."

"Nope. But good for her."

"Agreed."

19

———

"Three hours? I mean, seriously? Three hours? It sounds good in theory, but can you imagine the chafing?" Elise asked us at book club on Sunday.

The rest of us hooted with laughter.

"I don't think I'd be able to have more sex for three months after that," Goldie said. Her face said even more how much of a disappointment that would be.

"Same!" Anna said. "Then again, with kids in the house, I'd be happy with three minutes alone sometimes."

"Oh, please tell me Hudson is better than that," Finley said. "I always thought he'd be one of the good ones. The kind of man who makes sure the woman he's with is plenty satisfied before he lets himself go."

"He's definitely that," Anna said. "But when all you have is the time between a kid coming home from school and arriving back in the kitchen to ask what's for dinner, you do your best."

Goldie and Valentina laughed loudly and nodded their agreement.

"Teenagers are a whole new kind of challenge,"

Valentina said. "Of course, with Dawson, they never had to worry about walking in on something. Brantley is a whole different kind of man."

"You're also still in that cute, affectionate, hands-all-over-each-other phase of your relationship," Blake said.

"We are," Valentina agreed with a huge grin.

I laughed with all my friends, happy so many were able to be there for book club. It had been a long time since so many of us were there. Even as much of an introvert as I was, I was happy with the crowd that was overflowing our usual area at the back of Finley's bookstore, Book Boyfriends Unlimited.

"She's not the only one in that honeymoon phase," Chelsea said, giving me a pointed look.

"Oh, no, don't drag me into this," I argued. "What about Haley?"

"I'm old news," Haley said. "Tell us how things are going with Daniel."

I shrugged. "I actually haven't seen him much lately."

"Really? You two were together almost every day for a while," Piper said.

I nodded. "Yeah, but I haven't seen him in a week. It's really weird."

"Since we all met your dad?" Finley asked.

"I saw him that night and spent time with him the next day. I left to help Chelsea pack and haven't seen Daniel since."

"I'm sorry. I didn't mean to create an issue," Chelsea said.

I shook my head. "Nope. Not you. If things have run their course, I have to be okay with it. I always knew it was temporary."

"He's still here for another two months," Piper said.

"I saw him at Cracked a few times this week," Blake said.

"He's still texting me, but we just haven't seen each other. It's fine, guys. I'm not stressing about it. I can't."

"Okay," they said, none of them believing me.

"How's your dad?" Elise asked. "He was really nice."

I smiled. "He's good. Things between us are better, too."

"Is he sticking around a while?" Trinity asked.

"He hasn't decided yet. I'm trying to talk him into going back to the woman he wants to marry."

"Whoa, what?" Finley blurted.

I laughed. "He was telling me about this woman he met. They were dating a while ago, and he asked her to marry him. He said she turned him down because he's not willing to make space for her in his life."

"And you don't agree with that?" Trinity asked.

I grinned at her. "You know I do."

The others looked at us like we were crazy.

"The night we all met Jensen, Sofia was parking in front of our building when James and I walked out. Jensen had her drop him off in front so he didn't have to walk down the street. That's why he ended up with those bro-dudes at O'Kelley's. He thought they were Sofia's friends," Trinity explained.

"No, he didn't," Finley said.

I shrugged and nodded. "He's self-centered. He hasn't ever had to think of anyone else."

"What about you? You're his kid," Valentina argued.

"I only lived with him a few years. I was fourteen when my mom died, and I left as soon as I turned eighteen. I was sort of independent when I was with him. Plus, we were on tour most of the time I lived with him so it's not like he was monitoring curfew or keeping up with what I was doing."

"You didn't go to school?" Goldie asked.

"I had a private tutor. She was in charge of all my education through high school. She served as a sort of guardian, too. If I wanted to do something, usually I asked her instead of my dad."

"I had no idea," Piper said.

"It was a weird life. And people were always trying to get close to me to get to know my dad. When I went to college, it was weird because it became popular knowledge really fast who I was. I hated the attention."

"I'm not surprised," Haley said. "You're pretty private."

I nodded. "I always was, but not as much then as I am now. I learned not to trust anyone."

"That sucks," Valentina said.

"It did. A lot. I had a few boyfriends and a few friends, but once I told people I couldn't introduce them to my dad, most drifted out of my life."

"We're not going to do that," Haley assured me.

I smiled and hugged her. "I know. And I'm sorry I didn't tell all of you about my dad before."

"You don't have to explain yourself," Finley said. "You saw what I went through with Trent. I didn't understand it at the time, but money makes people crazy. It's not fair that everyone isn't entitled to the same level of privacy and personal life."

"That's part of why I moved here. I knew no one cared. There are plenty of rich people here, but they're treated the same as everyone else. For the most part, at least," I said.

The others nodded, knowing I was right. MacKellar Cove wasn't perfect, but there was no such thing as perfect. Our home was pretty damn amazing.

"Okay, I need to get back to this book," Elise said. "How would you even make three hour sex work? I mean, honestly, is there any possible way this book isn't complete crap?"

We laughed at her questions and launched into brain-storming ways a woman would survive three hours of sex without ending up in tears and pain.

I loved my friends. They were wild and crazy, but they were mine, and I was happy to have them.

AFTER WORK MONDAY NIGHT, I sat on the couch and stared at the last text I got from Daniel. Two days ago. He'd reverted to one-word answers. He never reached out first anymore. He only replied when I sent him something.

I didn't know why I was torturing myself. The writing was on the wall. Maybe he figured out I was falling for him. Or maybe he just decided he didn't want to spend his entire three months with me.

I thought about texting him, but I stopped myself. I wasn't into making a complete fool of myself. Instead, I sent a message to Gioioso from Book Boyfriends Wanted. Maybe he had some insight.

TALKNERDYTOME

> I've been ghosted again. Ugh. Maybe it's time to give up men completely.

GIOIOSO

> What makes you think you've been ghosted?

TNTM

> The guy I was seeing has disappeared. We were getting together regularly, and in the last ten days, it's been texting only.

G

> Maybe he's just busy.

TNTM

Or maybe he's just not interested.

G

I'm sure that's not it.

TNTM

I'm not, but I can't dwell on it.

G

You should try again. Give him one more
chance.

TNTM

At what? I've been texting him for days and
barely getting any response. Why do guys
do things like that? Ugh. I shouldn't be
asking you.

G

Why shouldn't you be asking me?

TNTM

Because we were matched. Isn't that
supposed to mean we should meet one
day? And here I am complaining that all the
men I date end up disappearing on me. Not
putting my best foot forward.

G

I'd rather know the real you.

TNTM

I'm afraid the real me is not all that exciting.
I'm a pretty boring person.

G

Boring means different things to different
people.

TNTM

Boring means I don't go out a lot, I am not outgoing or fun, and I would rather spend an evening home on the couch than in a club or bar or anywhere with a ton of people.

G

Sometimes we need that option. Time along to figure out who's really going to be there for us. Remember I said I got into it with a friend recently? Found out our friendship was because of work.

TNTM

Yeah. I'm sorry. That sucks.

G

It was a pretty big blow. Realized he's not who I thought he was.

TNTM

Have you been friends for a while?

G

Forever. Half my life. But it wasn't the same for him. I thought of him like a brother. It's really messed with me that I was so wrong.

TNTM

Ouch. And I'm sorry. That's one thing I will never understand. Lies and deceit are the worst kind of behavior when you say you care about someone.

G

Yeah. And that's why I need to be honest with you. I think we know each other.

TNTM

What makes you think that?

G

Because I know for sure the guy you were seeing is still interested. Just an ass who was wrapped up in his own shit. But I'm home, I'm upstairs, and I'm sorry I have been ignoring you.

I sucked in a breath as I deciphered his message.

"Daniel?"

"What about Daniel? Is he coming to dinner?" my dad asked.

I'd forgotten he was so close. I shook my head. "No, I just…"

"You haven't seen him lately. You should invite him to dinner. We can go out. My treat. Unless you two have other plans."

"No, we don't. Um, yeah, let me go ask him. See if he's free."

Dad nodded. "Sounds good. I'll get ready to go."

I nodded woodenly and stood. Dad went to his room and closed the door. I faced the front door like it was going to attack me.

Daniel was Gioioso? Was that possible?

There was only one way to find out.

I walked out the door before I stopped myself again. I took the stairs up to his unit and knocked, not thinking about what I was doing before it was done.

He didn't answer right away, and I started to second guess what I thought. I was about to leave again when the door swung open. He stood in front of me, his phone in his hand. He turned it to show me the conversation we'd been having.

"How long ago did you figure this out?" I asked.

"The night you went to help Chelsea pack. You told me

she was manifesting the house, and then TalkNerdyToMe said the same thing. I knew it had to be either you or someone else who knew Chelsea and was there packing."

"Wow. Is that why you stopped replying to my texts? Did you think I'd be mad or something?"

He shook his head and stepped back for me to go into his apartment.

I looked around, seeing the mess he'd created since I'd last been there. "Are you okay?"

He shook his head again. "My friend I mentioned... We met when my brother was sick. I thought... It doesn't matter what I thought, I was wrong. He's not really a friend. We worked together, and I thought we were friends, but he made it clear last time we talked that he doesn't feel that way."

"I'm really sorry, Daniel."

He nodded and sucked in a breath.

"Look, this is shitty timing, but my dad asked if you want to go to dinner with us. His treat. You can say no, and I'll make up an excuse for you. He just said he hadn't seen you in a while."

Daniel looked around the apartment like he was seeing it for the first time. "Yeah. I should probably eat. It'll be good to get out of here, too."

"I stopped by last week. You weren't home."

He avoided my gaze. "I've been trying to get out a little bit. Enjoying the town and the water. Clear my head. Sitting here all day is getting to me."

I nodded, letting the excuse stand. "I don't blame you. MacKellar Cove is beautiful, especially in the summer."

"Yeah, it is," he said, his gaze landing on me.

"Um, so, dinner?"

"Yeah, good. Thanks. Um, can I take a little while to clean up? Jump in the shower?"

"Sure. Just come down when you're ready."

"Sounds good. Thanks, Sofia. And I really am sorry for ignoring you and not telling you sooner you were talking to me."

I chuckled, laughing off the irony. "That last one is no big deal. Kind of funny, actually. And I'm sorry about your friend."

"Thanks."

I smiled at him and walked to the door. I was a little disappointed he didn't kiss me or touch me, but after more than a week of almost no contact, I had to admit it was just good to see him.

I went back to my apartment to get ready and talk to Dad about where we should go for dinner.

It didn't take me long to get ready, and when I came out of my room, Dad was in the kitchen getting a glass of water.

"Is Daniel coming?" he asked when I walked in.

"Yeah. He was going to take a quick shower and come down when he's ready. I was thinking we could go to Gino's."

Dad wrinkled his nose. "Have you ever been to The Boat House? It's a seafood place about twenty minutes from here."

I shook my head. I had heard of it, but it was a little fancy for me. "I've never been there."

"We should go. I heard great things. And I'm buying, so money isn't a big deal."

"You don't have to spend a lot on dinner, Dad."

"I know, but I want to. I've been wanting to try this place, and I figured Daniel would appreciate it as much as I will."

I narrowed my eyes, trying to understand why he thought he knew Daniel well enough to make that estimation. A knock on the door stopped my line of thinking as I went to let Daniel in.

All thought definitely stopped after that. He'd showered and trimmed his beard, and he looked like a model. He wore a dark green button-up shirt with the sleeves rolled up to show off his forearms. He had on three black bracelets I didn't remember him wearing before but suited him. His jeans were dark and hugged his legs all the way down to his black canvas shoes.

My dad was right. Daniel definitely looked like someone who would appreciate a fancy restaurant. I, on the other hand, did not.

"Um, hi. Dad wants to go to a seafood place, and I'm underdressed. Give me five minutes to go change." I rushed off before either of them could say something.

I almost slammed my bedroom door. Holy crap. I wanted to jump Daniel right there in the doorway. He looked amazing.

And I immediately felt frumpy and boring and nowhere near good enough for him.

I hated that feeling. It was the feeling I usually got when I went out on dates, but I hadn't felt it so far with Daniel.

I leaned against my door and took a few deep breaths. He wasn't ignoring me. He got into it with a friend. It wasn't because of me.

My closet was full of clothes I wore to work, and none of them would be good enough for a nice restaurant like The Boat House. I shoved past all the things I wore on a regular basis to the clothes that were shoved in the back. I pulled out a black dress I didn't remember buying and tossed it on the bed. A blue one followed it. A green skirt went next. Then a purple dress. Finally, a teal dress I found myself unable to toss on the bed.

I took the teal dress off the hanger and laid it on the bed when I realized I was still wearing my other clothes. I stripped quickly and pulled the teal dress over my head. The fabric was cool from neglect and soft over my skin. Black and silver accents dressed it up a bit and made what could have been a simple dress a bit more elegant.

I smoothed the skirt down and moved to the mirror on the bathroom door. I sighed. It fit. And it looked good. My bra was covered so I didn't have to change that. No panty-lines were showing. It accented my figure in the right places and gave me curves where I usually didn't see any.

It was perfect.

I changed my handbag for a small black one and slid my feet into a pair of silver kitten heels and left my room, ready for dinner with my dad and Daniel.

"I'm ready," I told them, joining them in the living room.

"Okay. Let's go." Dad headed toward the door.

I started to follow him and realized Daniel hadn't moved. He was staring at me. His gaze slid up and down my body, hunger and possession in his eyes.

"Wow," he breathed.

I couldn't stop my smile. "Yeah?"

He nodded and moved toward me. "Yeah. You're always gorgeous, but this dress is so different from your normal. I'm not sure which look I like more."

I laughed at his honesty, wondering if he meant it. "Most men would prefer the dress."

Daniel shook his head. "The dress is hot, but I know it's not you. You're tool belts and t-shirts and jeans. I love that look."

I smiled and tried not to fall over the word *love*. He didn't mean it like that. I knew he didn't. So there was no reason for my heart to skip. No reason at all.

"Thank you."

He winked and glanced over at my dad, waiting by the door for us. "I've missed you. I know it's my fault, but I hope we can see each other more than just dinner with your dad."

I grinned. "I'm sure I can find time in my day for you."

He chuckled and followed me to the door and out to my SUV. I never thought I'd be going on a date with my father and the guy I was seeing, but stranger things had happened.

20

TREY

Getting the *what are your intentions* talk from Jensen Carmack was the last thing I ever expected to have happen in my life.

But worse than getting the talk was not knowing how to participate in the talk. Not only had I never been asked what my intentions were with a woman, but my intentions had never been more complicated and messy than they were with Sofia.

One minute, I was sure I was ready to walk away from her. The next, I was following behind her with my tongue hanging out. I was a mess. I knew what I needed to do, but I couldn't make myself do it.

Jensen and Sofia carried the conversation on the way to the restaurant. It was a relief for me, a chance to get my head on straight before I spent the next few hours with them.

Avoiding Sofia wasn't a conscious choice. Not entirely. After finding out she was the woman I was talking to on the app, I knew I was keeping too many secrets. Then my fight with Seth made me raw in a way I'd never felt before. Not even when Michael died did I feel so exposed. Maybe because I knew my brother was going to die. I knew the end was coming.

I had no clue Seth was going to tell me he'd been using me for the last two decades. That we were only friends because of what he could get from me.

Just like the women I slept with and the fans who wanted to be friends and the other musicians who tried to worm their way in. Everyone in my life always wanted something from me. I assumed Seth was the one person who not only understood that but would never do that to me.

But he was the first. Without him, I wouldn't be a musician. I would have gone to college and done something else. Maybe. Probably. I'd never know for sure because I met Seth. I fell for the fantasy. I let him manipulate me into the choices he wanted me to make.

I shook my head. No. I couldn't sit there and blame him for my entire life. I went into it with my eyes wide open. I knew what I was doing. I wanted it. I fought for it and worked for it and dreamed of it.

"Daniel? You ready to go in?" Sofia asked, turning in the front seat.

The interior lights were on, her door open. Jensen was already on the sidewalk in front of the vehicle.

I nodded. "Sorry. Just lost in my thoughts."

She smiled kindly, like she understood. She didn't, but I couldn't fault her for trying.

Then again, maybe she did. Her relationship with Nate was miles different than Seth or Nate had ever led me to believe. They made it sound like she was a fling, someone Nate had a short thing with but it was never serious and ended amicably.

Knowing the truth, at least as much as Seth's words could be truth, painted a very different picture. One I still knew was a fabrication, but it was closer to the truth than what I believed when I arrived in MacKellar Cove.

"Welcome to The Boat House," the hostess said with a bright smile. Her gaze scanned the three of us, no recognition at all lighting up her eyes. "Three tonight?"

"Yes, thank you," Jensen said, capturing her attention.

She grabbed three menus and led the way, Jensen right behind her and carrying on a conversation. When she steered away from whatever table she'd intended to sit us at and headed straight toward the windows that overlooked the Saint Lawrence River, I knew he was talking her into a good view.

"Thank you, Cindy. It's so beautiful here," Jensen said as we took our seats.

Cindy smiled at him and told us a server would be right over.

I lifted my menu and scanned the pages of selections. Jensen and Sofia did the same, leaving our table in silence for a few minutes.

"Good evening," a man said. "I'm Roy, and I'll be taking care of you tonight. Can I start anyone with a drink?"

"Could you recommend a red wine for the table?" Jensen asked.

"Of course, sir," Roy said. "We have a wonderful chianti right here if you prefer something full-bodied. We also have a light pinot noir that's well suited for just about anything on the menu. Those are our two most popular bottles."

Jensen studied the options Roy pointed to like they held the keys to a good life. If only it was that easy.

"I think the pinot noir is a good choice. Thank you, Roy."

"Of course, sir. Would anyone like anything else? Water for the table?"

"Please," Jensen answered for us.

Roy, to his credit, waited for Sofia and me to nod before he smiled and walked away to get the water and wine.

"Everything is expensive," Sofia whispered.

"I told you, it's my treat. Don't worry about the price. I've been living off you for almost a month."

Sofia smiled at her dad. "And I'm happy you came, Dad."

Jensen grinned back, looking like a proud father instead of the rockstar jackass I'd known him as.

"Thank you for the invite, Mr. Carmack," I said, not wanting to take away from the moment but feeling like I needed to acknowledge his generosity.

"Happy you could join us, Daniel. And please, call me Jensen."

I nodded my thanks and went back to my menu.

Roy brought the wine back, opening the bottle table side and presenting it to Jensen for approval. Jensen swirled the sample in his glass, looking like he knew what he was doing. He sipped the wine and nodded approvingly. "Excellent suggestion, Roy. Thank you."

Roy worked his way around the table with a smile on his face. He poured wine for Sofia, me, then Jensen before setting the bottle in front of the seat we weren't using so we could finish it on our own. "Are you ready to order your meals? Or can I start you with some appetizers?"

Jensen looked at us, eyebrows raised for approval.

"I'm ready," I said.

"Me, too," Sofia said.

"Please begin with my daughter," Jensen said.

Roy turned his attention to Sofia. She ordered crab cakes as an appetizer and seafood medley pasta for her dinner. I chose the appetizer sampler and broiled salmon for dinner. Jensen requested shrimp cocktail and surf and turf for dinner.

Roy assured us he'd return with appetizers soon and left us to talk.

Joy.

Jensen raised his glass as soon as Roy was gone. "A toast. To Sofia, for your kindness and generosity, and for encouraging an old man to never give up on what makes me happy."

Sofia blushed and clinked her glass to her father's before turning to me and doing the same.

I reached across her to touch my glass to Jensen's, wondering what he wasn't going to give up on but not feeling like I should ask.

"We should all be happy," Sofia said. "Have you spoken to Andrew?"

Jensen nodded, his face showing pain. It was a new look on Jensen. "Andrew's not ready to stop fighting, but it's only a matter of time."

"Are you going to go see him?" Sofia asked.

Andrew could only be Andrew Oscar, one of the members of Four on the Floor. And from the sound of it, he wasn't doing well.

Jensen nodded. "I need to."

"You should."

"You trying to get rid of me?"

Sofia chuckled. "Of course not, Dad. I just know you'll kick yourself if you don't go see him again."

"I know. I will. I will reach out to his wife and find out when would be a good time."

"Good. Because regrets don't make a happy life any easier to live."

Jensen chuckled. "No, I imagine they don't."

Roy came back with our appetizers. We all dug in, sharing food and marveling at how good everything was.

When we finished appetizers, dinner arrived. Jensen refilled his wineglass, but Sofia and I waved off more, switching to water only.

Dinner was replaced with dessert, and the check disappeared as quickly as it was brought over. Before I knew it, we were heading back to MacKellar Cove with full stomachs.

And a full mind for me.

I thought spending time with Sofia would help me to decide what to do. If I stayed, I continued to manipulate her to get a song. If I left, I hurt her with my disappearance. I didn't know which was better. Or worse.

There was no good answer for me. I needed to find a way to tell her the truth. To confess my connection to Nate and Seth, and to tell her why I really came to MacKellar Cove. And why I was no longer willing to go through with it.

"Are you okay?" Sofia asked, her voice interrupting my thoughts once more.

I looked around and realized we'd made it all the way home without my even noticing. And once again, her dad was out of the vehicle and she was waiting for me to follow.

I shook my head and told her the closest thing I could to the truth. "Not really. I'm sorry I wasn't very good company tonight. I... I guess I shouldn't have come out with you."

I opened my door and got out. She hurried around the SUV and met me on the sidewalk. Her dad went inside, leaving us alone for the first time since she invited me to dinner.

"I don't care what kind of company you are. I care about you, Daniel."

My middle name on her lips was just one more reminder

that she didn't know me. We were virtual strangers. And it was all my fault. I was the one who kept everything from her. The one who made this whole situation happen.

"Do you want to talk?" she asked. Her face pleaded with me to say yes, which told me what my answer needed to be.

"Not tonight," I said, hedging. I couldn't walk away from her yet. I was an asshole for it, but I couldn't. I hated myself for it, but she was the only person in my life, the only person ever in my life, who saw me for more than Trey Ryan. Who wanted to spend time with me.

"Okay," she whispered, disappointed and hurt.

"Soon, okay?" I said before she could go inside and disappear.

She nodded, not stopping. She slid her key into the lock on the outside of the door.

The possessive, base-level asshole who commanded my dick moved me forward. I spun her around and pressed her back to the door. I covered her body with mine and sealed my lips over hers.

She responded to me instantly, her hands sliding up my chest and wrapping around my neck. I cupped her ass and dragged her against my erection. I couldn't have her walking away thinking I didn't want her. Even if I shouldn't want her, I did. And she needed to know that.

I kissed her until it was almost impossible to resist her. Until my hands curled against the fabric of her dress and ached to pull it off her and unwrap the treasures beneath. Until I was aching and hated myself for kissing her again. For giving us both hope.

Because the truth was there was no hope for us. She would hate me once she learned the truth. And I'd go back to my life and hate myself, too.

And I'd lose her. Forever.

"Good night," she whispered against my lips.

I kissed her softly. She deserved so much better than me, but if I couldn't be that man, I at least wanted her to know she was desired.

"Good night," I whispered back.

I finally moved, letting her away from the door.

She turned and unlocked it, then let us in. I went toward the stairs, pausing to watch her go into her apartment. She turned back to me and smiled, waving like it was any other night.

Her door closed, and I made the only decision I could at that moment.

I went to my apartment alone. I locked the door and opened a new bottle of whiskey and set about drowning my truth in the liquor.

Sofia texted me the next day. And the day after that. And the day after that.

I ignored them all.

It was the chickenshit thing to do. I should have been honest with her, but I couldn't do it. I couldn't tell her the whole truth and see the look on her face when she learned all the ways I'd deceived her for weeks.

The whiskey I drowned myself in brought one truth to the front for me. I'd fallen in love with Sofia. And after decades of writing, listening to, and singing songs about love, the only thing I knew was when you loved someone, you did everything in your power not to hurt them.

And I'd done the opposite. I'd done everything to hurt

her. But I was a selfish asshole and hadn't been able to leave town yet.

It was the equivalent of breaking up via text. It was low and shitty, and she'd hate me. But it was my best option. Because I couldn't face her.

Sofia wasn't the only one trying to reach out. Seth had sent me a few messages about music. No apology or explanation. Just demands about the music. Why wasn't I calling the label? Why hadn't I sent them new songs? Why wasn't I answering him?

He could kiss my ass. As soon as I got back to LA, I was going to my lawyer, not the band's or the label's but my own personal attorney, to find out how I could get out of my contract. I couldn't perform with Seth anymore. I couldn't write for the label. And I couldn't accept the way they treated people.

I didn't know what I was going to do after that, but it wasn't a today problem. It was a later problem.

A knock on my door sent me to my feet before I could think about what I was doing. I peeked through the peephole and sucked in a breath when I saw Sofia outside my door.

"I know you're in there," she said. "Let me in, Daniel."

I hesitated. I looked through the peephole again. She looked sad. Not angry like I expected. Resigned maybe.

"You're not going to ghost me while living in the same building as me. Open the damn door, Daniel."

I sighed and unlocked it, knowing she could have let herself in if she really wanted to.

She strode into my apartment with her head held high. She walked over to the couch and stood next to it, arms crossed over her chest, the notebook full of her songs clutched in one hand.

My heart ached to reach for her. To pull her into my arms and tell her everything. I wanted the last time I saw her to be a good memory. A moment when she was smiling and happy and didn't hate me. But I waited too long.

"I know you're done. What I don't know is why you can't be a grown-up about it and tell me the truth to my face. I'm not going to break. You're not going to take me down. I promise you, I've been through worse than you."

"Sofia," I began, reaching for her without thinking about what I was doing.

She didn't back away from me. The second my hand touched her arm, she sank into me, like her bravado was the only thing keeping her upright. "Just be honest," she whispered against my neck.

"I'm not good enough for you," I said, knowing it was the only truth I could give her.

She exhaled a laugh and shook her head. "Don't give me that. I deserve better than a line like that. If we're over, just say it. Please."

She found her strength and pulled away from me, standing on her own once more. She crossed her arms again. It took everything not to let my gaze fall to her plump breasts.

"I didn't follow the rules, Sofia."

"What rules?"

"The one where I said this was a fling."

"Daniel, what are you saying?"

"I'm saying I'm falling for you, Sofia. I'm saying I don't want to leave. I can't stay, but I want to."

"You can't or won't?"

"Does it matter?"

She nodded. "It matters to me. If you're serious, we will find a way to make it work. If you're just telling me this, that's different. I don't do well with people who say one thing and mean another."

"I'm telling you the truth, Sofia. I'm falling for you." I shook my head. "No, that's not true. I already fell for you, Sofia."

21

———

The breath she drew held my heart in it. Was that an angry sound that said she was getting ready to storm out because I changed the rules, or was that a hopeful sound because she was right there with me?

I didn't dare move. I stayed locked in place, trying my best to be invisible so she didn't lash out or run or—

Leap into my arms and climb me like a monkey?

"I broke the rules, too," she cried. Tears streaked down her cheeks. "I fell for you, too."

"Yeah?"

She nodded.

That was all it took. I was gone. I couldn't stop myself any longer. Love healed. Love fixed things. Love made everything okay, even when it wasn't.

I carried her to my room, knowing we'd have time to figure out the rest another time. I needed the woman I loved right then. Not in five minutes, or an hour, immediately.

I let her fall to the mattress, hardening when she gasped as she hit the bed. Her eyes dilated. She reached for me, and I went more than willingly to her.

We crashed together, like the crescendo of a song. Everything hummed inside me. Vibrating like I'd finally hit the right note.

"Daniel," she whispered against my neck.

The name still made me pause, but I'd explain it all later.

"I love you, Sofia," I whispered. I kissed her hard, stopping her from saying the words back. Stopping her from using the name that didn't feel like me.

Except it was me. It was the me that Sofia fell in love with. It was the me that decided to live my own life and to stop hiding from my mistakes and my regrets.

She moaned and wiggled against me, rubbing her core against my dick and nearly setting me off far too early.

I pulled back with a curse and tugged at her clothes. Shirt first, so I could bury my face in her supple breasts. Then her bra because I needed to lick them. I worked her shorts off while I kissed and teased her nipples, setting her hips in motion, begging me for more and more and more.

I pried her bottoms off and followed them down, settling myself between her thighs. She'd always pushed off my advances to taste her, but she was too far gone to argue, and I was too far gone to stop.

One lick and I groaned. She cried out. I'd only made a woman come on my tongue a few times. It wasn't the quick fuck kind of move, but Sofia wasn't a quick fuck. She was the woman I loved. And I wanted to see her in all her beautiful glory.

"Daniel," she whimpered.

She was already close, but I wasn't ready for her to lose her mind yet. I needed to draw it out. To make her beg.

I retreated, licking her folds and tasting her body. I wanted to memorize everything about her, to keep those little sounds and the way her body shook with me. I'd never seen something as beautiful as Sofia naked and open to me, not hiding herself in any way as she let me have her.

"Oh, God," she whispered.

I flicked my tongue over her clit and teased her with circles just outside where she wanted me. She shifted her hips to catch my tongue, but her movements were uncoordinated and clumsy.

I pushed her thighs wider and leaned back so I could look at her. She was soaked, dripping and ready for me. I licked the droplets trailing down her body and thrust my tongue into her.

She moaned long and loud, fucking my tongue with each stroke into her. "Oh shit, that feels so fucking good."

I murmured my agreement and licked through her folds again, unable to hold back any longer. I slammed two fingers into her and sucked hard on her clit, shocking her sensitive body into an orgasm she wasn't ready for.

"Oh, fuck! Yes!" She shook and screamed, coming hard and fast.

"More," I demanded, adding a third finger to her channel and flicking her clit rapidly.

Her hips moved to meet my tongue, her body completely on board with my plan to make her boneless so she couldn't run when I told her everything. If she was too weak to leave, she'd have to listen to me.

That and I loved her and wanted to make her feel good. Really fucking good.

She came again, this one drawn out and making her moan. She reached down and wove her fingers through my hair, holding me where she wanted me while she rode my face and carried herself to her third orgasm.

"Daniel. I need you."

I withdrew from her and grabbed a condom from the nightstand. I went to roll it on and realized I'd never taken my own clothes off. She reached to help me, both of us tugging until I was naked enough to get the condom on and slide inside her.

"Oh, my fuck, that feels so damn good," she said on a moan. "I want to feel you."

I stilled inside her and yanked my shirt over my head. She grabbed at me, pulling me to her for a kiss. I devoured her, needing her lips. All I could manage were short strokes into her with her lips on mine, but it was enough to send the message to my dick that it was go time.

She pulled back from our kiss with a gasp and a roll of her hips that did something to me that I couldn't explain. It was like a massage on my dick that took me from ready to there in half a second.

"Oh, fuck, Sofia," I growled, slamming into her.

She lifted her knees and let me sink in deeper, hitting her g-spot and rubbing her clit at the same time. She panted, racing for the same place as me.

"Daniel!" she called out. Her channel rippled around me, clenching and releasing me as she came. "I love you. Oh shit, I love you so much."

I couldn't speak as her orgasm carried me over the edge. I slammed in hard and everything tingled as my balls let loose and I erupted into her.

I collapsed onto her, unable to hold myself up for another second. She wrapped herself around me, holding me to her as our breathing slowed and returned to something close to normal.

"I love you," I whispered.

"I love you," she said with a content smile.

"We still need to talk, though."

She nodded against my shoulder. "I know. But first I need to use the bathroom."

I chuckled and let her up, enjoying the view of her naked walking to my bathroom. A knock on the door had me calling out to her, and thankful the bathroom opened to the bedroom and the living room. "Someone's here. I'm going to close the bedroom door so you can go back in there when you're done."

"Thank you!" she called back.

I grabbed my shorts and stepped into them, then picked up my tee as the person knocked again.

"I'm coming!" I called out, hurrying to the door and dragging the shirt over my head.

They knocked again, a steady rap of knuckles against the door that set my teeth on edge and sent a shiver up my spine a few seconds too late. I opened the door as I realized why.

"Yo! I've been out there for like ten minutes. What the hell were you doing?"

Seth pushed his way past me and into the apartment. I stared after him, frozen even as I knew everything was about to blow up.

"This place is a dump. Shit, is this how big it is? Dude, I don't know how you've managed to survive here."

"What the fuck are you doing here?" I demanded.

He flopped onto the couch and put his feet up on the coffee table. Shoes and all, not caring a bit about the furniture. "I figured you needed some help."

"Help with what?"

"The song. Duh. You said you were making progress, but you haven't sent anything in. The label's getting anxious."

I shook my head. "The label can go fuck themselves."

Seth raised a brow. "You might want to watch saying things like that."

I glared at the man I thought I knew as well as I knew myself. The cocky tilt of his brow, the dismissive way he stretched out on the couch that wasn't his and propped his boots up on the furniture. He glared right back at me, not backing down for even one second.

"You need to get your head on straight. We've worked too fucking hard for you to piss it all away." He glowered at me, standing and facing me.

Gone was the easygoing jokester who barged in and tried to behave like nothing had changed. In his place was the hard-ass he brought out when opening acts tried to pretend they were bigger than us.

"What do you care? You told me I'm no different than any other dude. I'm just the lucky one you plucked from oblivion."

"Oh, fuck you, asshole. I was pissed, and you were being a dick."

"You meant that fucking shit."

"Yeah, I did. You know why? Because you needed someone to pull your fucking head out of your damn ass! Because you came up here to fucking nowhere and you forgot who you are. You're Trey fucking Ryan, you son-of-a-bitch. You're a goddamn rockstar. You're better than this fucking place, and you're better than getting your dick all twisted up over some pussy who means absolutely nothing."

"She doesn't mean nothing."

"Yes, she does. She walked away from our world. She didn't want to be in it. She could have had everything we have. She wiped us from her fucking shoe and shook her fat ass on the way out the damn door."

"Shut the fuck up," I growled at him. I got up in his face, ready to punch my best friend over a woman I'd known for five weeks.

"You want to hit me? You want to take a fucking swing at me? Let's go, asshole. Try me."

I exhaled and took a step away from him. The dumbest thing I could possibly do was hit him. He would press charges, and it would be bad.

"You're not fucking worth it," I breathed.

Seth shook his head. "I came here to help you, asshole. I came here to get you back on track and get you back to LA with a song so we can get back into the studio. We have a fucking job to do, and it's time you get back to it."

"I don't need help. And I don't want it from you. It's time for you to go. Now." I glanced at the bathroom door. I hadn't heard any noise, but Sofia was in there. And Seth needed to be gone before she came out and saw him. That she wasn't out already surprised me.

"Why?" Seth caught my look and glanced at the door. "Dude, you got a girl in there?"

"Get. Out."

"You do! You got a chick in there. Who is it? Wait, no. It's not Sofia, is it? Oh, shit. I thought you were joking about screwing her. You don't usually go for the big ones. I've never seen you with someone who wore a double digit dress. Let alone a double-double digit dress size. Unless she got skinny. Wait, did she? Is she hot?"

Seth jumped over the back of the couch and headed for the door.

I vaulted to him and grabbed his arm before he could make it to the door. I pulled him away, clamping my hand over his mouth.

Seth laughed his ass off. He licked my hand, getting me to move my hand from his mouth.

I shoved him toward the couch. He fell onto it and laughed. "Man, you really are fucking her. She must be some kind of magic to get you and my brother. Maybe I should take a spin in her."

I was on him so fast he didn't have time to react before my hand was around his throat. I lifted him from the couch, squeezing his throat as I dragged him to his feet.

"Stay the fuck away from her. You put one hand on her—"

"Oh, hey, Sofia," Seth rasped.

I released him and spun. Seth fell to the couch and bounced. He stood behind me as I moved around the couch to Sofia.

Her hands came up in front of her before I could get to her. She was dressed, her cheeks flushed and damp. Her beautiful blue eyes sparkled with fury and pain.

"Sofia—"

Her hand went up again, stopping my words before I could even try to explain anything to her.

"Seth," she said, her voice colder than a polar ice cap.

"What's up, Sofia? Been a while."

I glared at him, noting the humor in his eyes.

His gaze slid down her body. His nose wrinkled. He pursed his lips like he was holding back the urge to hurl.

"I see you haven't changed," Sofia said, her own gaze loaded with disgust. "Still spreading your own personal brand of toxic everywhere you go."

Seth grinned. "You know you love me, Sofia."

She snorted.

"Well, you love my boy here. I tell ya, never thought I'd see the day you were fucking another one of my brothers."

"Brother?" she gasped.

"Eh, not blood. Me and Trey Ryan are bandmates. Broken Record? Maybe you've heard of us." Seth's chest puffed out as he slid the last piece of the puzzle into place for Sofia.

Her gasp was loud and sharp. Her gaze snapped to mine. I tried to plead with her with my eyes, but she turned away from me, pinching the bridge of her nose.

"Sofia, I was going to tell you everything."

She turned on me, taking two steps toward me and getting in my face. "When? When were you going to tell me? After you said you loved me? After you made me fall for you? After you took everything from me? You know what, Daniel or Trey or whatever the fuck your name is, fuck you. I wish I'd never met you."

"Sofia, don't—"

She sidestepped me, avoiding my touch and moving around me toward the door. "No. You don't get to tell me anything anymore. You knew my history. You knew what I'd been through. And instead of being a decent person, you used my past and manipulated me. I hope you got what you wanted. I hope you got it all. And I hope I never see you again."

I stared after her, at a loss for words to get her to stop.

Then she did. She looked back at me. "I wish I'd never met you."

I closed my eyes, agreeing with her. I wish she'd never met me, too.

The door closed softly, the click a shot through me. I drew a breath, needing a minute to figure out what I was going to do next.

"Damn, dude, you really took one for the team," Seth said with a big laugh. "I mean, when Nate fucked her, she was big but at least she was young. And he was getting closer to her dad. You don't have any excuse."

"Shut up, Seth."

Seth clapped me on the back. "Forget about her, man. It's time to go home. It's time to get back into it all."

"You have no idea what the hell just happened," I growled at him.

"No, I don't. But I know you, man. You're not a one-woman kind of guy. And you're not a small-town kind of man. It's time to get back to us, dude. It's time to go back to who you are."

I nodded, feeling broken and numb and empty. "Yeah, maybe you're right."

"Yeah! Hell yes, I'm right. Let's go. Get your shit packed up and let's get the hell out of here."

I nodded, unable to come up with an argument. "There's no reason for me to stick around here, anyway."

"Yes, man. Let's go. We'll get back in the studio and make some new music, and you'll forget all about Sofia. I promise."

"Sounds good. All good."

Seth made his way around my apartment, collecting things and starting to pack it all up. I went to my room, ignoring him. The sheets were still tangled, scented from us coming together. My throat closed up, and my eyes tingled. I swallowed back my emotions and worked on getting out of there.

I'd overstayed my welcome. It was time to leave.

22

SOFIA

I held it together almost all the way to my apartment. Almost. Tears ran down my cheeks, but I didn't sob until I was at my door. I jammed the key in the lock, since my dad still insisted it wasn't safe to leave the door unlocked, and turned it roughly. The lock clicked open, and I pushed my way inside, needing the door on the other side in case Daniel came after me.

Not Daniel. Trey. Trey fucking Ryan.

How in the fucking hell did I not see it?

I sank to the floor on the inside of the door and buried my face in my hands.

"Sofia? What happened? Are you okay?"

I'd forgotten about my dad.

He put his hands on my shoulders, not trying to move me but letting me know he was there.

I shook my head. "No. I'm not okay. I... Daniel is actually Trey Ryan from Broken Record."

I looked up at my dad to catch the shocked look on his face, except there wasn't one. He took a step back and looked around.

"You knew," I said.

Dad rubbed the back of his neck with one hand. "Well, yeah. I mean, I recognized him. I thought you knew who he was. You were spending all this time with him and I just figured that was why."

"You thought I was spending time with a man who is a famous rockstar just because he's a famous rockstar?" I pushed to my feet, fury replacing my pain. My own father thought so little of me that he expected me to be no better than all the brainless groupies out there who wanted a rockstar just so they could say they fucked one.

"Sofia, I don't know what you want me to say. I mean, you dated Nate when you were younger, when he was on tour with me. Broken Record is one of the biggest bands right now. Trey or Daniel or whatever name he wanted to go by didn't do a lot to disguise who he was. He changed his style a little, but it's not like he went blond or shaved his head or told people he was an accountant." Dad crossed his arms over his chest and rocked back on his heels.

"Yeah, but..." I trailed off. Dad was right. It was right in front of me the entire fucking time, and I didn't see it.

Because Daniel didn't want me to see it. He used a different name, he pretended he didn't know anything about writing music, and he never once said he was in one of the hottest bands in the world at the moment.

I stumbled to the couch and fell onto it. "You really thought that's who I am? That I'm the kind of person who's going to be friends with someone or involved with someone because of their career?"

Dad stood next to the couch, not close enough for me to reach him, but in my view. "Sofia, we don't know each other. I have no idea what you're like. I don't say that to be nasty, but because it's true. I wanted to come here because I was never a good father. Seeing Andrew... If that was me, you wouldn't drop everything to be there for me. I wouldn't ask you to. Andrew's kids are there every day. They're in his life. Seeing that made me accept that I'm the reason we aren't close. I'm the one who refused to accept you when you were born. I'm the one who didn't make an effort when you were little. I'm the one who didn't get to know you when you came on tour with me. Or who didn't leave the damn tour to be there for you. There are so many things I should have done differently. Things I'll always regret. But who I think you are?" He shrugged. "All I've ever known is people who want something from someone because they're famous."

"That's not me. It's never been me. I've never asked you for anything."

"You did once," he said softly.

I looked up at him. He was right. One time I asked him to choose me over his band. To choose me over the career that meant everything to him.

"And you refused," I replied.

Dad nodded and moved to sit next to me on the couch. "I did. When you asked me to have Nate removed from the tour, there was nothing I could do. If I pushed the issue, we would have lost our opening act. They said as much. So I let it go. I didn't realize how you felt about him. That you were in love with him."

"I wasn't—" I broke off because it would have been a lie to say I wasn't in love with Nate Catalan. "He hurt me, Dad. I fell for the oldest trick in the book. And his brother turned around and used that against me and fed all that to Daniel. Trey."

"Do you know that for sure?" Dad asked. He finally looked shocked.

I nodded. "Seth showed up at Daniel's, Trey's, just now. I

was in the bathroom and overheard their conversation. Seth said…" Pain welled up inside me again as I replayed Seth's hurtful words. Seth was always a jerk. He joined his brother on the road one summer. Spent three months with us and made my life hell. Seth was two years younger than me, but he was always hot, which meant he considered himself above me.

When Nate introduced us, Seth thought his brother was joking about us dating. Nate told him who I was, and Seth understood. I should have realized then how Nate actually felt, but I was too blinded by grief and love. I told myself Nate wasn't like his brother. That Nate was sweet, and he loved me. That Seth was just a stupid kid who didn't know anything about love.

Unfortunately, I was wrong. Not about Seth, but about Nate.

"Seth was always an asshole," my dad said when I didn't continue.

I nodded. "Yeah, but he wasn't wrong before, and I have no reason to think he'd be wrong now. Nate was exactly who Seth made him seem like. Why am I going to think Daniel is better? Why should I think he's decent when he spends all his time with someone like Seth?"

Dad shook his head. "Maybe you can't. Maybe he's finally showing you exactly who he is."

I huffed a mirthless laugh. "Then I guess I should listen this time."

Dad nodded. "That doesn't make it easier, though."

I shook my head. "Definitely not easy."

I closed my eyes as the pain of the day rolled over me. Tears leaked out. I couldn't stop them. I just let them fall, knowing it would be a long time before I considered trusting another person again.

"Should I order food for us?" Dad asked after a few minutes. "And alcohol."

I snorted and nodded. "I think I'm going to need lots of both."

"Best break-up cure," Dad said.

MY HEAD POUNDED. Someone was inside with a jackhammer. A jackhammer that was calling my name? "What the—?"

"Sofia, wake up."

I groaned and covered my head with a pillow. "Go away."

"I'm not going to do that. Wake up."

The pillow flew off my head. Bright lights glared at me, sending blinding pain through my skull. "What the hell?"

I swung my hands, trying to catch the evil person who decided I needed to be up instead of wallowing in my misery. My hands were captured, and someone laid down on top of me.

"Oof," I breathed. "I'm going to be sick."

That got her off me.

I scrambled from the couch to my bathroom, closing doors on my way in hopes I could avoid further interrogation.

No such luck. She followed me.

"Are you okay?" she asked through the door.

I finally realized it was Piper's voice. Then I felt bad for being so mean to my best friend. "No," I cried, all the emotion from the day before rising to the surface with the copious amounts of alcohol I consumed.

I sat on the floor in front of the toilet, but I didn't feel as sick without Piper laying on top of me. I still didn't want to talk to her, though.

"What happened, Sof?"

"He lied to me."

"Daniel?"

"Whose real name is Trey."

"Okay. So, you're mad he didn't tell you his name?" she asked.

"No!" I shouted through the door. I pushed to my feet and yanked it open.

Piped stepped back, startled by my sudden appearance and anger.

"I'm mad because he's a famous rockstar and pretended he was a regular guy. I'm mad because his best friend and bandmate is Nate Catalan's brother. And Seth knew all about me and Nate. And he shared all of that history with Daniel, with Trey, and *he* used it to manipulate me. The asshole even told me he loved me before we slept together yesterday."

"Are you sure he was lying?"

I scoffed and pushed past her. I needed coffee. Or more alcohol, but I'd never been a hair-of-the-dog kind of person. I glanced at the empty bottle of whiskey and sneered. Guess today wasn't the day to start.

I started the coffee, making a full pot since I knew Dad and Piper would both drink some coffee.

Piper gave me my silence while I let the coffee brew. She got cream and sugar from the fridge, plus my caramel syrup, and set it all on the table with two mugs and a spoon.

When the coffee was ready, I couldn't delay all of it any longer.

"I told you about Nate."

Piper nodded.

"Seth is Nate's little brother. He was there for a few months during our relationship. He was an asshole. Always looked at me like I wasn't good enough because I was overweight."

"Asshole."

"Yes, but it was more than that. Seth always saw the whole music industry as his right. Like he had a little bit of talent so he was entitled to everything the industry had to offer."

"Sorry I didn't get to meet him."

I rolled my eyes and sipped my coffee. The heat and caffeine soaked in and made me feel marginally better. "He's a real peach, let me tell you."

Piper snorted. "Okay, so he told Daniel all about you and Daniel came here to seduce you?"

I shrugged. "I don't know. I haven't heard much from him lately. We started writing a song together... Shit."

"What?"

I shook my head. "I just remembered I took my notebook to his apartment yesterday and left it there."

"What notebook?"

I looked at my best friend and realized just how many things I'd been keeping from her over the years. "I write music sometimes. It's always been just for me and for fun. I've never considered selling any of it. It's too personal for that. But I told Daniel. Trey. Fuck, you know who I mean. Anyway, I told him, and we were writing a song together."

"Really? That's kind of exciting," Piper said, not upset at all that I kept my hidden talent from her.

"It was. I... I thought it was. I had fun working with him. He was working on a melody, and I had lyrics. We would text and talk. It was... It doesn't matter."

"Yes, it does matter. If you enjoyed it, there's no reason you shouldn't keep doing something like that."

I laughed. "No. For one thing, it was always a hobby. Something I did when I was stressed or when I needed to get my emotions out. I never wanted it to be something I shared with anyone else. That's why I never told you."

"Oh, please, don't worry about me. After Nate Catalan and your famous father, you writing music is a small shock. Maybe not even a shock. Music is in your blood, literally, and it seems like it's in your soul, too."

I sucked in a breath. Music was in my soul. It was always something that brought me peace. Even since I went on tour with my dad and I realized I wasn't weird for loving music the way I did, I let it sink in and wrap around me.

When things ended with Nate, I lost music for a while. It hurt to think about it, to lean on it, when it had caused me so much pain. But after a while, I realized it wasn't music that was the problem but Nate. And my dad. That was when I started writing music.

But again, I let myself sink into music and I lost a piece of myself. A piece of my heart again.

"Daniel is the only person I ever told that I wrote music. And he used that. Seth said Daniel was there to get a song. That's why he came here. I'm guessing he was looking for my dad and lucked out when my dad was here, but he never spent time with my dad. I confessed my secret to him, and he used it to get what he wanted. I was easier to manipulate. A few sweet words and a ride on his dick, and I was putty in his damn hands."

And there went the tears again. God, I hated how dumb I was. How easily I fell for his lies and him.

"We all get stupid when love is involved," Piper said. She grabbed my hand and rubbed my knuckles with her thumb.

"Yeah, but it was all lies. I fell for the guy I thought he was. I can't say I'm not in love with him, but the man I fell for isn't the real Trey Ryan. Daniel doesn't exist. He was a figment of my imagination."

"He was real for a while."

I exhaled a long breath and swallowed the pain filling me. I wanted to go back to bed and forget all about Trey Ryan and Daniel. I didn't want to have anything to do with either of them ever again.

"I'm not sure if this makes it better or worse, but I came here to find out what happened because Daniel left the key for his apartment in the Inn's mailbox. It must have been overnight sometime, but I'm guessing he's gone."

"He's gone?" I blurted. Fresh pain lanced through me. I laughed mirthlessly. "I hate that I'm hurt that he didn't say goodbye."

"I felt the same when Gavin left. Even though we'd had a fight and I thought things were over, it still hurt like hell when he left."

"Yeah, but Gavin came back. Daniel's never coming back."

Piper stood. "Let's go see. If he left the keys, I assume he's saying he's not there, but maybe I'm wrong."

I shook my head. "I can't. I..."

Piper took my hand and pulled me to my feet. "It's not going to be any easier to go in there tomorrow or the next day. You can stay in the hallway if you don't want to go in, but I need to find out for sure if he's gone."

I sucked in a breath and finally nodded. I finished my coffee and set the mug in the dishwasher. If Daniel was there... It didn't matter. We were over. And whether he was there or not wasn't important.

I followed Piper upstairs to the third floor, not in a hurry to see the empty apartment. She stopped in front of the door and knocked. No sound came from the other side of the door, but she knocked again before she pulled out the key.

She unlocked the door and opened it. "Hello!" she called out. "Is anyone here?"

Piper left the door open while she went into the apartment.

The kitchen was cleaned up. No dishes were on the counter. The living room was clear of personal effects. Daniel's guitar was gone.

I stepped into the apartment. Nothing was on the table near the door. No shoes were on the other side. The bathroom door was wide open, and the counter was clear.

I went in farther and stopped short when I got to the living room. There was one thing still there. One thing that said it all.

My notebook was on the coffee table.

"There are no clothes in the dressers or closet. No personal effects anywhere. He's definitely gone." Piper looked up at me. "What is that?"

I held my notebook in my arms. "It's my songs."

"He didn't take it."

I shook my head. "Nope. Apparently he does have a conscience."

"That or he's smart enough to know your dad has just as good of lawyers as he does and you would sue him for the rights," Piper said.

I nodded. "Or that. But either way, he's gone. I never have to see him again."

Piper nodded and stared at me. Then she held me when I crumpled and sobbed and let the last pieces of my heart shatter.

23

TREY

I WAS GOING THROUGH THE MOTIONS. ON AUTOPILOT. Disconnected from everything.

After Sofia walked out, I packed my shit and left. I left the key at the Inn because I couldn't bear to see anyone, especially Sofia. It was a dick move, but it's who I was.

Seth was doing his damnedest to remind me of that.

As soon as we got on a private jet to fly home, he was the guy I remembered. The easygoing, casual guy who was only worried about one thing. Where the next party was. He spent the whole flight telling me all about the women he'd slept with since I was gone and the parties I missed. It didn't matter that I wasn't cheering him on or lamenting what I'd missed out on, Seth was too self-involved to give a shit.

When we landed, he dragged me back to his place where a party was in full swing. Women, liquor, and drugs were plentiful. All were offered freely. I took a bottle of whiskey and found a chair to sink into.

It was the same thing for weeks. Seth had a party, I drank a bottle of liquor, and I woke up the next morning and for about three seconds, I forgot about Sofia.

I was barely functional. I didn't want to do anything. So when Seth shoved me into the shower and told me to get dressed because we were going out, I didn't argue. I didn't care. Nothing mattered anymore.

Until his driver pulled up to the studio.

"What the fuck are we doing here?"

Seth looked at me like I forgot something. Like we had a conversation that was missing from my memory. I searched for it, but nothing was there.

"We're recording today," Seth said.

"What the fuck are we recording?"

"Come on, dude, we're already running late."

I sighed heavily and followed Seth out of the vehicle. I was wearing his clothes and used his bathroom stuff, so I smelled like him and looked like him. Everything felt itchy and off, but it wasn't the clothes. It was me.

I dragged my feet behind Seth. It didn't matter that he was an asshole, he was the only person I had left.

"Yo, yo, yo!" Seth called out to someone ahead of us. He stopped in the middle of the hallway and high-fived someone, then hugged him.

Our drummer. Adam moved past Seth to me and high-fived then hugged me. Right behind him was our bass guitarist, Ricky, and Nate, Seth's brother and Sofia's ex.

Nate smirked at me. "How's Sofia?"

"Fuck you," I growled at Nate.

Nate snorted. "Rumor has it I'm too small for you these days."

I slammed Nate against the wall and pulled my arm back to hit him. Someone grabbed me, yanking me off Nate before I could get in the hit I desperately wanted to give him.

Nate laughed as he was shoved away from me.

"He's trying to get your spot," Adam hissed. "Leave him alone."

I glared at Adam, not processing his words.

Adam dragged me forward, toward the studio. I hadn't picked up my guitar since the day Sofia walked out. Since we were working on the song together. I couldn't stand the thought of it.

But there it was. In the corner of the studio, waiting for me to play like an abandoned lover.

I walked over to it, touching the neck and debating my next move.

"Okay," the producer said from behind me, "we have the new song ready to go. The guys have been working on it for weeks now, so we should be ready to play and go."

"What new song?" I asked.

I turned and found all of them avoiding my gaze.

Dread slithered up my spine. "What song?" I growled.

"The one you wrote, dude," Seth said.

I turned my attention to him. "What fucking song, Seth?"

"Make You Stay," he said simply, the *duh* on the end silent but still there.

"I didn't write that song. And I never gave it to you. How the fuck do you have that song?" I snapped. I took in the others in my glare, making sure every fucking person in the room understood they were included in my anger.

They didn't have permission to use it. To record it. It wasn't mine, and even if it was, I needed to sign off on it.

"Seth sent us pictures," Robert Miller said from the door. "Since you never did. Weeks ago. We've spent that time getting everyone up to speed on the song."

"You don't have the rights to that song," I growled at the man who held my entire career in his hands.

Robert stared me down. No one challenged him. No one pushed back. He was in charge because when he said something, shit happened. But I wasn't going to let him walk all over me or steal the song Sofia wrote. It wasn't legal, and it wasn't right.

"We will have the rights to it. You are our artist, which means everything you write belongs to us unless we pass on it. We want this song."

"I didn't write it alone. Sofia Frank—"

"Paperwork has been sent to Ms. Frank. We've reached out to her father as well. We expect to get signed contracts back any day now. Until then—"

"You sent her a contract?" I barked.

Robert Miller tugged down the sleeves of his dress shirt, then repeated the move with his suit coat. It was a power move to show off the diamond studded cufflinks he wore. He was the most successful person in the room. It didn't matter that no one outside the music industry knew who the fuck he was or cared, he created bands. And he destroyed them if he wanted.

The barely restrained look of fury in his gaze told me he didn't like being interrupted. But he was going to get the fuck over it because I didn't like being fucked with.

"I don't answer to you, Mr. Ryan. Not today. Not ever. You can either get yourself ready to record this song, or you can get the fuck out of my studio."

I held his glare for a long moment. He didn't back down, but neither did I.

Not at first.

I cursed under my breath and stalked to my guitar. I picked it up, and the entire room let out a collective sigh.

Then I walked to the door.

"This is illegal. We don't have the rights, and until we do, I'm not recording one fucking note of that song."

"You're making a mistake, Mr. Ryan."

I shook my head. "The mistake I made was thinking any of you had my best interests at heart. Thinking any of you gave a shit about me. Fuck you, Mr. Miller. And fuck you, Seth. How could you?"

Seth snorted. "We have a goddamn job to do. You were going to throw it away for some fat bitch who means nothing. I saved this band. Like I've been doing for years."

I set my guitar down gently and walked over to Seth calmly. I didn't hesitate or pause.

He smirked as I approached him. The cocky son-of-a-bitch crossed his arms over his chest and waited.

He thought I was going to apologize.

The look of shock on his face right before my fist connected with his cheek was so fucking worth it.

Seth went flying, his balance gone with the surprise blow. He flailed his arms, searching for something to grab onto, and found a microphone stand. The stand hit the drums and clashed against the cymbals.

The cacophony of sound was drowned out by the shouting.

I turned, grabbed my guitar, and fucking left. "I quit, fuckers!" I shouted as I walked out, feeling like I made the first right decision in weeks.

MY PHONE BUZZED with texts and messages, but I ignored all of it. I didn't want to hear what any of them had to say. There was nothing that would make all of this right. They were going to pressure Sofia into signing away her rights to a song she created, and they were probably going to lowball her.

I knew she wouldn't listen to me, but I hoped someone else would. I looked up the one person who might be able to get through to her, knowing it was a risk.

"MacKellar Cove Inn. This is Piper. How can I help you today?"

"This is Daniel," I said.

The sharp intake of her breath said I didn't have to explain anything to her. She knew the entire story.

"Don't hang up," I blurted, realizing that was the likely next move for her.

"And why should I listen to anything you have to say?" Piper's formerly friendly voice was cold and cutting.

"I need you to do something for me."

She scoffed.

"It's for Sofia."

"Oh, now you care? If you're calling to tell me to make her sign that ridiculous contract, you can kiss my ass."

"Shit. No. I'm calling to tell you to convince her not to."

"Already done, asshole. Bye now!"

"Piper, wait!"

She sighed heavily, but she didn't hang up.

"They're going to try to force her into it. They'll do whatever it takes. They're trying to record the song already."

"You're doing what?"

"Not me. The label. I walked out. I can't do that to Sofia."

Piper snorted. "But lying to her for weeks, sleeping with her, and telling her you love her to get the song in the first place was within your moral code."

"No! No. I... It doesn't matter now. What matters is she needs a lawyer and maybe protection."

"Protection?" Piper squeaked. "Are you saying they'll hurt her?"

I shook my head and rubbed my eyes. "I don't know, Piper. But if they think this song could make them millions, which is possible, they will do whatever they have to do."

"How could you do this to her? How could you steal her work?"

"I know you won't believe me, but I didn't. I didn't give them the song. I left her notebook in my apartment because I couldn't. Not after... Seth took pictures of it. I didn't know until today. He's the one who sent the label the song."

"Sofia said he's an asshole."

I nodded, hoping she was going to help. "He is. I didn't see it before. But I can't go through with any of this."

"You know this doesn't mean she's going to take you back, right?" Piper said. The harshness was back in her voice.

"I know. I don't deserve her. I don't deserve a lot of things. Protect her, Piper. Please."

"I will." Piper was silent for a long moment, long enough that I wondered if she hung up. "For what it's worth, for a little while, I thought you might be the one for her."

"She deserves so much better than me," I breathed, knowing it was the truth.

I hung up without saying another word. I couldn't. Everything that happened the last few months rushed back to me.

And it all started with Avery Power. With her pregnancy. With the baby who could be mine.

I needed to know. I needed to make things right. I needed to be the man Sofia thought I was. Not the rockstar with an ego the size of a small country, but the man who was better than someone who neglects their child.

AVERY POWER WALKED down the street pushing a stroller. She smiled at one of her neighbors. She was pretty. Her long, dark hair was pulled back in a bouncy ponytail that swung with every step.

She looked happy and healthy. And so did the baby in the stroller. The one who could be mine.

I waited until Avery turned up the path to her house before I got out of my rental. She glanced back, her smile fading as she recognized me.

"What are you doing here?" she blurted. A smile lifted her lips again, but this one was strained.

"I need to talk to you."

She put herself between me and the stroller. "There's nothing we need to talk about. I haven't said anything to anyone. If anyone said they know something, they're lying. I promise you, I haven't said a word."

"Can we go inside?" I asked her, my brows high. I hoped I looked nonthreatening.

She looked up and down the quiet residential street and nodded. She parked the stroller next to the stairs up to her porch and locked the wheels. She spoke softly to the baby as she unbuckled the harness that kept her in the stroller. Avery lifted the baby from the stroller and held her in one arm, the other protectively on the baby's back even as the little girl tried to get a look at me.

Avery climbed the steps to her front door and pulled a key from her pocket, unlocking the door. She left it open for me to follow her inside and went to the right.

There was a small mesh crib looking thing with a few toys in it. Avery put the baby down, then moved to sit right next to the crib, her hand on the edge.

I closed the door and took a seat across the room from Avery and the baby.

"How are you?" I asked after a minute.

She snorted.

"Okay, I guess not great." I drew a breath and stared at the little girl. I'd never wondered if a baby was mine before. "What's her name?"

"Why are you here?" Avery demanded.

The little girl, sensing her mother's anxiety, whimpered and scooted closer to Avery.

"I... I didn't know anything about you being pregnant until after the label paid you off."

She stiffened at my choice of words but didn't argue with them.

"I wasn't behind that decision. I wanted you to know that."

"Okay. Thanks for letting me know." Avery stood like she was going to see me out.

"Is she mine?" I blurted.

Avery sat down hard, nearly bouncing off her seat in the process. She swallowed roughly, her throat moving slowly. "I..."

"I'm not going to tell anyone, Avery. I... I want to be here for you."

"Why?" she exhaled.

"I'm not the kind of person who would abandon my child. I don't... I don't remember us being together, but you do look familiar, and I wouldn't be able to live with myself if I abandoned..."

"Sara," Avery whispered.

I smiled and looked at Sara. She was beautiful. She had her mom's dark hair and hazel eyes that could have come from me. She had a tiny nose and chubby fingers that were jammed into her mouth. The outfit she wore was all pink, from her socks to her bib. Even the stroller outside was pink.

"I know I wasn't there for you before, and I can only imagine what you went through, but—"

"She's not yours," Avery blurted.

"What?" I breathed. My gaze flipped from Avery to Sara, trying to piece together what she said. It wasn't complicated, but it still didn't make sense.

Avery started crying. Her face crumpled like she'd been holding back the emotion that overwhelmed her. She didn't bury her face in her hands, though. She met my gaze steadily.

"We did meet, but we never slept together."

"Then why did you tell the label she's mine?" I whispered. My heart cracked. I wanted her to be mine. To know I did something good, even if I didn't mean to. To believe in miracles.

"I knew the actual father would never step up. He's... selfish. I didn't mean to get pregnant. I was stupid and drunk and I don't remember much of the night. But Seth—"

"Seth's the father?" I barked.

Avery jumped. Sara cried out.

I drew a deep breath and let it out slowly. "I'm sorry."

Avery nodded. "I will pack up this week and we'll be gone by the weekend."

"What? Why?"

She looked at me like I should know the answer to that question. "I know telling you violates the NDA I signed. I'm assuming that's why you're here. To trick me into admitting Seth is the father so the label can stop paying me."

"The label knows Seth is the father?"

Avery nodded. She looked as confused as I felt.

"And Seth knows?"

She nodded again.

I ran a hand through my hair and leaned back in the chair. I went there to be a decent man and step up for my child. But she wasn't my child. Everyone lied to me and let me believe she was while protecting Seth.

"You didn't know any of this?"

I shook my head. "No. Seth said something months ago about the label paying you off, but he never mentioned all of this. He was covering his ass."

"My dad walked out on my mom and I when I was six. He was the one who worked, so my mom had no income. He drained their accounts and left us with nothing. Before then, she'd been a stay-at-home mom. It was right before summer, and all the camps were full and she didn't have money for it, anyway. Every day was a struggle. I didn't want the same for Sara. I wanted her to have options. But I shouldn't have lied and told the label she was yours."

"I understand why you did."

"You do?"

I nodded. "How did they find out she's not mine?"

"They insisted on a paternity test. Said what they paid me would only be good until Sara was born, and that when she was, they needed proof. If I refused, they were going to sue me to get the money back. When she was born, I told a nurse the truth. I was alone and scared and it all just came out one night when Sara was a few hours old. They paid off the nurse to get the information, and they tested Seth. The NDA was changed, and the agreement was they'd pay for us to live here as long as I don't tell anyone who Sara's father is."

"I'm sorry you went through all that," I said. "The worst

part is you're probably not the first, and I'm sure you won't be the last."

"I don't care about any of that. As long as Seth never comes here, never tries to take her away from me, I'll be fine."

"You don't want her to have a father?"

"I'd rather she has no father than him as a father," Avery snarled.

I thought about it for a minute and nodded. "That's probably the best thing you can do for your daughter."

I looked at Sara again. She was watching me, her big hazel eyes tracking my movements.

I stood. "I'm sorry for interrupting your day, Avery. No one will know I was here. And I'm sorry Sara isn't mine. I came here to apologize to you in person for not being around, but Seth... keep her safe from him."

She tilted her head and gave me a questioning look.

"He's exactly who you think he is."

Avery swallowed thickly again and followed me to the door. "I wish she was yours."

I looked past her to where Sara watched us. "I do, too." I kissed Avery's cheek. "If you don't mind, I'd like to stay in touch."

She smiled. "You don't have to do that."

I shook my head. "I know, but if you ever need someone on your side, I want you to know I always will be."

"Seth is your best friend. Why would you do that?"

"Because he's not the person I thought he was. And you and Sara deserve better."

"Thank you, Trey. That means more than you know."

I nodded and let myself out. Avery closed the door behind me.

A weight lifted from me as I walked down the steps from

her house to the rental car I had. I felt the tingle of music again. But it was all tied to Sofia.

I looked up at Avery's house and knew the woman I loved deserved the same as the woman I thought had my child. I just hoped Sofia would let me say sorry in person. Without maiming me.

24

SOFIA

"ARE YOU SURE YOU'RE OKAY?" DAD ASKED AS I PUT HIS LAST suitcase in the trunk of his rental car.

I slammed the trunk and nodded. "I'm good, Dad."

"But—"

"Dad, I'm not going to hide, and I'm not going to sign that contract."

Dad sighed heavily. When the offer from Trey Ryan's label arrived to buy my song, Dad was excited for me. He was proud and thought it was a good opportunity.

But it wasn't right for me.

"Hearing your song on the radio is a really cool thing, Sofia. To know your words connected with others. It's powerful."

I shook my head. It didn't matter that we'd had the same conversation a dozen times over the last few weeks. "It would hurt too much," I confessed for the first time.

He pulled back, like he never guessed that part of it.

"I wrote that song with Daniel. I thought we were doing something together. Something for us. Knowing it was part of his manipulation taints the whole thing. If I heard it on the radio... I just can't, Dad."

He pulled me into a rare hug and held me close. His hands rubbed up and down my back. "I'm sorry, Sofia. I didn't realize that was the reason."

I shrugged and hugged him back. "I didn't want to admit it."

"You can admit anything to me," he said, pulling back to look into my eyes. He held my shoulders and smiled at me. "There's no wishing pain away."

I nodded.

"And there's no shame in forgiving someone you love for hurting you."

"Dad," I whined.

"I'm just saying you talked me into asking Monica for a second chance. I messed up with her, but I'm putting it all out there and hoping she's willing to give me another chance. I can't go there and hope for that without also thinking you should consider giving Trey a second chance."

"It's different, Dad."

"Why is it different?"

"Because you didn't lie to her about who you are and try to steal something from her."

"It sounds like he changed his mind about that second part. As for lying to you, I don't think he was lying about loving you."

I snorted, but his words hit me in the heart. Hard.

"I don't want you to live a life of regret, Sofia," Dad said, hugging me again. "Trust an old man when I tell you that's no way to go through your days."

"You're not that old yet," I told him.

He chuckled and shook his head. "Yeah, well, I'm older than you and am trying to impart my wisdom on you."

"Uh huh."

Dad walked around to the driver's side of the car. "I love you, Sofia."

"I love you, too, Dad."

"I'll let you know how things go."

"You better. I get the first invite to the wedding."

"Deal."

I smiled as my dad lowered himself into his vehicle. He started it up and eased away from the curb. He honked the horn and waved before he turned the corner and disappeared.

I wiped a tear from the corner of my eye. My throat was tight. I was going to miss him. More than I thought I would when he first arrived.

The apartment was quiet when I got back inside. I'd gotten used to the steady hum of him being there. It was strange to be alone again, especially since I'd been wishing for it when he arrived and used to love it.

I walked into his room and smiled when I found the sheets had been stripped from the bed and left in the hamper. The dirty towels were out of the bathroom and clean ones were in their place. On the dresser was an unopened bottle of my favorite caramel syrup, with a bow tied around the top.

I chuckled and picked up the syrup just as someone knocked on the door.

I set the syrup bottle on the kitchen counter on my way to the door. I opened it with a smile, assuming it was my dad. "Did you forget— Daniel. I mean, Trey."

He shook his head. "Daniel."

I crossed my arms and stepped back. "What are you doing here?"

"I owe you an explanation."

"You don't owe me anything, Trey. We don't know each other."

"Sofia, please."

"Please what? You had plenty of opportunities to tell me what was going on. To ask me to write a song with you. To confess who you were and why you were here. Instead, you lie to me, get me to fall for you, then do exactly what your buddy Nate did and stab me in the back."

"Nate is not my friend."

I rolled my eyes. "Whatever."

"I quit the band."

"Yeah, sure."

"I'm serious. I walked out of the studio. I couldn't record your song."

I laughed mirthlessly. "Not without permission. So that's why you're here. You want me to sign this contract so badly?" I turned and walked into the apartment. The contract was on the coffee table, taunting me every fucking time I tried to sit down and relax.

I picked it up and started to go back to the entrance but ran into Trey. "Oof."

He caught me, his arms coming around me. He held me against his body.

Everything inside me felt like it was finally back in the right place. My eyes slid closed. I leaned into him.

Then my brain kicked in, and I pushed back.

"I didn't invite you in."

"Don't sign that contract, Sofia."

"Why? You have a new one? Less money? More money? Need more songs? You here to steal my notebook so you can just say they're all yours?"

"No! Dammit, listen to me. I don't want you to sign anything. They don't deserve your song. I quit because I realized who I was working with, and what they were doing to people. They paid off a woman who said she was pregnant with my baby."

I gasped. It wasn't true. He couldn't be using my own story to get my sympathy.

"I went to see her. She lied and said the baby was mine because she wanted more for her kid and thought I'd do the right thing. Seth's really the father, and the label paid her off to keep quiet. He's also the one who gave them your song. He took pictures of your notebook, not me. He's a complete asshole, and I never saw it before. He's manipulated me since we met."

"Sounds familiar," I snapped.

Trey nodded. "I deserved that." He swallowed and took a step away from me. "When I came here, I knew I couldn't tell you who I was. I came to find out where your dad was. Seth told me your name, even though you were never in the spotlight. I've always written our songs, but when I heard I might have a child, my muse left me. I couldn't write anything. I thought your dad could help. That he would be willing since he hadn't released anything in a while. He was one of the best songwriters of his generation, and I needed that spark from him."

"But you got me instead," I snarled.

"Daniel is my middle name. It's a family tradition. All the men in my family since my great-grandfather have the same middle name. Including my dad and Michael."

I sucked in a breath. I knew that was important.

"No one has ever called me Daniel, but when you first said it, it felt like you were seeing a piece of me no one else ever got to see. I thought Seth saw it, but I was wrong."

Trey took a breath, visibly working through his emotions.

"Michael was at the end when I met Seth. He overheard me singing to Michael in his hospital room. Seth was visiting the hospital with Nate and Nate's band. Outreach and giving back. Stuff the label encouraged to the point of it being forced on a band, especially when sales dipped."

I'd seen reports of bands doing things like that. Four on the Floor had done some of it, but when their sales declined, they all decided they were done. When they did charity events, it was out of the spotlight. It didn't surprise me Nate only did things like that when he was forced to.

"Seth walked into Michael's room and joined me singing to Michael. I had no idea who he was, but it had been months since Michael had been awake long enough to sing a song with me. It was good to hear another voice with mine. Seth and I hit it off after that. He reached out regularly to ask how Michael was doing and came to Michael's funeral. We stayed in touch and got together sometimes to play around with music. One day, Nate came with Seth."

"I bet you thought it was the coolest thing ever."

Trey breathed a laugh and nodded. "I did. He was famous. He was huge. And I'd been hanging out with his brother all that time and had no idea. Seth said Nate wanted to get us in front of his record label. That they were looking for new bands and Nate thought we were good enough."

"Turns out he was right."

"He was. But I didn't know the rest of the story until recently. Seth tried to make a go of it on his own. The label didn't want just him. Nate's little brother wasn't good enough. They wanted something new. Seth tried to pass off some of the songs I'd written as his own, and the label liked them well enough that Seth decided to bring me in."

"Wow."

"Yeah. All these years, I was completely in the dark. The

label didn't care. They would have stolen my music and left me with nothing if Seth had been enough alone, but they shot themselves in the foot. I didn't know any better at first and signed contracts that gave them more rights than they should have had, but it's too late for that. I don't want the same to happen to you."

"Why do you care?" I asked. His story was good. It got him the sympathy vote. It kept my attention and drew me in again. But it wasn't going to change anything. He still lied to me when he said he loved me. I could consider overlooking the rest of it. I could maybe understand the pressure he was under. But telling me he loved me was low. It was Nate Catalan low.

"I punched Seth. I almost punched Nate. I quit my band, Sofia. I lied to you about my reason for being here, but I never lied about how I felt about you."

I shook my head and took a step back from him. Being in such close proximity was messing with my head. Making me think he was saying things I knew he wasn't saying.

"I love you, Sofia. I know you can never forgive me. I know we're over. I know this is the last time I'll ever see you, but I couldn't sit back and risk letting you make the same mistake I did."

"You can't love me. Stop lying to me!" I cried.

He walked closer to me, but I moved away from him. If he touched me again, I'd be done.

"You don't have to feel the same. I know you don't. But I do love you. And I came here to tell you not to sign the contract. Did Piper tell you I called her? You need protection. You need a lawyer and someone to make sure you're safe. I'll pay for both."

"No. Daniel, no. I..."

He smiled.

"Why are you smiling?"

He shrugged. "You called me Daniel."

"I..." I closed my eyes and drew a breath. "Daniel doesn't exist. The man I fell in love with wasn't real."

"I am real," he breathed. "God, Sofia, I am more myself when I'm with you than I've been since Michael died. I didn't see it before because I couldn't. I had no one after my brother died. My parents fell apart. They divorced and forgot about me. They weren't around for me. I lost my brother, and they lost their son, but they were so in their grief they didn't notice me. I don't blame them, but it was true. I needed a family. I needed someone. Seth took advantage of that. He knew he could use Michael's death against me. And he's been doing it for twenty years. I never saw it. Not until I came here and I was no longer Trey Ryan. I was Daniel. I was the guy you saw. The one you fell in love with. The guy your friends welcomed in without a second thought, because of you."

"But you're not Daniel."

"I'm not Trey Ryan either. I walked away from that life. I am probably going to be broke after I have to buy my way out of my contract."

"I happen to have a second bedroom," I whispered.

He inhaled sharply. His gaze blazed. He took a step closer to me. "Is that for when you're mad at me?"

"Considering I'm mad at you now..."

"Mad is better. Mad means there's a chance you'll forgive me one day. And if you let me move into your second bedroom, maybe I can convince you with massages and ordering takeout for you and singing your songs whenever you want."

I closed my eyes and let him pull me into his arms. "I'm

not sure you can afford to sing my songs. Rumor has it they'll sell for a pretty good price."

He exhaled a laugh into my hair. "They definitely would. Maybe I can get a job as a music teacher. Then I can afford one note."

I snorted. "Or you could go solo."

He shook his head. "I burned my bridges when I punched Seth. I'll never get another contract again."

"You do know Trent is Trent MacKellar, right?"

Daniel pulled back from me and narrowed his brows. "You mean MacKellar Investments?"

I nodded. "And MacKellar Cove. He's probably richer than you are. And he probably has contacts that can get you a new contract if that's what you want to do."

Daniel shook his head. "I don't... I don't know. I got as far as walking away from Seth and the label and all their lies, finding Avery, and coming here to apologize to you. I haven't thought past that. Hell, I never let myself imagine you might forgive me."

"You still have some groveling to do."

He nodded solemnly. "I know. And I'll do whatever you want me to do to show you how sorry I am. I was an asshole. I came here with the intention of using you and walking away. I never bothered to consider the consequences of my actions. For years, I've thought I was above it all. You showed me it doesn't take much to be a decent person."

"You are a decent person."

"I'm working on it. And I hope to keep improving with your help."

"Then I guess you should rent that room from me," I teased him.

He chuckled softly and nodded. "As long as you know I'm going to do everything in my power to convince you to forgive me. Sleeping naked. Buying you extra caramel syrup. Massaging your feet. Carrying groceries for Mrs. Watson."

"You had me at sleeping naked," I whispered, lifting on my toes.

He smirked and closed the distance between us. "Yeah?"

I nodded. "Yeah."

He kissed me, both of us sucking in a breath the moment our lips touched. I never thought I was going to see him again. Not in person. But having him come back, apologize, and tell me he loved me snapped all those broken pieces back into place.

Tears leaked into our kiss, and Daniel pulled back. "Oh, shit," he whispered. "What did I do?"

I shook my head. "Nothing. These are happy tears."

He swiped at my cheeks and smiled. "Yeah?"

"Yeah."

"I love you so much, Sofia. I will spend the rest of my days making everything up to you and loving you."

"The rest of your days? That's quite a commitment."

He shook his head. "Not to me. It's the only thing I'm sure of right now. I will love you forever. Whether you feel the same way or not."

"You think I don't?"

He shrugged. "You haven't said it. And that's okay. I don't want you to tell me you love me because I said it. I want you to wait until you are in love with me again."

I laughed and shook my head. "It hurt so much because I love you. I forgave you so easily because I love you. I'm asking you to move in with me because I love you. I love you, Daniel or Trey or whoever you are and whatever you want me to call you. I have for far too long, and I will for the rest of my life."

"Well, thank God for that. I was starting to get worried."

I slapped his shoulder playfully. "Did you really think I didn't love you?"

He shrugged. "When you said it before, everything was different. The truth changes things. I was hoping it didn't change your love for me, but I wasn't going to count on that."

"I love you. So much. Whatever your name is."

"Daniel. I'm definitely Daniel."

"Then I love you, Daniel."

"I love you, Sofia."

EPILOGUE
CHELSEA

Moving was a whole lot easier with a huge group of people to help. Especially when I didn't have that much to move to start with.

"Where does this go?" Elise asked as she walked by with another box.

"Bathroom upstairs," I told my cousin.

Elise nodded as she headed for the stairs. She'd come through for me big time. I hadn't gotten to know all of her group of friends, but Sofia and Haley were bringing me into the fold and Elise was there to help them. And a whole bunch of their friends were at my new house to help me move.

And to help me get set up.

Blake and Ian gave me furniture and bedding from their guest room that was being turned into another nursery. Laura gave me a couch she and Nico had in storage for a while since my old one smelled like smoke. Trinity and James gave me a kitchen table and chairs because I didn't have one in my old apartment. Willow gave me end tables. Goldie, Anna, and Valentina bought new things to make sure my much bigger kitchen was fully stocked and ready, then volunteered to cook for all the movers so I didn't have to buy everyone food.

I'd never felt so welcomed, and I'd lived in MacKellar Cove my entire life.

It just proved to me that buying the little house was the right move. From the day I saw it, I knew, but having the move-in go so well told me everything was going to be okay.

"Knock knock!" my mom said from the doorway.

"Come on in, Mom!" I called out. I knew unpacking was going to happen later, but I was trying to get a few things settled when I had a minute in between trips.

"We brought a guest," Mom said.

Panic welled up inside me at the tone of her voice. If Mom was unsure about whoever she brought to my new house, I was unsure about it.

Then I heard a whimper.

I rushed toward the door, wondering what in the world was going on. Until I saw the cutest face ever.

"Oh, my God, he's beautiful!" I cried.

My mom let go of the leash, and the brown and white dog rushed toward me. I sank to my knees so I could wrap my arms around him. He licked my face and barked excitedly.

"We knew you always wanted a dog. He was at the shelter and the lady said he's very friendly, great with kids, but does well when he's left home alone. He's mostly trained, and we knew you had a doggy door, but we hoped you wouldn't mind."

I hugged the beautiful animal and felt him settle against me like he'd been waiting to meet me. "I love him," I whispered.

I'd planned to get a dog, but I wanted to wait until I

moved. This guy was perfect. He was big enough that I wouldn't worry about hurting him if he slept in my bed, which was totally going to happen, and I rolled over onto him. But he was small enough that I felt like I could keep control of him.

"The lady said he's probably three or four. She recommended taking him to see Dr. Harris when you have time. He sees all the dogs that come through the shelter. He can get you registered as the owner and will microchip him and keep everything set with shots and all that."

I hugged my dog one more time, then stood and hugged my mom. "Thank you. I adore him." I hugged my dad, who'd been standing behind my mom and likely hedging since buying me a dog could have gone either way. "Does he have a name?"

"No," Dad said. "He just came in so they didn't have time to give him a name."

I looked at my dog and tilted my head. He tilted his to match mine.

"He looks like a tank," Daniel said from the stairs. "Where did he come from?"

"He's mine. My parents got him for me."

"He's adorable," Sofia cooed.

The dog heard her voice and turned to her. He looked up at me, as if asking permission. I nodded. "You can go meet Sofia."

He took off toward her, licking her and barking happily.

"He's well trained," Daniel marveled. "And very sweet."

I nodded, watching my dog. Elise and some of the others came downstairs, distracted by the dog who said hello to everyone. People came in from outside, including Valentina's daughters and Goldie's son. The teens circled around the dog and rubbed him until he flopped on his side, his tongue hanging out like he had never been more content in his life.

"Can we take him to the backyard?" the kids asked.

"Yeah, that's a great idea," I told them. "While you're out there, see if you can think of a name for him."

"Okay!" they chorused.

"You're going to let the kids name your dog?" Goldie asked.

I shrugged. "I don't know. Daniel said he looks like a tank, so anything's better than that."

Ian scoffed at Daniel. "You call yourself a creative." Ian shook his head.

Daniel shouted, "Hey!" and chased Ian out to the driveway to get more stuff.

"I'm glad they get along so well," Sofia told Blake.

"I am, too. Ian was really disappointed when he found out Daniel wasn't who we believed him to be. It's good to know that wasn't entirely the case, and that he's back. Has he decided if he's going to talk to Trent about going solo and getting another contract?"

Sofia shook her head. "He's still thinking about it. The music industry wasn't really great to him. We've also talked about writing songs and putting music online ourselves. He's not sure what the best thing is. But I told him everything is different when you have someone looking out for you."

"That's very true. And doing things yourself is a cool idea," I said.

Sofia nodded. "I think he's leaning toward that. No one to answer to, no labels to take all your rights. It means a much smaller platform, but I think he's ready for that."

"Oh, hey, Chelsea, Melody said they know one of your neighbors," Blake said.

"Really? I haven't met my neighbors yet. Hopefully they're nice."

Blake nodded. "Melody said the guy is really great. Single dad."

"I'm happily single," I told her, and my mother before Mom could ask more.

Blake chuckled. "Not trying to change that. Just telling you what Melody said. She's sorry they couldn't be here today to help."

I waved off her concern. "I didn't expect this much help, and I'm grateful for it."

Blake smiled. "We take care of our own. And you're ours, so stop fighting it and come to book club."

I chuckled. "Thanks. I guess I have to."

"It'll be fun."

I nodded. "Thanks. I'll be there Sunday."

"Chelsea, Chelsea!" the teenagers called, running inside. The dog was right behind them.

"Yeah?"

"We came up with a name for your dog," Samantha, Goldie's younger daughter, said.

"Good. What is it?"

"Bulldozer," they all said together.

I looked at Blake and Sofia. They looked as shocked as me. "Bulldozer?"

"Yeah," Bianca, Valentina's oldest, said. "Because he ran right through all of us like a bulldozer."

"You can call him Bull for short," Goldie's son, Paul, said. "Or Dozer. That would be kind of cool."

We all looked at the dog, who was passed out next to the couch, sound asleep despite all the noise in the house.

"He definitely looks like a Dozer right now," Sofia teased me.

I chuckled and shook my head. "I guess he has a name. Bulldozer. Also known as Dozer."

"I just hope he doesn't knock down anything else. Like your house," Dad said.

"You got him for me!"

Dad laughed. "You can blame your mother. I think she's hoping getting you a dog will mean you meet your neighbors. Especially the ones who are single."

I groaned. "Tell me you're joking."

Dad shook his head. "Sorry, pumpkin. Your mother's biological clock is ticking, and she wants grandkids."

"That's not how it works, Dad."

He snorted. "Try telling her that. I dare you."

I looked over at my mother, who was talking to Dozer. Whispering something to the sleeping dog.

I was in so much trouble. My mom bought me a man-catching dog. And was giving him tips.

All I could do was shake my head and hope he didn't listen.

THANK you for reading Sofia and Daniel's story! Sofia is a character I've been thinking about for years, but it took a long time to find the right man for her. Daniel needed some work, but I love the two of them. I hope you feel the same!

The next book in the series is Chelsea and Derek's story. Chelsea loves everything about her new house, except her rude neighbor who keeps leaving notes on her door about the problems she's causing. She finally has enough and goes to give him a piece of her mind, but she gets a lot more than she bargained for. Preorder His Curvy Surprise now!

. . .

Wᴀɴᴛ ᴍᴏʀᴇ from Sofia and Daniel? Daniel gets an offer he never expected, but he's not the only one with a decision to make. Bonus epilogue is only available to subscribers. Sign up now!

Sᴛᴀᴄᴇʏ ᴛʜᴏᴜɢʜᴛ Wray was her forever. He picked her, but he lied and he stole and he broke her. There would never be anyone else for her, but without trust, what did they have? Wray won't give up on them so easily, especially when he learns someone is threatening their family. *FURY* is available now!

ABOUT THE AUTHOR

USA TODAY Bestselling Author Mary E Thompson spent most of her childhood wishing she had a few less curves. She hid in the pages of books because her favorite characters never cared what size her clothes were. Now, neither does Mary, and she writes stories that celebrate women like her. Real women who have curves, chase dreams, and find love, because we should all be happy, no matter our dress size.

Mary spends her non-writing time with her husband and two kids, watching too much TV, cheering for her hometown football team (Go Bills!), and hiding chocolate from her family.

Visit https://MaryEThompson.com/ to sign up for Mary's newsletter, **Romancing the Curves**. Subscribers get free ebooks and other fun stuff, like exclusive, members only content and giveaways, plus are the first to know about new releases and sales!

www.ingramcontent.com/pod-product-compliance
Lightning Source LLC
Chambersburg PA
CBHW030803200726
48285CB00014B/545